OVERLOOK

This is a work of fiction. Names, characters, businesses, places, events and incidents are either the products of the author's imagination or used in a fictitious manner. Any resemblance to actual persons, living or dead, or actual events is purely coincidental.

Winterfield Press

For Ted

Also by Elizabeth Hein

How To Climb The Eiffel Tower

Overlook

Elizabeth Hein

WINTERFIELD PRESS

ONE

Kitty Haskell felt itchy and dirty. Again. The sticky discharge in her white cotton panties had come back, even after scrubbing her skin raw after her morning jog. It felt like as soon as she rid herself of one nasty infection, another appeared. Kitty changed into fresh panties and a clean track suit before dropping the offensive panties in the laundry room sink to soak. *Maybe I'm having an allergic reaction to the laundry detergent.* She held the bottle of detergent at arm's length and stared at the tiny print on the back. *It says gentle enough to use on baby clothes but, you never know.* She tossed the bottle in the kitchen trash can.

Becky, her seventeen-year-old daughter stood at the high kitchen counter struggling with a bag of granola. With her feathered hair and bright red bathing suit, Becky looked like a young Farah Fawcett.

"Are you life guarding again tonight?" Kitty asked.

Becky poured half a bag of granola into an orange Tupperware bowl and added a scoop of yogurt. "I'm picking up as many hours as I can before school starts." She wrinkled her nose and dumped the bowl in the sink. "I think this yogurt has gone bad."

"How can you tell?" Kitty rinsed out the bowl and put it in the dishwasher before wiping the stainless steel sink dry with a linen dish towel. "I don't see why you eat that hippie food. I'd be happy to make you a ham sandwich."

Becky rolled her eyes. "I'm a vegetarian now, Mom."

"You're difficult. That's what you are."

Becky flipped her long strawberry blonde hair over her shoulder. "When is Dad coming back from his trip?"

"Thursday."

"I can't believe he's making me pay for the car insurance on the Bug."

"You'll have to take that up with him, honey. Just be glad you have a car. You could drive the Volvo instead."

Becky rolled her eyes again. Kitty inspected her daughter's face; a pink tinge peeked out between the freckles on Becky's nose. "Make sure you put on plenty of sunblock today. You need to protect your skin or you'll get all wrinkly. I wish we had Coppertone when I was your age."

Becky smeared some of the coarse peanut butter she bought at the local health food co-op on some whole grain bread. "Aunt Rose told me you never went to pools when you were kids because your mother was afraid you'd get polio."

Kitty followed Becky around the kitchen wiping crumbs from the orange Formica. "We swam in the ocean and the occasional lake when we got the chance. I was always a strong swimmer. You take after me in that respect." Becky kissed her mother indulgently on the cheek before gathering her towel and sandals and heading out the door.

The moment Becky was gone, Kitty called Lake Tate Medical Center. "I'm sorry, Mrs. Haskell," the nurse said. Kitty imagined her standing in the reception area filing the days patients into the multicolored wall of floor to ceiling shelves. "Dr. Bukalis put a note in your file. We can't call in any more refills for you. You'll have to come in and see him."

"Put Paul on the line, will you?" Kitty replied.

Paul Bukalis came on the line. "Hey, Kitty? What seems to be the problem?"

"That nasty itch is back. It doesn't hurt to pee or anything, but I am seriously squirming in my shorts. Could you call another refill into the Kerr Drugs for me?"

"Sorry, Kitty," Dr. Bukalis replied. "That discharge means there's something going on. You can't just ignore it and hope it goes away."

"That's why I need some more of that cream."

"Look, my next appointment canceled. Can you come in right now?"

Kitty had planned to knock a few balls around the tennis courts behind the Overlook clubhouse before lunch. At forty-three, she feared underarm jiggle more than nuclear war. The tennis courts would have to wait; she needed to get rid of the awful itchy feeling in her nether regions more. She made a mental note to conveniently drop Dr. Bukalis' wife from the Overlook Book Club phone tree. Kitty had invited Patsy to join the club. She could just as easily uninvite her.

"I'll be there in ten minutes."

ᘏᘏᗋ

Hours later, dark clouds brooded over a shard of orange sunset. It reminded Kitty of a painting by El Greco. She laid a bowl of air-popped popcorn on the coffee table beside her husband's feet. "Seth, I'm going for a quick jog before the storm hits."

"Leave the dog here," Seth said without taking his eyes off the television. Daisy stinks when she gets wet."

The family's golden retriever rolled over and looked up at Kitty with a sleepy smile. "Don't look so disappointed," Kitty chuckled as she laced up her running shoes. "I'll be back in half an hour or so." Seth grunted in her general direction as she slide the door open to the deck.

Kitty scrambled down the path cut through the poison ivy and brambles to the raised wooden trails that hugged the shoreline like an articulated collar tracing the curves of a woman's neck. After being subjected to a full poke and prod by Dr. Bukalis, she couldn't resist the chance to take an evening run in the rain. No one else would be out. During her morning runs, Kitty had to pick her way through a confluence of neighbors walking their dogs before the oppressive August humidity forced them into the air-conditioned isolation of their splendid constructions of wood and glass. Now, with fat raindrops polka dotting her path and thunder rumbling in the distance, Kitty was alone.

Lightening cracked open the sky over Lake Tate causing Kitty to quicken her pace. She wanted to get to the gazebo behind the Overlook Swim & Tennis Club to watch the storm approach. Unlike the sleek modern homes designed to blend into the wooded lakefront, the faux Victorian gazebo, set high on the side of the ridge, reminded her of the house she lived in as a child. She and her sister, Rose, would sit in the attic windows and watch storms roll in over Narragansett Bay.

A few hundred yards before she reached the gazebo, the clouds burst. She lifted her hands and face to the sky and did a little dance before sprinting to the shelter to enjoy the concerto of raindrops hitting the leaves. Kitty watched a wave of heavy rain advance across the lake and engulf a small red canoe out in the water.

Kitty's first thoughts were of Bobby and his friends camping out on the island. *The boys wouldn't be crazy enough to come back during a storm, would they?* She leaned over the railing and tried to make out the figure frantically bailing rainwater from the canoe. It was then that she saw a psychedelic orange flash in the water beside the boat. *Holy Moly, that's Stacia in the water! She must have been training for one of her long distance races and gotten stuck in the storm. It's nice of Lana to spot her mother from the canoe, but this is ridiculous. Get in the damn boat, Stacia. Put your daughter out of her misery.*

As much as she thought her friend's training regimen excessive, Kitty didn't turn back and run the half mile back to her house. If Stacia could swim across the lake during a thunderstorm, she could run around the neighborhood during a thunderstorm. Also, the hamburger she ate at lunchtime with Bobby and his friends still weighed heavily on her mind. She was disgusted with herself for giving in to its charms. She wasn't a kid; she couldn't eat thick juicy burgers anymore. She should have been satisfied with just a TaB. She hadn't allowed herself anything else for the rest of the day. Despite the now pounding raindrops, Kitty completed the entire four mile loop without seeing another soul and returned to the house cold and wet.

TWO

Stacia Tate Curran looked out over Lake Tate, her lake. It was stunning from her vantage point on the tip of Sweet Gum Ridge. The thunderstorm that had rattled the windows and sent the dog whimpering under the bed the night before had washed the August humidity from the air. It would be back. For now, the mosquitoes were still drying their tiny wings and a chorus of tree frogs were harmonizing like a passage from *Peer Gynt*.

Stacia tucked her goggles into the leg of her neon yellow bathing suit and tickled the ears of the fluffy white dog in her arms. "Now, you be a good girl while I go for a swim to check on the boys."

She put the dog down and wheeled her high-powered telescope from its waterproof cabinet. Stacia didn't use the telescope to look at the stars; she used it to keep tabs on any and all activity on Lake Tate. She trained the viewfinder on the island in the center of the lake. Three sets of gargantuan adolescent feet hung out of the flap of Bobby Haskell's tent. He was the only one of the boys who set up his tent properly so it wouldn't leak in a downpour. Stacia liked Bobby. He had the same pleasant demeanor and efficient precision that Stacia so admired in his mother, Kitty. She adjusted her focus to the boat tethered to a nearby pine tree. The boys hadn't properly covered the runabout. It now had three inches of rainwater in it. *Typical. All their things will be soaked through.*

"What are we going to do with that boy, Baillie? I warned him it was going to rain and he went out there anyway. Now he's going to be grumpy and overtired all day. Remind me to make him take a nap before his camp. We can't have him falling behind the other boys on the soccer field, now can we? Everyone would notice." She slid the telescope back then gave the dog a kiss on the top of her head. "Okay, no barking now. Daddy's sleeping."

Stacia descended the long staircase from the patio high on the ridge to their private dock. She adjusted her goggles on her head, tucked a stray blonde lock into the strap, and dove in. Fifteen yards from the dock, she surfaced and set out for Mill Island. Stacia wanted to get three miles of training in that day. The island was a little over a mile from the ridge; she could check on her son and get most of her training in at the same time.

Within a few hundred yards, Stacia fell into a comfortable stroke rhythm and let her mind wander. She wondered if the boys knew the island they were camping on was once the high ground of a thriving mill town. For seventy years, the Bradford Falls Mill made the poplin fabric that once clothed Confederate soldiers and employed the local people, both black and white, after Reconstruction. The mill and dozens of homes had all been washed away, first by a brutal hurricane in 1927 and then by the hydroelectric dam, to make way for progress and a New South. All that remained was a pile of rusting machinery and crumbling bricks beneath a jungle of poison ivy.

Stacia knew the history of how the town of Bradford Falls was drowned beneath Lake Tate because Stacia was a Tate. Her great grand-daddy had been one of the men who bought up the ten miles of hardscrabble land covered with sweet gum and river birch so Carolina Power could build a hydroelectric dam. When she was a little bitty girl squirming in her church pew, she heard the preacher say that God made all the earth and the water and the sky. She knew that wasn't altogether correct. People could change the world. Her family created her lake and she created Overlook.

When Stacia and Weldon got married in 1958, while he was still in the service, they had returned to North Carolina with nothing more than their love to create the three-hundred home oasis that would become Overlook. The Curran family had farmers and laborers in it, like every other black family in Magnuson, but they were primarily a family of bankers. Weldon's father had made his money on Parrish Street up in Durham and had taught his children to seek out opportunity. When the two hundred acres of stony ground became available, the young couple jumped on the development trend and took a chance on Overlook. Like so many residents of Magnuson, most of the homeowners came from somewhere else. Only a handful of them remembered when Sweet Gum Ridge was a place for teenagers to do the things that teenagers do in the woods or when Stacia Curran was not queen of all she surveyed.

❧

The boys were fine. Stacia helped them bail out the boat and made sure it would start before swimming back to shore. She wanted to get back before her husband woke up and found her gone. Weldon was obsessed with her safety.

A hundred yards from the dock, Stacia lifted her head to judge her distance from the shore and saw Weldon pacing back and forth at the end of the dock. She slowed her pace when she noticed he was clenching and flexing his giant fists. At forty-eight, he was still as fit as he was at eighteen. Decades of swinging hammers and climbing ladders had kept him as strong as the day he came home from Korea. When she surfaced beside the dock, Stacia could see the muscles around Weldon's eyes twitching.

"Good morning, honey," she said as she peeled off her goggles and flung them on the surface of the dock.

Weldon inhaled a ragged breath and barked, "What do you think you're doing?"

Before Stacia could slide back beneath the water, Weldon grabbed her arms and hauled her out of the lake like a fluorescent trout.

"What do you think you're doing?" he repeated. "We agreed! You promised not to go out alone." Stacia pedaled her legs and twisted in her husband's grip as he scolded, "You could have drowned!"

Stacia stopped squirming and went limp. "Please put me down," she whispered.

Weldon blinked and seemed to realize for the first time that he was holding his five-foot tall, a hundred and five pound wife at arms length and a foot off the ground. He put her down then pulled her to his chest. "What am I going to do with you?"

"I'm sorry, Weldon."

"You promised."

"I went to check on the boys."

Weldon released Stacia and picked at the wet patches she'd left on his faded Army T-shirt and shorts. "So, how are the boys?" he asked.

"Fine. Grumpy. Damp. They'll be heading back soon." Stacia retrieved her goggles from the dock and started up the stairs to the house. "Can I make you some toast?"

Weldon picked up his binoculars from where he had laid them down on an Adirondack chair and followed Stacia. With his long legs, he took two steps at a time and quickly caught up with her. "Don't think you're off the hook here, Stacia. Why didn't you ask me, or Lana, to spot you from the boat?"

"Lana went out with me last night and was such a great sport when it started raining that I wanted to let her sleep. This is one of her last days before she leaves for school."

"Don't remind me," Weldon sighed. Stacia felt doubly guilty for worrying Weldon now. In two days, they would be taking their daughter to start her freshman year at the University of North Carolina. Weldon was having a hard time of it. He put on a brave face in front of Lana, but Stacia knew he was dreading the drive to Chapel Hill.

They heard a yelp and Weldon sprinted past Stacia to intercept Baillie from tumbling down the stairs. "I must've left the gate open when I saw you out in the lake."

Stacia paused on the stairs to compose herself. Baillie was her precious but she couldn't justifiably yell at Weldon for leaving the gate open when he was so upset at her for doing something she had promised not to do. She took a deep breath, bit her lip, and climbed the last few steps.

On the patio, Stacia could feel the day's humidity beginning to weigh down the air. She walked inside and pulled the heavy floor-to-ceiling drapes over the wall of windows that made up the back of their A-frame. Baillie danced around her feet until Stacia picked her up.

"Has that little dust mop been fed yet?" Weldon asked from where he stood pouring them both mugs of coffee.

Stacia scratched Baillie's chin and cooed at the little dog, "Did Daddy call you a dust mop? Bad Daddy!"

She put the dog down and scooped dog food out of a ceramic canister on the counter into a monogrammed bowl. Stacia held the bowl up until Baillie sat at attention then put it down on a placemat in the corner of the parquet floor. Not until Stacia gave the signal did Baillie scamper to her bowl. With Baillie happily crunching away at her kibble, Stacia turned her attention back to her husband. The glass and brass table was strewn with ledger books. Weldon sipped from his chipped and spackle-marred Howard Alumni mug and stared at the ledgers despondently.

"Are you still obsessing about the house on Serenity?" Stacia asked.

"Of course I am," Weldon replied. "If they go into foreclosure, it will affect the entire community." Weldon had channeled his anxiety about losing his beloved daughter to adulthood into worrying about his beloved subdivision losing value in an economic downturn. He wanted Overlook to remain the preeminent community on Lake Tate. It was.

When northern scientists began migrating to the area as more and more technology companies moved to North Carolina, Curran Construction had been there to offer lake front homes with all the amenities. A family could get a four bedroom air-conditioned house on a wooded half acre for the same price as a two bedroom cape in Connecticut. Weldon enjoyed talking to the homeowners on the phone but he was also pragmatic enough to let Stacia be the face of Curran Construction. Her ballerina's grace and southern drawl made the buyers overlook their being an interracial family. Her eye for detail and his careful management had kept the housing values in Overlook rising year over year.

Stacia poured milk into her pink glass mug and gestured with the container. "Don't you even think about loaning Liam and Deirdre any money, Weldon Curran."

Weldon took a sip of his coffee and curled his lip at its bitterness. "I can't just let them lose their house."

"Yes, you can. You helped them build their house; you didn't promise his company would succeed."

Weldon got up from the table, poured his coffee down the drain, and rinsed out his cup. They had been having this conversation for two weeks and didn't seem to be coming to any resolution.

"Let it go, Weldon. One foreclosure will not ruin the whole subdivision. They are not our responsibility."

"What if I talked to the bank for them?"

"Would your brother be cool with that? I don't think so."

"I just feel so awful for them."

Stacia kissed the scar on the side of Weldon's neck. He told their children it was from catching his shirt on a rusty nail while replacing a roof but Stacia knew it was the result of flying shrapnel during his third tour in Korea. He smelled good, like a little boy waking up from a nap. "I know, honey. You've got a big heart. That's one of the things I love most about you, but you've got to use your head."

Weldon picked up Baillie and wiped some dog food off her little face. "You are such a slob, girl. You don't have to bolt down your food like that. You'll get a tummy ache."

Stacia took the dog and put her on the floor. "Why don't you take the dog for a walk along the trails? Get some fresh air before it gets too hot."

Weldon ran his fingers over his shaved head. Stacia thought he was looking a little tired these days but he was still as handsome as ever. If she didn't love him so much, she would have been jealous of how supple his cocoa colored skin still was and how few wrinkles he had around his big brown eyes. She had to be careful when out in the sun and slathered herself in potions to keep her pale skin looking youthful.

"I guess you're right. Brett isn't worried about the property values. Then again, he stopped caring about Overlook as soon as the last lot was sold. He's moved on." Weldon pulled a bottle of Coke from the refrigerator. "Did Eulalie tell you they are thinking of selling their house and building a new one across the lake?"

"No, I hadn't heard that." A shudder of joy ran through Stacia. Her sister-in-law, Eulalie, was the crabgrass in Stacia's pristine lawn of life. Just when Stacia thought she had gotten rid of her, Eulalie would pop up in a new place. "You know your brother. He can't relax. He needs the excitement of a new project, a new challenge."

"Sounds like someone else I know," Weldon teased. "I'll sure be happy when you're done training for this race. You're not planning on going back out there today, are you?"

"I'll go do some laps at the club. I don't have the heart to ask Lana to go out in the boat after the soaking she got yesterday."

"Thank God. It always makes me nervous to see you out there dodging the boats."

Stacia poured water into the kettle for a pitcher of iced tea. "They are supposed to dodge me, but thank you."

"Still, I'll be happy when this race is over. I'm getting too old for this kind of thing."

Stacia threw a dish towel at her husband. "I'm the one who is doing the swim, not you."

"I think it's more grueling for the spectators." Weldon gathered the papers from the kitchen table. "So what are you up to today?"

Stacia helped Weldon pick up the ledgers. "I'm meeting the other Lookers in an hour to finalize the PTA budget."

"PTA stuff, already? School doesn't even start until tomorrow."

❧

Anyone could attend official PTA board meetings and state their opinion. Stacia couldn't do anything about that. On the other hand, she could convene a core group of Overlook moms, otherwise known as The Lookers, the morning before an official PTA meeting to decide which teachers would get their special projects funded and what equipment the PTA would donate to the school that year. How one became a member of The Lookers was not as simple as owning a home within Overlook, although that was a prerequisite. There were plenty of women, like Kitty's good friend Molly, who lived in Overlook but were never invited into the inner circle. The Lookers were polite to these other women at the pool or in the grocery store, but there was never any doubt as to who was in and who was out of Stacia's favor.

The Lookers had initially come together to launch a relentless campaign of phone calls and emails until the Magnuson Public School system buckled under the pressure and allowed school buses to pick children up at each street corner within Overlook. Until then the children were forced to hike, or be driven, the two miles from the tip of the ridge to the landscaped granite sign that heralded the subdivision's entrance. On the heels of that early success, The Lookers had taken over the local PTAs. Of course, Stacia had been PTA president since her daughter, Lana, was in first grade and intended to remain so until her son, Marcus, graduated in four years. Committee chairs changed as people's children moved from the elementary school, to the junior high, to the high schools, but the faces were always familiar.

Stacia pulled Deirdre Logan aside outside Bella's Brew before their not-so-impromptu unofficial PTA meeting that morning. If Deirdre and Liam were going to lose their house, they needed to hurry up and move on. Foreclosures were bad for Overlook, yards weren't maintained, paint was allowed to peel, marriages frayed. Stacia needed to revoke Deirdre's membership in The Lookers right away. The school year was starting and the holiday social season was not far off. Talk of real estate showings and job searches would be awkward. Better to rip the bandage off now, than let the wound fester.

"Look Deirdre," Stacia said as she leaned against the door of Deirdre's wood-paneled estate wagon. "I think it would be better, for everyone, if you don't participate in PTA this year. You've got other things to worry about than the membership numbers of Lake Tate Junior High's PTA."

"But...I've been..." Deirdre stammered. She dropped the heavy file box in her arms on the pavement between the cars. Rage colored her freckled face as she spat, "Really? After all the hours I've sat behind that damned membership table, you're gonna just kick me out of PTA? Really?"

"Of course, if you and Liam are still here next fall," Stacia drawled. "You'd be welcome to take the committee over again."

Deirdre yanked open the driver's side door and hurled her white pocketbook across the seats before rearing on Stacia again. "You and I have been friends for—" She sucked in the oppressive August air like a goldfish unceremoniously dumped out of its bowl. "I thought we were friends!"

Stacia couldn't look at the woman who had been her tennis partner for the past five years. They were friends. Stacia truly cared for Deirdre, but the health and prosperity of Overlook were more important than her personal feelings.

"My affection for you has nothing to do with it. I'll miss you terribly."

At that moment, their conversation was cut short by Kitty Haskell nosing into the parking spot next to Deirdre. Kitty tooted her horn and waved. Only Stacia waved back. Deirdre jumped into her station wagon and roared out of the parking lot, nearly toppling a man coming in on a bicycle.

"Goodness!" Kitty said as she climbed out of her green Volvo. "Is everything all right?"

"It'll all work out in the end," Stacia sighed. She clamped her cigarette between her pink lips and opened the tailgate of her gleaming Jeep Wagoneer. Weldon joked that Stacia bought the giant vehicle because it made her feel tall and chose the fawn color because it matched her hair. He wasn't far off the mark. The Jeep did make her feel powerful and the neutral color didn't clash with her colorful wardrobe.

"The others aren't here yet," Stacia said as she kicked the file box to the back of the vehicle with a bright pink sandal. Because she still wore a child's size shoe, she had a wardrobe of fun sandals. Today's pink sandals had sky blue polka dots on them that coordinated with Stacia's pink and blue paisley tank dress.

Kitty discreetly pulled at the crotch of her black linen shorts. "What are we meeting about today?"

"Just typical starting up a new school year kind of stuff. We need to prepare for the official board meeting tomorrow night." Stacia kicked the box again. Actually, Kitty," Stacia said. "Maybe you could help me out a little. Do have an hour or so?"

"Sure, what do you need?"

"I have all these membership forms that need to be put in the teacher's boxes before school starts. Want to stick around after the meeting and help me count out class sets?"

After the meeting, over cups of black coffee and a pack of cigarettes, the two women put together packets of thirty-two membership forms per homeroom. "Thanks for helping me do this, Kitty," Stacia said as she tossed a stack of fliers back into the box. "Why is it always the same ten people who do all the work?"

"I'm surprised Deirdre Logan isn't Membership Chair again this year. Why isn't she doing this?"

"She's going to have to step down from the PTA. I'll have to recruit a new person for the job."

"What happened?"

Stacia took a sip of her coffee and changed the subject. Deirdre was definitely out of The Lookers but Stacia would let her go quietly. "So, where's Becky going to apply this fall?"

"We're still not sure," Kitty sighed. "Seth wants her to go to a state school and study something practical like business. Becky won't hear of it. She wants to go somewhere where she can sit on a tree-lined quad for hours and debate books and big ideas." Kitty tossed another packet into the box. "When we were up in Rhode Island in May, my sister was driving me crazy fussing over every detail of our mother's funeral, so the kids and I toured a whole bunch of schools in the area. Becky fell in love with Brown."

"Do they let girls go to school there now?"

"She has better grades then most boys her age and she did very well on her national tests, but Brown would still be a long shot. Still, there are plenty of other liberal arts schools where she can sip coffee for hours with professors in corduroy blazers with elbow patches."

Stacia smiled into her coffee. She wondered if her Lana would sit on the quad and debate ideas at Carolina. She doubted it. Lana was more of a sleeping through class and cramming before the test kind of girl. "You sound like you know what that's like."

"I spent my share of hours hanging out in the library stacks and staying up all night staring at light boards. I was an art history major." Kitty wistfully tapped a stack of papers on the table before paper clipping them together. "Applying to schools is different now. I don't remember the application process being so arduous. I wrote a few essays, went on an interview or two and that was that. You got in, or you didn't. Do you remember it being like this?"

Stacia tapped another cigarette out of her pack of Benson & Hedges. "I never did the whole college search thing as a kid."

"You probably always knew where you wanted to go," Kitty said with a self-deprecating smile.

"I didn't plan on going at all." Stacia unconsciously stroked her left knee. "I was going to go to New York and get a place in a dance company, or die trying."

Kitty paper clipped another pile of forms and absently asked, "New York didn't pan out?"

Stacia held her cigarette midway between the table and her mouth and stared at Kitty slack-jawed. It took Kitty a moment to notice anything had changed between them. "What?"

"The accident."

"Accident?"

Stacia winced as she flicked her Bic to life. It was a testament to Kitty's disdain for petty gossip that she didn't know the story behind the ten inch jagged purple scar running down Stacia's leg. It was impossible to miss. Stacia could have a plastic surgeon make the scar less noticeable or hide it under pants, but she made a point of wearing miniskirts year round. It was always visible.

It was the least she could do.

Stacia considered how much to tell Kitty about the night her life, and the lives of everyone in the Curran family changed forever. A group of them had gathered out at Sassy Leveritt's farm to celebrate the graduating class of Northwest Magnuson High School, the area's "colored" high school. Everyone was drunk on pitchers of Sea Breezes and the hope engendered by Von Curran's rousing valedictory speech. Von was Stacia's best friend and fellow ballerina. Stacia was not going to miss her speech no matter how uncomfortable she was being the only white girl at the party. Von's classmates had been gracious and, ultimately, happy she was with them.

Long past midnight, Stacia, Von, and six other girls crammed into the back of an old pickup truck to make the long drive back to

Magnuson. As they crossed back into the city, a blue Studebaker came out of nowhere and slammed into the side of the truck. When the truck careened into a giant oak tree, the girls in the back were all thrown from the bed. Liza Brown flew into a fence and broke her pelvis; Stacia had heard that she still walked with a limp twenty-five years later. Stacia had landed in a muddy gully beside Von. Her friend couldn't move and could barely breathe. Stacia dragged herself a quarter mile to the closest farmhouse for help before passing out from the pain. If she were not a member of the influential Tate family, the farmer might not have called for an ambulance for the five injured girls. Nevertheless, it was too late. Von was dead and Stacia would never dance again.

"I was in a terrible car accident. A bunch of girls, including Weldon's little sister, were killed." Stacia took a deep breath before she could continue. "I broke both my legs and was in rehabilitation for months." Stacia lit her cigarette with shaking fingers and took a deep drag. "Anyway, my Daddy made a few phone calls and I went off to Carolina the next fall."

"Did you study dance?"

"Oh no, finance."

THREE

A swarm of chocolate cupcakes cooled on the wood-trimmed Formica waiting for Kitty to turn them into bees and sunflowers. Her wrists already ached from transforming three-dozen vanilla cupcakes into ladybugs. As Hospitality Chairs, she and her tennis partner, Marni Kaur, were responsible for the bake sale during that evening's general PTA meeting. Kitty and Marni had been a team for four years and usually spent the day of the bake sale together. Kitty would bake all the sweets and Marni would keep her entertained while she frosted. She had forgotten how tedious it was alone.

Kitty rinsed yellow frosting off her fingertips and dialed Marni's number on the black princess phone hanging on the kitchen wall. There was no answer, again. *Where is she these days? I hope she made those brownies for tonight.*

The house felt too quiet without someone to talk to. Every August, it took Kitty a few weeks to adjust to being alone all day while Becky and Bobby were in school. Kitty turned the radio on for company. The curator of the latest traveling exhibit of Rodin's *The Gates of Hell* was blathering on about how the exhibit was especially relevant in this modern era of terror threats. He said that sculpture was more accessible than ever because we are moving away from the written word and are becoming a visual society again. *Blah blah blah. That guy doesn't know what he's talking about. When I saw The Gates of Hell in Paris, I wasn't thinking about world politics. I stood in front of it and was sucked in by all that suffering. All that death made me feel more alive.*

The show went to a news break, and Kitty was pulled back to what she was doing. She picked up a cupcake, spread brown buttercream across the top then, expertly piped a yellow buttercream sunflower on

16

top of it. *This is what my life has come to – making pretty cupcakes. I should be talking about art and artists. I'm smarter than that guy.*

When the phone rang, Kitty assumed it was Marni finally calling back. She picked up the receiver with her least frosting caked fingers.

"Kitty? It's Pam at Doctor Bukalis' office."

"Hey, Pam. What's up? Did I forget to pay my bill on the way out?"

"He'd like you to come in for a follow-up appointment."

He's seen more than enough of me already, missy. I can't believe the way that man was poking around my breasts the other day. Even Seth doesn't touch my breasts like that!

"That won't be necessary, Pam. The cream cleared the problem right up." She finished the flower with a brown star center and plopped the pastry bag in a glass. "I am feeling much better now."

"He'd like you to come in anyway."

Kitty picked up another cupcake. "I understand that you want to be thorough, but it seems silly to make me come back in." She appraised the expanse of unfrosted cupcakes in front of her and considered the whoopie pies she still had to make. "I really don't have time to come in for another exam right now, Pam."

The sounds of shuffling papers and the scratching of a pencil against paper came through the phone. *Why are they making such a big deal out of this? How serious can a little itch be? It's not like he was testing me for cancer or anything.* "Just tell me over the phone," Kitty demanded as she smoothed brown frosting across another cupcake.

"Okay." The nurse cleared her throat. "I'm sorry, Mrs. Haskell. You have gonorrhea."

Kitty stabbed the offset spatula through the cupcake into her hand. "What?"

"You heard me, Kitty. You have gonorrhea. ... It's treatable with a course of antibiotics, but you will need to speak to all your sexual partners—"

"Excuse me! I've only ever had one sexual partner. My husband!"

"Be that as it may, all your sexual partners will need to see a doctor." Dr. Bukalis's nurse cleared her throat again. "Would you like to come in and talk about this now?"

Kitty was tempted to hang up and pretend the conversation had not happened. The Rodin expert was talking again. Kitty wanted to think about art, not the sticky mess.

Oh my God! Seth gave me gonorrhea. She tossed the ruined cupcake in the sink.

"Do you want me to call the prescription in to the pharmacy on Bradford Falls?"

"No!" Kitty knew the pharmacist there. He was a neighbor. "I'll come pick it up in a few minutes."

∽◦∾

The receptionist at the Lake Tate Medical Center must have been keeping an eye out for Kitty because Paul Bukalis stepped out of his office seconds after the glass doors to the clinic whooshed closed behind Kitty. He looked near Kitty, rather than at her, as he said, "Why don't we talk in my office?"

Kitty walked past him and stood in the center of the tiny journal-lined office. Dr. Bukalis closed the door behind them. "Would you like to sit down?"

"No, I'm not staying." Kitty couldn't help but notice the smell of rotting food coming from the collection of half eaten sandwiches and cans of Coke in the trash can near her feet. The life of a doctor didn't seem remarkably glamorous at that moment. "You could have left the prescription at the front desk."

"I thought you might want to talk," Paul replied. He took a folded piece of paper out of his medical coat pocket then hung the coat on the back of the door. "Did you know we have an in-house pharmacy now? You can have the prescription filled right here."

Kitty stuck her hands in her pockets to keep from grabbing the half-eaten tunafish sandwich from the top of the desk and shoving it in her mouth. *There is no way I would ever have that prescription filled here. All I need is for some nosy Nellie figuring out why I am taking it. If anyone gets wind of this, I will be laughed out of Overlook.*

"You can't tell anyone about this, can you?"

"Of course not," Paul said. His eyes darted to the stack of open files on the desk as if worried Kitty could read them.

"But it will be in my file?"

Paul nodded with a frown, keeping his eyes on the desk. "Do you have any questions?"

Kitty thrust her hand out, palm up, for the prescription. "This is embarrassing enough. I don't want to talk about it!"

Paul looked down at the slip of paper in his hand and said, "Before I give you this, you need to understand that you must inform ALL your sexual partners about the infection and they must inform ALL of their partners."

"I told you people—"

"You don't just get gonorrhea out of the blue, Kitty. If Seth's your only partner then you must have gotten it from him and he got it from—"

Kitty didn't wait around for the doctor to take his statement to its logical conclusion. She snatched the slip of paper from Paul's hand and ran out of the office. She didn't slow down until she had bolted down two flights of stairs and out into the blazing sunshine of the parking lot.

���

The prescription burned a hole in the front pocket of her crisp Bermuda shorts as Kitty drove north. Three serviceable pharmacies flew by but she didn't pull over until she crossed the Virginia state line. She didn't remember any of the drive. She kept repeating, "Paul can't tell anyone about this. Paul can't tell anyone about this." She pulled off the highway and followed the blue signs promising civilization to the right past an abandoned textile mill and fallow fields until she hit a town that appeared stuck in 1944. There wasn't a modern store in sight. Beyond a post office and boarded-up furniture store, Kitty found a strip of stores with a pharmacy nestled between a men's clothing store and a religious book store. She stepped inside and slid the prescription across the counter. The pharmacist put down the box of bandages he was restocking and asked, "Have you had prescriptions filled here before?"

"No," Kitty replied daring the man to give her a hard time.

The pharmacist looked at the prescription and handed her a form to fill out. "I have these in stock. Will you be waiting for it?"

Kitty filled out the form and walked away to peruse an aisle of dusty vitamins and supplements. Her heart was dancing a jig in her chest. *The pharmacist didn't bat an eye when I gave him the prescription. Maybe he can't tell what it's for. Maybe people take that antibiotic for lots of things. Maybe it's not such a big deal. I can just take the pills and no one need ever know.*

Kitty might have been able to hide the fact that she had gonorrhea from everyone else, but she still knew. She wished she didn't, but she

19

did. She couldn't unknow this. She'd suspected that Seth had extracurricular interests over the years and had chosen to ignore the clues. A pink blouse had showed up in the laundry that did not belong to either her or Becky. There were the phone calls that Seth ignored when Kitty was in earshot. She didn't want to know. The deal was he not let his improprieties interfere with their marriage, and she would not ask too many difficult questions. Giving her a disease was definitely a deal breaker though. *What am I supposed to do now?*

A parabolic mirror hung over a display of disposable diapers. Kitty could see the cashier watching her pace up and down the aisles. She picked up a tube of lipstick, but her hands were shaking so violently, she quickly shoved it back in the display and moved to the greeting cards aisle. When the prescription was ready, she paid the full amount. She didn't want it showing up in her medical insurance records. She also bought a pack of cigarettes as if it were perfectly normal for her to be shopping in that podunk town that day.

Outside, the smell of chicken frying in hot grease spewed from the restaurant with a ten-foot chicken standing in front of it at the far end of the parking lot. Kitty loved fried chicken but ate like a rabbit because that was what she was supposed to do to stay slim and keep her husband happy. That plan obviously hadn't been working. She marched across the broken pavement and ordered a fried leg quarter with mashed potatoes and gravy, two biscuits, slaw, and a tall glass of sweet tea. This was no time for salad and TaB. She sat at one of the sticky tables and ate with a voraciousness that she would consider extraordinarily unbecoming in someone else. Kitty hadn't had a piece of chicken with the skin on it, never mind golden brown deliciously fried skin, in years. She had forgotten how succulent fried chicken could be. She would normally feel guilty about how long it would take the Earth to decompose the little styrofoam bowl of gravy, but she didn't care today. She dumped the gravy over the fluffy mound of mashed potatoes and watched it form a puddle. She took a bite and let the creamy starch coat the inside of her mouth and push Seth out of her mind.

After her initial food frenzy, Kitty felt somewhat satiated. She gazed out the front window of the restaurant while she savored the fluffy biscuits slathered with butter. It was a beautiful clear day. The humidity had finally broken and people were emerging from their summer exile. Across the busy road, an old woman in ratty slippers and a housecoat was standing in her front yard. She didn't appear to care that everyone driving by could see her varicose veins and balding scalp. Japanese beetles flew in all directions as she cut a pile of mixed roses from the bushes lining her oil-stained driveway. The canes were as tall as she was and showed signs of black spot, but she didn't seem to notice. She buried her face in each blossom before adding it to the trug. Kitty thought they would make a beautifully eclectic bouquet.

Kitty had three shades of yellow tea roses growing along the side of their dark stained house. They were pretty, but had no scent at all. Her mother had every known color of rose in her own garden in Rhode Island and had tried to hybridize a few more. Roses were her obsession. Mother's year was dictated by the cycles of her garden. She would not travel if it was time to trim the canes, or treat the leaves for black spot, or mulch and wrap each bush with burlap before the first frost. Consequently, she had only visited her daughter twice in the eighteen years she had lived in North Carolina. Now, she never would again. Kitty's mother had died between her Mister Lincolns and Double Delights earlier that year. It had been an unseasonably hot, humid day and there was a storm coming. Kitty guessed that her mother was trying to save her beauties from the coming rain when she had a massive stroke. It was awful for Kitty's sister, Rose to find her that way yet Kitty felt Mother would have been pleased to go quickly and efficiently while doing something she loved.

Kitty enjoyed the fried chicken so much that she stopped at a Krispy Kreme before leaving town. She enjoyed watching the doughnuts come out on a conveyor belt still dripping with hot glaze and recalled how she and Seth had taken Bobby to a Krispy Kreme like this one after his pee-wee football games, whether his team won or lost, then pushed any thought of Seth back out of her head. A half dozen doughnuts and the remains of her sweet tea propelled her back to Magnuson. The sugar high allowed her to forget about the gonorrhea for an hour and sing along to the FM rock station. Unfortunately, by the time she was back in sight of Lake Tate, the doughnuts were gone, her blood sugar was crashing, and she was running behind schedule. The clock in the Volvo's dashboard said 2:24. She needed to be parked inside the yellow loading zone in front of the junior high by 2:21 to avoid getting stuck in the line of cars snaking down the street. She was already late and still ten miles away. She pictured Bobby, decked out in his practice uniform and cleats, standing in front of the school with the crowd of miscreants whose parents wouldn't pull up until 3:00, cars vibrating to the bass beat of

KISS. Then, she thought of her friend, Molly. *Molly will be just leaving for the school. She's a good mother.*

Kitty pulled into the rutted parking lot of a north county Food Lion and stopped at a pay phone. She dialed Molly's number and, after the usual pleasantries, asked, "Can you grab Bobby and take him over to the soccer field?"

"Sure," Molly replied. Kitty heard the sounds of Molly gathering her keys and purse. "You know I'm always willing to take him. It's silly for both of us to wait in that stupid line every day."

Kitty agreed but also knew that Molly would no sooner skip one of her son's practices than Kitty would. "Thanks Molly, I owe you one," Kitty said. "I'll see you at the fields. I shouldn't be long." Kitty hung up and got out of the car. She gathered up the evidence of her misdeeds and disposed of it in the battered garbage can outside the Food Lion.

By the time Kitty got to the soccer field, the boys were already doing drills and Stacia Tate Curran was already holding court beside the field. From a distance, Stacia's pink Lily Pulitzer dress made her look oddly flamingo-like. Kitty appreciated that Stacia swam every day, but no one should be allowed to have such slender legs. Kitty jogged every day and her legs felt like tree trunks.

Station wagons and compacts were squeezed into every available spot near the field. Kitty didn't want to park in the muddy overflow lot and ruin her white Keds lugging her camp chair through the dirt lot. She circled around and followed a young woman in hot pants and a tank top that showed off her red bra straps pushing a stroller toward a VW Bug. The woman left the stroller in the middle of the parking lot as she loaded the baby into his car bed. *Must be the babysitter. No self respecting mother would drive a cute little car like that with a baby.* The Lookers drove station wagons and land barges so they could carpool with confidence. Becky, on the other hand, drove a cute little yellow VW. Kitty was distracted by the wave of jealousy rushing through her body to head off an Impala from swinging into the young woman's spot.

While she circled the lot another time, she wondered if Seth would be home for dinner that night. She hoped not. She didn't want to sit across the table from him and make polite conversation. *He'll probably have dinner with the little floozy that gave him the gonorrhea.*

It hit her again. Her husband gave her gonorrhea.

There was a painful grinding sound as Kitty slammed the car into neutral without depressing the clutch. She slapped a hand over her mouth and sprinted for the ladies room behind the cinder block snack bar. Doughnuts on top of fried chicken had been a mistake. When she finally emerged, wasted and disgusted with herself, her car was gone.

Oh great, how am I going to explain this? I don't know how it happened officer, I left my car running in the parking lot and someone stole it. You see, I just found out that my husband gave me VD, so I ate a huge plate of fried chicken and half a dozen Krispy Kremes to deaden the pain, but then they made me nauseous and I lost my cookies.

Yeah right! That would really fly. She reached for her bag to find a dime for the pay phone then realized it and her wallet were still on the front seat of the Volvo. *Seth's going to kill me.*

"Kitty!" She looked up to see Blaire Morton, dressed in a pristine white tennis dress that would never see a tennis court, walking toward her. Even Blaire's hair was the size of her native Texas. "There you are!"

Kitty discreetly checked her Keds for vomit as she waved back. *Just what I need, another one of Blaire's my-kid-is-better-than-your-kid rants.* Kitty hardly knew Blaire's son and was sure he was a great kid, but Kitty was sick and tired of hearing about his perfect grades and perfect games and perfect social life. Even Bobby had commented on how tiresome Mrs. Morton was.

"Are you okay?" Blaire asked with a vicious gleam in her eye. "I saw you run into the bathroom ages ago."

Fabulous.

"I think I have food poisoning," Kitty replied. She hoped she looked half as nauseous as she felt. "I must have eaten some bad shrimp or something."

Blaire pursed her coral coated lips doubtfully. Kitty suspected that Blaire will have told the whole neighborhood that Kitty was bulimic before midnight. Kitty didn't care; that would be better than the truth. Blaire handed Kitty her keys. "I parked your car for you."

"Blaire, you're a life saver! Thank you so much!"

"Lucky for you, I was watching."

"Yeah, it's my lucky day," Kitty laughed. She stepped between two cars and looked down the slope at the field. "How's practice going? I don't see Marni down there. Is Connor sick?"

Kitty could smell Blaire's florid perfume as she came up behind her. "She called me earlier and asked me to give Connor a ride home. She has an appointment or something."

"I can take him," Kitty said. "I need to talk to her. I've been trying to talk to her for days actually. She's not picking up the phone."

"I bet," Blaire replied.

Blaire turned away but Kitty still saw her smirk. She wondered what juicy piece of gossip Blaire was bursting to tell about Marni. Kitty quickly spit out, "I hope she got the table decorations for the open house tonight."

Blaire took a step back and exclaimed, "You're worried about that silly open house? Bless your heart!"

On the way home, Kitty and Bobby stopped at Tony Tomato's and picked up a large cheese pizza. Kitty had planned to serve lemon caper chicken with scalloped potatoes and carrots for dinner but then again, she had also intended to be home to defrost the chicken and get the potatoes in the oven. She had planned to spend the day frosting cupcakes and preparing for the open house. Nothing was as it was supposed to be. The mere thought of food made her want to throw up again. Her children still needed to be fed though. Bobby held the pizza box on top of his backpack to protect his bare knees and told his mother about his day at school. She didn't process any of what he was saying - something about his English teacher giving him grief over the use of personal pronouns and Ryan Ney kicking him above the shin pad at practice. Kitty was wondering where her husband was at that moment. Did he take his pretty young thing to fancy hotels? Did they go to dinner and talk about their days? Did he listen to her when she talked?

At home, she opened the box to pop the pizza in a warm oven. There were foil packages lying on top of their pie.

"I can't believe this," she groaned, "they gave us someone else's food! There's stuff in with the pizza."

"They always give you garlic bread with a large," Bobby yelled from the laundry room. Like a good boy, he knew to leave his muddy soccer clothes in there. He kicked his backpack into the kitchen and emerged in the robe Kitty kept hanging on a hook behind the door. "When was the last time you had a pizza, Mom? 1930?"

"Try 1960. This cardboard crap can't hold a candle to the pizzas Mrs. Pinto used to make. She used six types of cheese and peppers she roasted herself over an open flame and ..."

"They were square, right?"

"Rectangular. She made them on these ancient black cookie sheets. The same ones she made pizzettes on and broiled vegetables on."

"You make your old neighbor out to be the best cook who ever lived."

"She was." Kitty rustled Bobby's hair. "Becky won't be home for twenty minutes or so. Why don't you jump in the shower and start your homework. I'll call you when she comes in."

"Can we eat in front of the TV since Dad's not going to be home and you're going out?"

"No. Maybe. Let me think about it. I've got to get these cupcakes over to the school so I'll need you to clean up after yourselves. And bring that robe back down when you come. I'm tired of carrying it back down for you."

Bobby disappeared up the stairs and a moment later, Kitty heard him put a record on his turntable. *I should go up there and tell him to do his math homework before playing a record, but he's young. Why can't he have a little fun before dinner? I miss fun.*

The three dozen unfrosted cupcakes Kitty had abandoned when the doctor's office called were dried out and the tips of the frosting bags had hardened into sugary rocks. Kitty made beautiful desserts because she knew, no matter how hard she tried, she could never make a tastier dessert than Mary Pinto, her landlord, neighbor, and surrogate grandmother.

The summer between Kitty's junior and senior years at Mount Holyoke, she had an internship at the Worcester Art Museum. She spent her mornings in the corner of the curator's office sweating over a grant proposal and her afternoons helping little old ladies choose between silk scarves in the gift shop. She loved every second of it. When the museum received the grant to launch a special exhibit of their medieval collection, the head curator offered Kitty the job of exhibit specialist after graduation. The curator, Mr. Mastrogiavanni made her feel it was her exhibit as much as his. The position came with beautiful business cards and a certain amount of prestige but demanded laborious hours researching each of the pieces for the exhibit guide, haggling with printers, as well as working twenty hours a week in the gift shop. Mr. Mastrogiavanni could not pay her very much and worried about her living alone.

That was where Mrs. Pinto came in. Mary Pinto was Mr. Mastrogiavanni's mother's fourth cousin and owned one of Worcester's ubiquitous three-deckers. Every evening, as Kitty walked up the forty cement steps from the street, Mrs. Pinto stuck her head out her kitchen window and yelled, "Go call your mother so she knows you're home safe, then come eat. I made too much for one old lady." Initially, Kitty thought she was merely being polite, but the invitations kept coming and the smells wafting through the floorboards were too irresistible. Mrs. Pinto was a fabulous cook. She could make the simplest ingredients into a banquet and opened young Kitty's eyes to the joy of cooking for the people you love. Her mother's repertoire consisted of cold sandwiches, boiled dinners and meatloaf. Even Kitty's birthday cakes came out of a box, although they were beautifully decorated with sugared flowers and frosting rosettes.

The smell of bleach hit Kitty like a swift slap as Becky came in and dropped her swim bag at the base of the stairs. "You okay, Mom? You look awful."

"Gee thanks, sweetie," Kitty replied. She slashed open the bottom of the yellow frosting bag with a chef's knife and slapped some frosting on the remaining cupcakes. They were not up to her usual standards, but they would have to do. She had nothing more to offer.

Becky swiped a finger full of frosting from the bag. Kitty swatted her away. "These are for the PTA meeting."

"I thought you were making Grandmonster's whoopie pies for the bake sale table." She rushed over to the oven. "Do I smell pizza?"

"Yes, and you and Bobby can eat in front of the television..."

"Awesome!"

"...if you clean up after yourselves." Kitty pulled a tray out of the wide cabinet drawers and put plates and napkins on it. "I was going to make your grandmother's whoopie pies, but it's far too late for that now. The rounds of devils food cake need to cool for several hours before you can pipe the whipped filling inside. I tried rushing the process once, and they became gooey globs not fit for the dog." The color drained from Kitty's face. "Oh my God, the dog! I forgot all about her."

Kitty had put Daisy out on the deck that morning, so she wouldn't get in the way while Kitty was baking. She had been out there all day without food or water. Kitty rushed out onto the deck, imagining her loyal golden retriever dehydrated and gasping for breath in the heat. Daisy bounded up the steps without an iota of reproach in her slobbery smile. She was fine. Filthy, but fine.

There was mud caked up to Daisy's elbows and in the fur on her belly. "Did she get down to the lake?" Becky yelled through the door.

Kitty looked for the source of the mud and discovered that Daisy had excavated the soaker hose beneath the rose garden and chewed it to bits. What used to be a neat bed was now a mud hole. The rose bushes had been upended and there were tiny fountains bubbling between the day lilies.

Daisy rubbed up against Kitty's legs, smearing mud across the hem of her shorts. "Daisy, look what you've done. What a mess!" Kitty pulled her by the collar to the corner of the foundation and sprayed her off with the hose. Daisy gave Kitty a wet kiss. "Thanks, girl. I needed that. It has been a pisser of a day and it's not over yet." She attached an old leash to Daisy's collar and slipped it under one of the legs of the deck chairs. "You're still kind of muddy, so stay out here for a bit. Becky will give you a warm shower after dinner, okay?"

"Mom," Becky whined from the kitchen. "She gets hair all over my bathroom."

"Then use my shower. Get Bobby to help you carry her upstairs. Her paws are muddy."

Kitty threw her muddy clothes in the washing machine with Bobby's sweaty uniform before pulling herself up the stairs to don her own uniform of a modest wrap dress and diamond studs. With enough foundation and rouge, she almost looked happy.

FOUR

The open house started at seven. Stacia arrived at the school by six. There were things only she could do properly. Custodians needed to be sweet-talked into carrying tables from the storage shed and set up in the lobby, traffic flows had to be managed so no one could avoid the membership and bake sale tables, and administrators needed to be flattered. Stacia stepped into the sixth grade girls' room, the only bathroom that had hot water, to dampen a rag to wipe down the dusty tables.

Von and Weldon had attended Lake Tate Junior High before the Magnuson schools were integrated. In the colder months, Von would arrive at ballet practice wearing two sweaters because the old coal furnace could rarely push heat to the second floor. The building was still a hodgepodge of corridors, but the furnace was new and the broken windows had been replaced. As a member of the city-wide PTA board, Stacia was lobbying to have the building torn down and replaced with a modern building that would both appeal to the northerners migrating to the area and the long-standing families of northern Magnuson. For now though, she would make Lake Tate Junior High the best school she could.

Once the tables were clean, she draped them with blue and yellow cloths and parked the membership table just inside the door where no one could avoid walking into it. Stacia had cornered Blaire Morton at soccer earlier that afternoon and asked her to take over as membership chair. Blaire had turned her down. She wouldn't even help out for that night's meeting. Her husband's car dealership was not selling as many little foreign cars as they were right after the oil embargo a few years back. Blaire was picking up more nursing shifts to make a little extra money. Word was, the Mortons were behind on their bills. Stacia was disappointed. She was counting on Blaire; she seemed to know everything about everyone, a handy trait in a membership chair. Stacia was desperate for someone to sit behind the table that night and had to settle for her sister-in-law, Euilalie. She left a money box and a stack of membership forms for Eulalie and hoped for the best. Stacia's place was standing at the door to the auditorium to hand out agendas and greet the parents. The bylaws mandated that the PTA provide the general membership a copy of the budget and an agenda, but the bylaws didn't say people need to be able to read it. She ran them off single spaced on half sheets of paper. Paper and ink were expensive.

Kitty thought she could pull off the bake sale. On the way over to the school, she ran into Hoppin' Frog Bakery and bought four-dozen chocolate chip cookies. If she dumped them haphazardly on a tray and broke the edges off a few, she could pass them off as homemade. She would screw on a smile and play the game, but as soon as she walked into the school lobby, she knew she would lose. She could not stand behind a table and pretend to be little-miss-happy-homemaker. She wasn't happy. Her home had been infected.

Kitty placed her tray of cupcakes in the center of the table and put trays of cookies on either side. Someone, Kitty assumed Marni, had draped blue and yellow tablecloths over the bake sale table. But where was Marni?

A girl walked up to the table holding her father's hand and asked if she could buy a cupcake. "After the meeting, sweetie," Kitty replied. The girl pouted for a second until her father whispered something in her ear and led her away. Seth would have refused to let Becky ever have a cupcake if she pouted like that. Kitty watched them walking away and take a handout from Stacia outside the auditorium doors. Stacia's sheath dress, with its cobalt blue fleur-di-lis on a sunny yellow ground, looked like it had started its life as a tablecloth in Nice.

I should go over there and ask Stacia to tell Marni I have a migraine and had to go home. She looks so busy though and the meeting is about to start. Kitty looked around the lobby again for Marni. The only PTA board member around was Stacia's sister-in-law. She walked over to the membership table. "Hey Eulalie, do you know where Marni Kaur is?"

"Sure don't," Eulalie replied with an empty-headed grin.

"Are you going to be out here while the meeting is going on?"

"Stacia told me to get people to sign up for the PTA when they come in."

"Good." Kitty looked around the lobby for Marni one last time. "When you see Marni, could you tell her I had to go home? I've got an awful headache. I left the stuff for the bake sale on the table, so all she'll have to do is sell them. Okay?" Kitty left, assuming Marni wouldn't let her down.

࿐

At 6:59, Stacia made her way to the stage. She passed a toddler with a rainbow crown of multicolored balls floating on the ends of her braids eating a Happy Meal. Food was not allowed in the auditorium but Stacia was not about to say anything. That poor mother probably worked a long thankless job all day, picked that child up from some dismal daycare center, and dragged her to her big brother's school function. Stacia let the child have her french fries in peace.

She retrieved the cordless microphone from backstage; a donation from Curran Development because Stacia despised being tethered while on stage. She stepped out to the podium, "Good evening parents, I'm Stacia Curran. I am your PTA president this year ..."

"Again?" someone shouted from the back. The room giggled.

"Thank you all for coming out tonight. We have a few brief business items to get through while the teachers open up their rooms ..." A collective groan rolled through the small crowd. "No really. I promise this will be quick and painless. Now, if you'll direct your attention to the overhead ..."

The second the perfunctory "ayes" were over, Stacia handed the microphone to one of The Lookers and cut up the center aisle like a Kingfisher through the swarm of parents exiting the auditorium. On her way to the lobby, she told another Looker to go around and pick up the agendas floating around like Bradford pear blossoms after a hard rain, and take them to the trash bins out back. The custodians had enough to deal with without having to pick up after rude parents.

The inevitable traffic jam in the main lobby as parents tried to find their child's class rooms was the perfect opportunity to snag people to join the PTA, but Eulalie was leaning against a pole gabbing with some nobody wearing coveralls and scraped-up work boots. Stacia tapped Eulalie's arm and said through a smile, "Sweetie? I thought you were working the membership table."

"Molly Blevins said she would do it."

"Did you think that was a good idea?"

"I don't know, Stacia. She seems to be doing a pretty good job." Stacia peeked around Eulalie's shoulder and, judging from the pile of completed membership cards in front of her, Molly had recruited over a hundred new members.

"Well, bless her heart."

"I was just telling Eulalie here," the woman said, "she should run for PTA president next year."

"And you are?"

"Martha Pickett. I work for your husband? Our daughters were in the same class since kindergarten?" Stacia didn't recognize the woman. She must have been from the other side of the lake. "Eulalie's got to run. Your boy will be at the high school next year, and a Mrs. Curran has been PTA president at this school for as long as anyone can remember."

"Fifty-six years," Stacia replied, "but there are a lot of Mrs. Currans in these parts." Weldon's family had lived in the area for generations. His granddaddy gave the money to build the school. His aunt Jean was a teacher there when they first opened and had stayed on when the white children integrated the school. A Mrs. Curran would be in charge next year but it wouldn't be Eulalie; not if Stacia had anything to say about it. Weldon's third cousin had a boy who would be in the sixth grade the next year and Stacia was grooming his wife for the job. There would be a formal election but no one would run against Stacia's choice once she put a name on the ballot.

Stacia sensed this Martha woman was fixing to argue Eulalie's merits when her little boy barreled into Stacia's side. "Look, cupcakes!" the little boy lisped through a mouthful of crumbs.

Martha's eyes widened at the smear of blue frosting on Stacia's dress. "Say excuse me to the nice lady," she scolded.

The little boy pointed at Stacia's leg and squealed, "Eww, what a gross scar!" Martha picked him up and scurried away leaving a trail of chocolate cake crumbs down the sixth grade hall.

"What a cutie," Eulalie chuckled.

Stacia ignored her sister-in-law and stepped over to the bake sale table. It was a disaster. The tablecloth had blue and yellow frosting smeared across one corner and there were cookie crumbs everywhere. The money box gaped open and every cent of change was gone. "Where are Marni and Kitty?"

"Oh yeah," Eulalie gasped. "I was supposed to tell you."

Stacia shooed a little girl with dirty little fingers away from the cookies before she managed to touch every one. "Tell me what?"

"Kitty brought the cupcakes and cookies while you were talking in there. She said she had a headache and told me, to tell Marni Kaur, that she couldn't stay."

The little girl circled around the table and stuffed another cookie in her mouth before Stacia could stop her. "Where is Marni?"

"I don't know. Don't you?"

Stacia was tempted to grab one of the cupcakes and smush it into Eulalie's face. She wiped at some of the frosting on her dress with a paper napkin, but it just smeared more. "How about you stand here so at least the kids stop eating all the profits?"

"Okay, Stacia," Eulalie said and bounced behind the table. *She is so stupid,* Stacia thought. *It's hard to be angry with her.*

Stacia stepped toward the ladies room when someone slapped her on the back. She reeled around ready to screech at some awful child and saw Weldon's second cousin, Jacqueline Ellis. She threw her arms halfway around Jacqueline; she had gained weight since high school. "Jac! What are you doing here?"

"Being a good auntie. I came down to make sure Glory started sixth grade okay."

Stacia looked around to see Jacqueline's niece giggling with friends on the other side of the room. You could spot an Ellis anywhere, taller than the other children, darker than the other children, with a wide, high forehead and narrow chin. Jacqueline and her brothers had stood out of the crowd. The class had once seen a series of ebony heads from Mozambique on a school trip that could have been busts of the Ellis children. Their classmates had taunted Jacqueline by calling her Jackie Moz for weeks afterward.

Glory was the spitting image of her aunt at that age. "Did I miss something?"

Jacqueline slapped her on the arm and replied, "Her father is fine. You always go to the worst-case scenario."

"Not a bad policy with this family," Stacia teased and slapped her back.

Jacqueline pointed to her dress. "What happened here?"

"I had a collision with a cupcake. Help me find a damp cloth."

"No damp cloth is getting that out. That Lilly P is toast."

"Don't say that. This is my PTA dress." Stacia tried to pick off globs of frosting. "So where are Glory's parents these days? Has your brother solved world peace yet?"

"Michael is in Germany training people how to maintain nuclear warheads without blowing them up, and Sondra has been deployed to a medical ship in the south Pacific for a few more months. With them both away, they thought it best for Glory to stay with Mama for a while."

"How is your mother?"

"She's starting to show some wear. You knew that Daddy had a stroke a while back, right?"

"Weldon told me he has the sugar. She always did love sweets. Remember how she used to sneak in cookies for us when we were in the rehabilitation hospital?"

"Sure do," Jacqueline shifted her weight off her right leg as if the mere memory of their months of rehabilitation made the leg hurt. "You still swimming?"

"I've got a race coming up. You still doing your exercises?"

"Used to but once Ianna went off to school, I got out of the habit."

"Weldon took our Lana over to Chapel Hill the other day. He's having a hard time with it." Stacia gave up on the dress and tossed the napkin in a trash bin. "Suddenly, he has a lot of work to do at the office. I think he can't stand knowing she's not in her room."

"Poor thing," Jacqueline sighed. "My cousin has always been such a softie."

"I'll be glad when she comes home over Labor Day weekend. He needs to know that she'll come back." Stacia lowered her voice to a whisper. "He called Lana Von the other day. It freaked her out."

"Don't worry. He'll get through it. We all do."

The two old friends hugged again then Jacqueline pointed across the room toward the bake sale table and gasped, "Is that Brett's wife, Eulalie?"

"You know it is."

"She's so fat. How fabulous."

FIVE

By the time Kitty got back from the school, the kids had eaten, put their dishes in the dishwasher, and were working on their homework. She'd trained them well. There was nothing left to do but run a dish cloth over the already crumb-free counters, open a bottle of Chardonnay and wait.

What am I supposed to say to Seth when he comes in? She was upset, but she wasn't about to dissolve into hysterics, or angrily pound her fists against Seth's chest, or throw things. The proper thing to do would be to take the children and dramatically storm out, but it was too much of a bother and she had nowhere to go. Other wives could yell and scream and carry on. Kitty loved Seth, in her own way, but theirs had never been a grand romance. He was a good provider and he loved their children, but hot blooded passion was not part of their arrangement.

Kitty wondered if they would ever have gotten married if they had met in 1976, instead of 1956. She doubted it. She had liked Seth, he was charming and handsome, but they weren't even going steady when Becky was conceived. Good girls weren't supposed to plan for sex in those days and abortion was still something "other" people used to deal with their problem. When Kitty discovered she was pregnant, she and Seth did what was expected of them. Mother was overjoyed. Seth came from a wealthy family, or at least wealthy by Mother's standards, and she wanted her daughter to be rich. Seth's parents found the whole mess embarrassing. His father arranged to have an old frat buddy, who owned a golf equipment company in North Carolina, take Seth on. Seth had done well and was now vice president of Golf Systems. They had not seen or spoken to Seth's parents in years.

How could I have let myself get into this mess? How could I have been so stupid? I should have told no one and just had Becky on my own. Life will be different for Becky. I' should take her to the clinic downtown and get her a prescription for the pill before she leaves for college next year. I don't want some man holding her back from her dreams.

Kitty had drifted off on the couch when the mantel clock struck midnight. The bottle of Chardonnay was empty beside her and Seth was still not home. She got up to get more wine and banged her hip on the edge of the new white leather sofa. Seth bought it because it was the most expensive one in the showroom. Kitty liked the old sofa better, it had soft round arms. She opened a bottle of Chablis and poured the pale liquid into a clean balloon goblet from the ready collection hanging above the wine rack.

She rested her back against the high counter top, took a sip, and felt thoroughly disgusted with herself for not being more upset. The idea of having gonorrhea made her want to scrub her insides with bleach and steel wool, but it wasn't terminal. She'd take the antibiotics and be fine in a week or so. It was not the infection itself that was bothering her, it was Seth's carelessness. *How could he think so little of me? What else could he have given me?*

The dog jingled down the stairs and stared at Kitty as if to say, "What are you doing down here while he's out having fun? Are you just going to take this kind of behavior?"

"You're right, Daisy. I don't need to do anything drastic over this, but I do need to do something." She pet Daisy's tea-tree scented fur; she was still damp from her shower. "Remember that time he kicked you, and you took a piece out of his ankle? That was amazing. I won't bite him, but I don't have to take his crap anymore either. If he wants to be a philandering pig, fine. I don't need to sleep next to his cheating ass anymore!"

Kitty shoved a cork in the wine bottle and calmly went up to their bedroom to gather up the toiletries on Seth's side of the sink. There was plenty of room in the guest room bath to accommodate his Water Pik, shaving things and assorted potions. She made sure there were fresh sheets on the bed and clean towels in the shower. She was transferring some of his clothes to the guest room closet when Seth finally came in. It was almost one in the morning. "What the hell, Kitty. What are you doing to my shirts?"

"You'll be sleeping in here from now on."

"What?"

"Keep your voice down," Kitty hissed. "The kids have school in the morning."

Seth pulled the pile of shirts out of her hands and threw them on the bed. "What are you doing? Are you drunk?"

"I saw a doctor today." She threw a hanger at him. "Your skank gave you gonorrhea and then you gave it to me."

"What? But I ..." The color drained from Seth's ruddy face. "I don't have ..."

"Yeah. You do."

Seth picked up the hanger from the floor. "Oh my God." He seemed genuinely surprised.

"You'll need to see a doctor and get some antibiotics. And that woman who gave it to you should go see a doctor too, if you even know her name."

Seth pushed his tousled blonde mop out of his eyes, a gesture Kitty once found endearing. "But Kitty. I ..."

"Save it!" Kitty picked up the shirts and hung them in the empty closet. "I can't talk to you about this right now. I'm tired and I need to think about how we are going to handle this, but I can tell you this much. I am never ... having sex ... with you ... again."

"But Kitty ..."

"No! You don't get to talk right now. I have let you crawl all over me every Tuesday and Friday, even though you know I hate every second of it, and this is what I get?"

"And that makes it so fun for me. I have to make sure you have plenty of wine at dinner to even get that much."

"Shut up! I've held up my side of the deal ..."

"Come on ..."

"No. No more. You go ahead and sleep with your little floozies. I am done." Kitty closed the closet door and stormed out with as much indignation as she could muster. "I hope your pecker falls off!" She hissed over her shoulder.

Kitty expected Seth to come running after her and plead for forgiveness. He didn't. He brushed his teeth and went to bed in the guest room. Around two o'clock, Kitty gave up trying to sleep in their bed. The pillows smelled of Seth. The bottle of Chablis called to her from downstairs. That and a self-involved memoir helped her finally conk out for a few hours. At dawn, the trash truck woke her as it did a seven-point turn in the cul-de-sac. Kitty climbed out of the couch, packed Bobby's lunch, and laid out bowls for cereal before taking her two empty wine bottles out to the box of recycling behind the garage. She nearly tripped over the upended rosebushes on her way back.

I should have come out and taken care of these last night. I can put them back in the ground, but I doubt they'll survive the winter. Once the roots have been exposed to the air like this, it's pretty dicey.

Kitty had planted the yellow garden under her mother's direction. When they built the house, Mother had Seth send her a site plan and designed the garden sight unseen. Gardening in North Carolina was nothing like gardening in Rhode Island. Digging a hole in Mother's garden was like scooping out a hole in a chocolate cake. Digging a hole in Kitty's garden required a pick axe. In order to plant the rose bushes in Mother's plan, Kitty had excavated holes three times the size the plants needed and refilled them with amended top soil before planting each bush. Kitty did all the work but had no say in the design. Seth gave his mother-in-law a budget to stay within and let her tell Kitty what to do. Mother loved Seth.

Kitty initially thought Daisy's misdeeds were a tragedy, but perhaps it was a blessing in disguise. It had been over fifteen years since she planted the garden. Specimens had been replaced if they died or outgrew their place, but she had not changed the basic design. She could start over now; Mother could not grouse from the grave.

Maybe I'll plant some pink peonies like Dad used to have. Kitty's father had been allowed a corner of Mother's garden to plant his flowers. In a three foot square he had a riot of peonies in varying shades of pink. Mother complained that they attracted ants, but Kitty loved their opulent nodding heads. Every spring, her father would cut a few choice blossoms and put them beside Kitty's bed in the middle of the night so she would wake up to the heady fragrance. Now that she thought of it, fragrance was the common thread that ran through her Dad's favorite flowers. He treasured the dark French lilac bush in the back corner of the yard. Its blooms seemed skimpy next to the lush lavender blossoms of the common lilacs but their scent was ten times more intense. He would fill Rose's bedroom with blossoms every year. *I wonder if lilacs would thrive here. The crepe myrtles look similar, but they are not the same. Even hydrangea is not the same here as it was near the ocean.*

She poked at the dried roots with the toe of her Dr. Scholl's. *These are ruined; I'll just replace them next spring.* She thought about the multicolored riot of color she had seen across the street from the chicken place in Virginia. *It would be fabulous to have a bouquet of multicolored roses in a bowl, like that painting by Fantin-Latour.*

By the time Bobby emerged from the kitchen with his backpack, Kitty had pulled up four more rose bushes and was hurling landscape plants into the compost heap.

"Mom, it's 7:08. We gotta go."

"I'll take him," Seth yelled from inside the house. "I'm leaving right now."

Kitty sat back on her heels and fought the urge to turn around and hurl a tiger lily at Seth's head. The calm she had gained from digging in the dirt had vanished the second she heard his voice. She held up a dirt-caked thumb over her head.

"Is that a yes?"

She shook her thumb several times in the air, sending a shower of red dirt over her pajamas and robe.

"Okay. See you tonight," Seth called from the deck. Then he was gone, without a word about what she told him the night before.

How can he act like nothing has changed? Well, maybe nothing has changed. What's really different about today? The only real difference is now I know I have the clap. That's my problem though, as far as he's concerned. I wonder if he'll even see a doctor. I doubt he even cares that he's got gonorrhea. For all I know, he's had it before. Can you get it more than once? Probably, especially if antibiotics clear it up.

Kitty was hungry. She wanted fluffy pancakes and maple syrup-glazed bacon and a thick mug of cocoa like she and Rose used to make themselves on Sunday mornings while their parents slept off their Saturday night. She had a drink instead. She poured herself half a glass of Seth's special orange juice that came in an elaborate glass bottle and filled the glass to the rim with the champagne she had bought to celebrate her forty-second birthday the following week. She and Seth celebrated their birthdays and anniversaries the same way each year, they would go to the Capital Steakhouse where he would order the biggest steak on the menu and she had a wedge of iceberg lettuce. She looked forward to the decadent blue cheese dressing all year. They would bring home a piece of chocolate torte to share with a bottle of champagne. Not this year. Kitty was not about to sit across a table from Seth and celebrate anything. She would drink the champagne herself.

Bottle in hand, she climbed the stairs to the master bedroom and collapsed, face down across the bed. She couldn't sleep though. She could smell Seth in the room. She sniffed the satin duvet; it smelled fine. She stood up, gently pulled it off the bed and folded it neatly in quarters at the foot of the bed. Then she sniffed the cotton blankets, they smelled vaguely of Seth's Old Spice cologne. They were pulled off and piled near the door. They could be washed. She chugged champagne until it made her nose tickle then dropped the bottle in the bathroom sink. She went back to the bed and sniffed the sheets and pillow cases; they reeked of Seth. She yanked the sheets and mattress pad off the bed and shook the pillows out of the cases before hurling them over the balcony. They landed on the new sofa with a satisfying whump. She could soak the linens in bleach then wash them twice in hot water to get the smell out, but she would have to throw the pillows away. No amount of hot water would get Seth's smell out of the down filling.

She stumbled down the stairs and threw the sheets in the washing machine. She poured half a bottle of bleach in, selected the hottest setting, and turned it on. She then grabbed the small vacuum and a can of disinfectant spray and head back upstairs. She was a little tipsy standing on the mattress, but she managed to vacuum every inch of it, steadying herself by hanging on to the high upholstered headboard. Once every inch of the master bedroom was vacuumed, from the ceiling fan to the carpet in the walk-in closet, she sprayed every surface with Lysol. No bacteria could survive her spray can of wrath.

The effects of a bottle of champagne on an empty stomach hit Kitty's system like a pillow to the back of the head. She needed to lie down. She pulled the silk duvet into the master bedroom closet and curled up like a kitten until the ever-present sound of lawn movers woke her, just in time to pick up Bobby from school.

SIX

A woodcut of vaguely Egyptian people sowing grain graced the cover of the Pinnacle Pointe Church bulletin in celebration of Labor Day. Few of the people tucking their bulletins in the pew hymnals had ever labored a day in their lives. Only the best Magnuson families attended Pinnacle Pointe. A parking pass with the outline of PPC's neo-gothic facade on a Mercedes window held as much status as the three-pointed star on the hood; not that anyone in the congregation, other than Kitty, would have known a flying buttress from a lancet window. Kitty didn't like the church - the theology was muddy, parking was a nightmare, and the public address system struck her as simply wrong.

Seth didn't consider his family's spiritual needs when he chose where they would spend their Sunday mornings. Seth had turned his back on their Catholicism when his parents turned their backs on him. When they had moved to North Carolina, he wanted a new life without all the rules and strict mores they had both been brought up under. Seth now considered church attendance a networking tool. The coffee hour presented an excellent opportunity to glad hand wealthy golfers and sell them his latest clubs. It further served Seth's purposes for the Haskell family to be seen as pretty, prompt and pious by the important people of Magnuson. Kitty and the children were in their pew in the first balcony by 10:40 every Sunday morning. It wasn't engraved with their name as it would have been in Colonial days, but it was the Haskell family pew just the same. A strange family tried to sit there one Sunday morning but after Stacia Tate Curran had a few choice words with the mother during the coffee hour, they never made that mistake again.

"Should I save a space for Dad?" Bobby asked as they slid into their pew that Sunday morning. Kitty didn't know whether Seth would slip in after the second hymn as usual, or not. They still hadn't spoken since their confrontation Thursday night. She had passed out long before he came in Friday night. Seth had left at the crack of dawn to host a golf tournament on Saturday and was still out when Kitty had gone to bed. She was beginning to wonder if the whole thing had been nothing more than a bad dream.

"I'm sure he'll be along shortly," Kitty replied. She brushed Bobby's hair out of his eyes. "You are getting a haircut this week, buster. I don't care if boys are wearing their hair in their face these days. You look ridiculous."

Kitty waved to Stacia and her family as they filed in next to her father in the Tate pew. Stacia's son, Marcus, looked as green as his willow-colored dress shirt. Kitty remembered the maid telling her that Marcus had been recruited to practice with the high school's soccer team. Kitty could appreciate Marcus wanting to play with the older boys, but the team was known for their drinking parties. She wished he would stick to his old neighborhood soccer buddies instead.

Weldon sat down and rested one of his long arms around Lana's shoulders. Their daughter had only been away at school a week or two, but he seemed to be hanging on to her as if she had been gone for years. Lana crossed her long toffee-colored legs and Kitty noticed that her miniskirt left no question that Lana was a woman. Kitty heard her mother's voice in her head, saying, 'That young girl should have more respect for the Lord's house. Do young people have no shame these days?' *They don't*, Kitty thought. *Shame has become extremely unfashionable these days.*

Kitty wouldn't have dared wear a short skirt to church as a girl, but no one batted an eye nowadays. When they were young, Kitty and Rose obediently wore a dowdy dirndl in either blue or brown with a starched, white Peter-Pan collared shirt to services in the drafty stone Our Lady of Assumption chapel. The only adornment Mother approved of was a single strand of fake pearls. When she was a girl, she dressed to worship God. As a woman, Kitty dressed to be seen. Seth didn't care how much she spent on clothes, as long as she looked fashionable and thin. Kitty ran her fingertips over the polished cotton of her black sundress. She bought it the week before to show off her pale shoulders amongst the sea of late-summer bronzed beauties and highlight the turquoise necklace and bangle Seth brought back from his golf junket to Arizona the previous winter. She slipped off the heavy bangle and dropped it in her woven jute bag. She couldn't wear it anymore; it felt like a manacle.

The offertory music changed from a Mozart piece to Bach and pulled Kitty back to the present. Pinnacle Pointe's organ was reputed to be one of the best in the Southeast, and the congregants were all very proud. Stacia's grandparents had donated it when the church was built in the 50's and left a generous endowment to keep it maintained and pay the organist's salary. He was a squirrelly looking little man, but he had gone to Juilliard.

At the end of the piece, an usher carried a red leather-bound tome to the altar. Before the service, people wrote prayer requests for their aunt's gallbladder surgery or their co-worker's cancer diagnosis at a walnut lectern discreetly tucked in a tiny alcove in a corner of the elaborate narthex. Those prayer requests were the most efficient way to find out who was sick, unemployed or dead. The young associate minister opened the book and intoned, "For Mary Osgood who passed away Tuesday following a stroke."

"Lord, hear our prayer," the congregation droned.

"For a friend, who is experiencing marital problems."

Kitty heard someone whisper her name and chuckle behind her. A flush rushed up her neck. *Is this some kind of cruel joke? Does someone know what's going on with Seth and me? How could anybody know?* She turned her head, trying to look casually at the crowd but couldn't see who had laughed. She tried to catch Marni Kaur's eye, sitting three rows behind them, but Marni was busily blowing her nose. A woman Kitty recognized as the parent of another senior smiled vaguely at her. Kitty smiled back and quickly turned back around.

A bubble of doubt rose in her chest. *Should I be asking for prayers? What would I write? Please pray for Kitty who has been unjustly cursed with a philandering husband? I don't think so. I don't want any of these people to know my secrets.* She looked down at the balding pates below and didn't want to know what awful things were going on in their lives. The moment passed. She was able to slip back into her role of wife and mother. If anyone looked up, they saw only the passive little smile of Mrs. Kitty Haskell. When the minister read out the next prayer request, Kitty mumbled, "God hear our prayer," as disingenuously as ever.

❧

"What time did you tell the bakery we would pick up Brett's birthday cake?" Weldon asked as the Curran family hiked across the Pinnacle Pointe parking lot to Stacia's behemoth Wagoneer. "Should we swing by now, on the way home from church, or do you want me to go out later and get it?"

Stacia opened the passenger-side door and let the blast of sweltering air escape before gingerly perching on the edge of the hot leather seat. "Marcus honey, hand me that canvas bag. I can't touch this seat belt buckle with my bare hands."

"You did order it, right?"

Stacia had not ordered the cake. She had conveniently forgotten that it was her brother-in-law's birthday, because she didn't want to host the yearly birthday cookout. Lana would be taking the bus back to Chapel Hill that evening and Stacia wanted to spend as much time as possible with her. She wanted to know every detail about Lana's roommates and her classes.

"Of course I did," Stacia replied as she adjusted her giant white sunglasses. They were almost as large as her head.

"Liar," Weldon teased as he started the car and cranked up the air conditioning. "Let's stop at that new bakery - Jumping Joe's, Bouncing Toad ..."

"Hoppin' Frog, Dad," Lana sighed from the backseat. "It's only like the raddest place in town."

"Like you would know," Marcus said. Lana shoved her little brother.

"You run in there and get a cake, and maybe a pie or something," Weldon continued, ignoring his children fighting in the back seat. "The kids and I will run into the Harris Teeter and get hot dogs and some burgers."

"Do we have to have them over to the house?" Stacia sniffed. She liked spending time with Brett, he was sweet and funny, but Stacia did not want his annoying wife, Eulalie, and their whiny little girl, Anita, in her house. "Couldn't we go out?"

"No, Mama always grilled hot dogs and hamburgers out back for Brett's birthday." Brett was a six foot tall, burly thirty-eight year old man but he would always be Weldon's little brother. After their mother passed away, Weldon took it on himself to throw his brother's birthday party every year.

"It has got to be a hundred degrees out today. I don't want to be standing over a hot grill this afternoon, and I'm sure you don't either.

Why don't we take Brett out somewhere where there is air conditioning?"

"No," Weldon said with uncharacteristic resolution. "We'll do it the way Mama did it."

"I'll grill the burgers this year, Dad." Marcus said from the back seat.

"Thanks, buddy," Weldon replied.

When they got to the shopping plaza, the Currans scattered. Weldon and Marcus went into the grocery store to get the food, Lana went into the Hallmark store to get balloons, and Stacia stepped into Hoppin' Frog Cakes and Treats. The sparkling glass cases displayed a rainbow of cakes and cookies lined up like soldiers poised to kill any dieter's resolve. Stacia picked out a small dark-chocolate torte and asked the perky salesgirl to write 'Happy Birthday' on it in white icing.

"Sure, ma'am," the girl replied as she carefully lifted the cake out of the case and disappeared into the recesses of the shop. When she came back, she said, "Can I offer you a cup of coffee while you wait? It's going to be a few minutes."

"I'll have a small black coffee and could you wrap up that chess pie for me?" Stacia studied the case. In the lower-left corner were some plain vanilla-looking cupcakes. Her sniveling little niece, Anita, seemed to be allergic to everything put in front of her. Stacia doubted the kid could have that many food restrictions and still manage to be so chubby. She suspected Eulalie made a big deal out of Anita's diet to get her extra attention. "And throw in one of those boring looking things too." Eulalie would have nothing to complain about now.

Stacia retrieved her coffee and sat at one of the bistro tables shoehorned between the refrigerated drinks case and the day-old bread rack to think through which serving pieces would be best for that afternoon's menu over a cigarette. She didn't pay attention to the customer entering with a blast of hot breeze. The prosaic black pants suit and flat black bob could have been any real estate agent or sales rep, until the woman opened her mouth.

"Are these tarts fresh?" Marni Kaur demanded in her grating Long Island accent. She tapped her garish red fingernails on the glass leaving oily fingerprints behind.

"We bake everything fresh every morning," the salesgirl replied with a smile. From her perch in the corner, Stacia could see she was making an obscene gesture at Marni behind her back. Stacia hoped Marni would make her purchases and leave without seeing her sitting in the corner. She would have to deal with Eulalie later on; one annoying woman was enough for the day.

"Then I'll take two key lime tarts, two ham and cheese croissants and two apple strudel. And throw in a blueberry muffin too. Those are his favorite." The young woman busied herself putting the smallest, least filled pieces of pastry in a bag.

Marni turned to pull a couple of bottles of Dr. Pepper from the cooler and spotted Stacia. "Hey!" Marni gushed as she tucked the bottles under her arm. "Imagine running into you here."

"Hello, Marni. You and Connor going on a picnic?"

"Oh no," Marni replied. She put the bottles on the counter and hurriedly thrust a few bills at the salesgirl. "I'm showing a house at noon then meeting a friend."

"We're having a cookout this afternoon. Connor is welcome to come have a burger with us," Stacia replied. She hated the thought of Connor sitting home alone while his mother was working.

"Connor is with his dad this weekend. It's his step-sister's second birthday."

Stacia had heard that Marni's ex-husband had married a young associate in his firm but she did not know they'd had a child. *To see him with a young new wife and child must be driving Marni bananas.*

The baker emerged from the back and handed Stacia her cake as Marni gathered her pastries. Marni peeked into the square white box. "I pegged you as someone who made homemade birthday cakes."

"It's a last-minute celebration," Stacia said through grit teeth. She turned to Marni with an imperious smile. "Did you get my message regarding the open house? With Kitty not feeling well, the bake sale was a no-go."

Marni rolled her eyes. "Kitty's fine. She's not really sick."

"Still as hospitality chair, you should have ...."

Marni opened the door and replied, "You know what, I can't do hospitality this year. Kitty'll just have to go it alone from now on."

"Excuse me? When were you planning to ...." Marni walked out of the bakery and hopped into her car as if Stacia were not even talking.

The nerve of that woman! She is definitely on my shit list now.

Stacia did her best to avoid Eulalie all afternoon. She played games with the kids, took an inordinate amount of time to make a simple cole slaw, then stood over the hot grill for an hour chatting with Lana while Eulalie sat in the shade nursing a beer. After all the cake was eaten and the ice cream put back in the freezer, Eulalie carried the empty platter into the kitchen. "It sure was nice for y'all to have us over this afternoon," Eulalie said.

Stacia took the platter and slipped it into the sink full of soapy water. "Weldon likes to see his brother on his birthday."

"Still," Eulalie picked up the brown terry cloth towel with *Baillie* embroidered on it that Stacia used to wipe the dog's muddy paws after their walks and wiped down the kitchen table. "It's nice to get together."

Stacia pulled the towel out of Eulalie's hand. "That is not a kitchen towel." She threw it toward the sink and wiped the table down with a soapy dish cloth.

"Maybe your people have special towels just for wiping down the table. A towel's a towel to my people." Stacia grit her teeth and dried the table with a clean linen towel. She was determined not to rise to the bait. Eulalie took every opportunity to remind Stacia that she was the odd man out in the Curran family. Eulalie didn't approve of Weldon marrying a white girl even though the Tate and Curran families had been business associates for decades. Nothing Stacia could say could yank Eulalie into the twenty-first century.

Stacia put the dish towel in the hamper under the sink. "What do you hear about the election? It'll be wild if Jimmy Carter wins, huh?"

"I don't follow the politics," Eulalie replied. "Hey, it's too bad about your friend, Kitty."

"What are you talking about?"

"Kitty and her husband. They're splitting up."

"Excuse me?"

"I heard from Kimmi Fitzgerald, that her cousin overheard Marni Kaur say something about it last week. I just about fell out when she told me but then, that Marni never showed up at the PTA meeting and ..."

"You don't know what you're talking about. If Kitty and Seth were having trouble, I would know."

"Would you? I heard ..."

At that moment Anita ran into the kitchen holding Baillie like a stuffed toy and Stacia was distracted from the thought of Kitty's marriage by the immediate need to save her dog.

SEVEN

When Kitty and the children pulled into Azalea Lane, Kitty's sister, Rose, was standing in their front yard with her stiff black purse securely clenched in the crook of her elbow like a bizarre lawn jockey. Kitty wished Seth had not persuaded the sisters to rent out their mother's house and Rose had stayed in Rhode Island. Rose and Kitty were getting far more for the seventy-five year old cape than it was worth - the cellar was damp, the bedrooms were small and the kitchen was pokey - but no amount of money could compensate Rose for losing the only home she had ever known. Kitty had left at eighteen. Rose had never moved out. She had taken a job in Providence after nursing school and had still slept in the same twin bed she had as a toddler.

Kitty liked her sister more when they only saw each other for a week each summer. Rhode Island was like another universe. She and Rose spent a week numbing their toes in the frigid water, capturing hermit crabs with the kids, and eating as many fried clams as they could stomach. Then, they didn't speak until the next visit. Now, Rose appeared every Sunday afternoon at noon expecting to be fed Sunday dinner. She hovered like a mosquito, always annoying and occasionally harboring contagion.

Kitty stopped in the driveway near where Rose was standing on the front walk and rolled her window down. The mid-day heat rushed in with a vengeance. "Rose. You're here. I hope you haven't been waiting long."

"I have been admiring your new day lilies. Yellow is such a lovely color. Mother would be appalled. You need to get out here and weed."

"It's just been so hot. I've let it go a bit."

Rose cocked one over-plucked eyebrow and replied, "I can see that." She tugged at her polyester blend blouse and gasped, "It's sweltering out here. I am dying for a glass of lemonade."

"You really should get a sleeveless cotton blouse or two. What do you say we run over to Trent's later? They're having a sale."

"At my age? I could never wear a sleeveless blouse."

Bobby tapped Kitty on her bare shoulder and whispered, "Isn't Aunt Rose younger than you, Mom?"

"Shut up, butthead. Mom has tennis player arms," Becky hissed. "Get out and open the garage door. It's your turn."

"If I had a key," Rose whined as she fanned herself dramatically, "I could have let myself in."

"Yes," Kitty said. "I keep meaning to make one for you." She pulled into the garage and jumped out to close the door behind them.

"You wouldn't give Aunt Rose a key to our house if it were on fire," Becky giggled.

"Don't I know it."

The kids disappeared up to their rooms while Kitty took her time walking through the house to open the front door. Rose was standing on the front porch holding a large empty Tupperware container. Not only did Rose expect a free meal including a dessert, preferably chocolate, she expected Kitty to cook enough on Sundays for Rose to take home leftovers to last until Wednesday.

"How was church?"

"Fine, how was Mass?"

"Beautiful. That Father Abrams is wonderful. Such a beautiful voice." Rose put her ratty old black purse on the foyer table on top of a stack of catalogs. "You and Seth should come next week and listen."

"We are fine at PPC. You know Seth makes good contacts there."

"I worry about your soul sometimes, Mary Katherine," Rose sighed.

So do I.

"I told you, people call me Kitty here. Seth thinks Mary Katherine sounds too nunny." A wave of nausea bubbled within her. *I'm not sure if taking the last of the antibiotics on an empty stomach was such a good idea.* Kitty turned to go into the kitchen. "Would you like a mimosa?" Rose murmured a distracted affirmative to Kitty's back. The JC Penny catalog on the foyer table would disappear into Rose's purse.

A few minutes later, Seth came roaring down the stairs. "Rose!" He enveloped her in a hug. "How's my favorite sister-in-law?"

"Hi, Seth," Rose sighed like a schoolgirl. She was a sucker for Seth's salesman's grin and smarmy charm. If Rose knew that Seth called her Frump-a-Dump behind her back, she would have been crushed. Kitty agreed that her sister needed to stop getting $2 haircuts and lose a few pounds, but Rose was not like Seth. She didn't care about looking attractive, just about being right.

"So, how's that couch working out for you?"

"Oh Seth, it's wonderful! Thank you so much for giving it to me." Rose touched him on the arm below the band of his sky blue LaCoste shirt. "I can't thank you enough," she gushed.

Seth shook off her touch and opened the hall closet door. He rustled around in the bottom of the closet. "Hey Kitty," he yelled. "Where is my tennis racket?"

"Not in there," Kitty yelled back from the kitchen. "Check the garage. I think Bobby used it when he did that clinic."

Seth flew through the kitchen and into the garage drifting a cloud of cologne behind him. Kitty followed him into the garage. "Are you really going to play tennis?"

"Hal Efland bet me $100 that I couldn't beat him at tennis and golf in the same day."

Kitty closed the door behind her. "Did you leave Rose standing on the lawn in this heat while you were upstairs?" she hissed. "And why weren't you in church?"

Seth found his racket hanging next to Bobby's baseball equipment. He leaned against the supply shelves and whispered, "I thought I'd give you a little ... you know... space."

Kitty was amazed; Seth was actually blushing.

"I thought you might need some time to talk to your sister, you know, without me."

"So you're going to play tennis? All day?"

"Mary Katherine?" Rose called from the kitchen. "I thought you were making me a mimosa?"

Kitty grabbed the racquet out of Seth's hand. "How 'bout I go play Hal and you stay here and make dinner for Rose?"

He tucked a stray strand of Kitty's auburn hair behind her ear and whispered, "Can we talk about this later? She'll hear you."

Kitty handed the racquet to him. "You owe me."

"Well, gotta go." Seth jumped into his Mercedes and sped out of the garage. Kitty walked back into the kitchen and slammed the door.

"Is he coming back?" Rose asked.

Kitty pulled one of the expensive bottles of champagne that Seth was saving for their anniversary from the extra refrigerator and handed it to her sister. "Why don't you make the mimosas, Rose? I could use a drink."

Kitty took the makings of a chicken dinner out of the refrigerator while Rose poured orange juice into a pitcher. "You know, Mary Katherine, the juice at Food Lion is two dollars less than this stuff."

"I don't care, Rose." Kitty dropped the chicken on the counter. "Seth likes the juice from the co-op."

"Well! If Seth likes the fancy schmancy kind, I guess that makes it worth the extra dollar. Us working people have to settle for Tropicana."

"Shut up and pour me a drink, Rose."

Rose added half the bottle of champagne to the pitcher and poured them each a tall flute of the bubbly liquid. Kitty sipped her mimosa and rubbed herbed butter under the chicken's skin while Rose blathered on about the other nurses on the maternity ward. Kitty was only listening with one ear. She was thinking about her husband. *Was he really going to play tennis with Hal? Did he even have his tennis clothes with him when he left? Did he go out just to avoid me? Is he with some girl right now?*

Rose was fussing over how complicated Kitty's oven was to set when Becky and Bobby came downstairs. Kitty could tell from their expressions that they were feeling guilty about something. "Mom?" Bobby asked. "Since Dad is out, would you and Aunt Rose mind if we went to go see *Silent Movie*?"

"But sweetie," Kitty said as she gave Becky a 'please don't leave me alone with her' look. "Your Aunt Rose is here. I'm roasting a chicken."

"Don't change your plans for little old me," Rose whined. "You two go ahead. You won't have time to do stuff like that once the semester heats up." The kids were gone before Kitty could come up with a decent excuse to keep them home. Now that it was just the two of them, the chicken went back in the refrigerator and Sunday dinner became a big salad, a batch of brownies, and a bottle of Merlot.

After dinner, Rose disappeared while Kitty slowly loaded the dishwasher. The pitcher of mimosas and several glasses of wine had left her tipsy. Kitty paused to let the room stop spinning and looked up at the ceiling. She could hear Daisy's collar jingling as she followed Rose from room to room. Five minutes later, Rose returned looking like the cat that caught the canary.

"What were you doing upstairs?" Kitty demanded.

"I had to use the bathroom."

"There's a bathroom down here."

"I like your bathroom. It smells nice." Rose picked up Kitty's wine glass and drank the remains her wine. "So, what's going on? Why is Seth sleeping in the guest room?"

"He has been snoring lately. I think he might have a sinus infection."

"Then why are you the one taking the antibiotics?"

"You looked through my vanity drawers?"

"What is wrong with you?"

"Nothing serious," Kitty said and slammed the dishwasher shut. "Everything's fine."

"Mary Katherine." It was spooky the way Rose could channel their mother's voice when she wanted to. "What did you do to make your husband leave your bed?"

"It wasn't anything I did. It was him. He went out and got gonorrhea and then had the nerve to give it to me." It was a relief to finally say it, like diving to the bottom of a lake and finally resurfacing to exhale.

"That's awful," Rose sighed as if Kitty were an errant child caught misbehaving.

"Yes, it is." Kitty reached for another bottle of wine. "Thank you."

"You should be ashamed of yourself. Why can't you satisfy him?"

EIGHT

The next morning, Kitty put a little extra effort into making her children's lunches, a salad with sliced chicken and grapes for Becky and three peanut butter and jelly sandwiches for Bobby. *If I can't satisfy my husband, at least I can make my children happy.* She slipped a cut up apple and a bag of pretzels into Becky's lunch box, and some chips and a cookie into a paper grocery sack for Bobby. He was too cool to carry a lunch box.

Kitty chugged down a bitter cup of black coffee hoping the caffeine would wake her up and make her head stop pounding. She hadn't slept well at all. Rose's question kept skittering through the recesses of her mind. Why couldn't she satisfy Seth? What was it about her that was so lacking? She had done everything that was expected of her and she still came up short. The same thought kept coming back to her mind - this was not the way her life was supposed to be. She was not supposed to be the pathetic middle-aged suburban housewife waiting up half the night for her cheating husband to deign to come home. On the other hand, she couldn't put her finger on exactly what she was supposed to be doing at this point in her life. If she had never married Seth, where would she be by now? Would she have stayed in Rhode Island and taken care of her parents, instead of leaving Rose to carry that burden herself? Could she have been a museum curator by now? Or, would she have married some other bozo and been in a similar situation somewhere else?

"Mom!" Becky shouted from the second floor.

"Come down if you want to talk to me," Kitty called back. She rubbed her aching head. "And stop yelling!"

Becky bounced into the kitchen. Her youth was galling. "Is Renee coming today?"

Kitty's hand slipped. Grape jelly smeared across her thumb instead of the bread. She had forgotten that the maid was coming that morning. She raised her thumb to her mouth, but resisted licking the sticky sweet goodness off at the last second.

Kitty wiped her thumb on the dishcloth then handed Becky her lunchbox. "Today is Monday. Right?"

"Can you ask her not to move the project I have laid out on my floor?"

"Sure, honey. I'm sure she will be more than willing to not vacuum your room. I'll just have her change the sheets. Pull your laundry out into the hallway, and she won't even need to go over to that side of the room."

Bobby poked his head over the banister. "Has anyone seen my calculator?"

"Here I come." Kitty ran up the stairs. She had to stop for a moment in the hall to let her stomach settle before going in to help Bobby rifle through his backpack and under his bed. On her way back downstairs to continue the search, she poked her head into the guest room. Seth was standing naked in front of the closet. "The maid is coming today."

"Good, I'm out of clean boxers."

Kitty walked into the room, pulled the last pair of white cotton boxers from the highboy and, handed them to Seth. She sat on the unmade bed. "This drawer was full the other day. How are you going through these so quickly?"

Seth took the boxers from her and stepped over a pile of dirty clothes into the bathroom. Kitty picked them up and folded them before putting them in the hamper.

"Why do you clean before she comes? Isn't that what we pay her for?"

"You need to hide your stuff under the sink, Seth."

"I am not hiding my things from the maid."

"But—"

"Make something up." Seth spread toothpaste on his toothbrush. "Say I snore and you just couldn't take it anymore," he said with his toothbrush in his mouth. "You're a smart girl. I'm sure you can pull off acting put out."

Bobby stuck his head in the door and demanded, "Mom, my calculator?"

"I'm sorry, honey. When did you use it last? Did you check the car?"

Seth emerged from the bathroom in navy chinos and a pink oxford. Kitty was struck by how much he still looked the same as he did when they were first married. "How's soccer going?" he asked Bobby.

"We have a game this afternoon. Are you coming?"

"I don't know." Seth fumbled with the buttons on his right cuff as he watched Kitty pull up the sheets and fluff the pillows on the bed. "I may need to work late. I'll try."

With a sigh, Kitty buttoned his cuff for him and straightened the back of his collar. "Can you run Bobby to school this morning? I need to get ready for Renee."

"I don't understand why you use her. She didn't vacuum my office last time and she always folds my pants wrong."

"Please Seth. It would be a big help. You drive right past the school."

Seth slipped his wallet in his pocket. He absently kissed the top of her head. She didn't protest. It was too much of an effort to push him away.

"Bobby, grab your stuff," Seth said. "And your calculator is on the coffee table. Right where you left it."

After they left and she sent Becky on her way, Kitty went back up to the guest room to finish tidying up before the cleaners came. *Seth is right. There is nothing so strange about a middle-aged man sleeping in the guest room. Lots of guys snore. The maid can't tell if we're still having sex. For all she knows, he starts the night in the master bedroom and then goes into the guest room in the middle of the night.*

In the bathroom, she made sure the toilet was flushed, tucked Seth's bottles of hair tonic under the sink, and threw away the used Q-tips he left on the side of the sink. She picked up a few wadded-up tissues that had missed the trash and noticed a pale-blue sheet of paper in the trash can. She fished it out and read the tiny type. It was a pamphlet from a walk-in clinic downtown on the possible side effects of getting a shot of penicillin to treat gonorrhea. Stapled to the sheet was the paperwork from Seth's appointment the day before. Kitty felt like she had been punched in the stomach.

This is really happening. He didn't play tennis with Hal. He went to some clinic to get a shot. How many other times has he gone to that clinic?

Kitty ripped the paper up into tiny pieces and flushed them down the toilet.

She staggered out to the hallway. Seth's cologne still lingered in the air. His voice echoed in the stairwell taunting her. His shoes threatened to trip her at the top of the stairs. She had to get out of that house.

Renee would be there soon. Kitty was in no mood to make polite conversation with the maid. She quickly changed into tennis whites, left the sliding glass door unlocked for Renee, and raced over to the tennis courts. She and Marni Kaur had a standing tennis date for 11:00, but she couldn't wait two hours. Kitty needed to hit something now.

The tennis pro for the Overlook Swim and Tennis Club was nowhere to be found when Kitty arrived, so she let herself in with the hide-a-key. Its location under a rock was a poorly kept secret. It threatened to be another scorcher of a day, but she barely noticed. She rolled the ball machine out of its closet and set it on high. The machine made for a good partner; it stoically kept her moving and allowed her to tease out her tangled thoughts. With each ball she connected with, another realization hit her.

Seth never even bothered to deny he is sleeping around.

Slam.

He wasn't sorry when I asked him about it. Surprised, but not sorry.

Kitty wiped sweat and tears from her eyes.

He didn't seem all that surprised that he had a disease. He was surprised I knew. He seemed more embarrassed than sorry.

Tears clouded her vision, but she managed to connect with each ball and launch it cleanly over the net. *He didn't do anything when I told him. I was expecting some kind of grand gesture of contrition - jewelry, flowers, something. Who am I kidding? That's never going to happen.*

He didn't even apologize.

Slam.

He's assuming that if he just gives me enough space, I'll just get over it and move on.

She recalled how that morning, Seth had left his shirts draped over the banister for her to take to the dry cleaners like any other Monday. She was going to take them.

He's right. I will just get over it and move on.

I am such an idiot.

She remembered Dr. Bukalis saying that she and Seth should contact all their sexual partners and wondered how many that would be. She smashed a ball with such force, it stuck in the fence at the far end of the court. *He's probably been cheating on me all along.*

The next ball grazed the top of the net.

I just didn't want to see it.

Kitty barely connected with the next ball.

Who am I kidding? This is my problem, not his.

"Hey! Kitty!" Molly Blevins called from the gate as Dana, Molly's ancient Irish Setter, lumbered onto the court and pawed at one of the bright yellow balls littering the far court.

Kitty blinked back into her surroundings. Sweat was pouring down her face and her mouth was bone dry. Far more tennis balls than she remembered hitting rolled around Dana's paws. A ball flew across the net and hit Kitty squarely in the gut, knocking her on her bottom.

"Oh my God!" Molly yelled. She sprinted to the machine and turned it off before it could hurl another ball at Kitty. "You okay?"

"Fine," Kitty grunted as she pushed herself to her feet again. She wiped her face with a towel and tried to take a deep breath. Dana meandered over to Kitty with a slobbery ball to get her grey-flecked muzzle rubbed. Molly brought the dog with her everywhere she could. The poor old thing was incontinent and half-blind, but she loved to be outside with people.

"What's gotten into you today?" Molly asked. "You were hitting those balls like you wanted to kill someone. Did you and Seth have a fight?"

"Of course not." Kitty bounced on her toes, wishing Molly would shut up and go away. She was feeling clear-headed and physically powerful for the first time in days and didn't want to lose the feeling. "We never fight."

"Every couple fights sometimes." Molly's upper arms flapped as she bounced a ball in front of her. Kitty made a mental note to add more push ups to her own upper-body workout. At the same time, Kitty admired Molly's spunk to wear a halter top and cut-off jeans out in public with those arms. Molly was what her mother would have disparaged as a free spirit.

"Come on, there's bound to be things you disagree on."

Kitty bounced a ball on her racket. "No, not really."

Molly caught the ball mid-bounce and tossed it toward the ball machine. She touched Kitty's shoulder and asked, "Kitty, what's going on with you?"

Kitty flinched. "I'm just distracted." Kitty wasn't about to tell Molly about what was going on between her and Seth, it was bad enough that Rose knew her shame.

"I'm just worried about Bobby. He couldn't find his calculator this morning. He seems so sullen and scatterbrained these days. I thought girls were the ones that act all hormonal at this age." Their boys were the foundation of Kitty and Molly's friendship. They became friends when they both signed up to be room parent for their sons' kindergarten class, both built houses in Overlook and, were the founding members of the neighborhood's on-again-off-again book club. They had supported each other through construction crews repeatedly cutting their power lines and inscrutable book club choices, as well as playground bullies and the boys' awful third-grade teacher who insisted they write everything in cursive.

Molly nodded pensively. Kitty rushed on, warming to her subject, "And, he's been acting all sulky lately. The other day, Seth wanted to go to the driving range and work on Bobby's swing but Bobby insisted on spending the afternoon reading *The Lord of the Rings*. Now I'm glad he's reading, you know I love those books, but Seth so infrequently wants to spend one on one time with Bobby that I was surprised."

"Are you sure nothing else is bothering you? You're obviously upset about something," Molly said. "Your eyes are all red and you're shaking like a leaf."

Kitty turned her back on Molly and took a long drink from her water bottle. "I'm fine. I'm just dehydrated and a little annoyed that Marni is late."

Molly stopped playing tug-of-war with Dana for the ball in the dog's mouth and looked at Kitty incredulously, "Marni? You're going to play tennis with Marni?"

"The fall round-robin starts in a few weeks and we need to practice."

Concern clouded Molly's open face as she tugged the ball away from Dana and tossed it in the machine. "I don't think she's coming. We saw her driving out on Sweetgum a few minutes ago."

"Really?" Kitty tried to pull off a casual laugh. "She must have gotten the schedule mixed up. She'll probably be here tomorrow wondering where I am. Well, I'm here now. Guess I'll just reload and practice by myself for a while."

Molly patted Dana's haunches with a frown. "Are you sure you're all right? Do you want me to stay and help you here?"

"No," Kitty replied. "You finish your walk before it gets too hot out here for Dana."

"Okay, but why don't you come by later and we can talk if you want. I made some lemon bars." Kitty loved Molly, and her lemon bars, but she didn't want to be with her right now. Molly knew her far too well. She would ask too many questions.

Kitty took her time fetching the tennis balls from along the fence. *It's true what I said to Molly. Seth and I never fight. He has nothing to complain about, and I just don't complain.*

NINE

Renee Navarone was as much a drug dealer as any Columbian cocaine boss or street corner pot pusher. However, her clients' drug of choice wasn't cocaine or marijuana. It was secrets. Renee didn't bother to move furniture when she vacuumed, rarely dusted base boards, and left cobwebs in corners. Not one of her clients ever complained. They would never fire Renee. Like any successful dealer, Renee started her customers out with a few free samples: why the principal at the high school left suddenly, when the new Harris Teeter would break ground, and which doctors gave generous prescriptions for diet pills and painkillers. She breached the houses in Overlook, one by one, by offering free cleaning in exchange for referrals. For the first year or so, she subtly cultivated a taste for gossip in The Lookers by weaning them on the secrets of people from outside Overlook and then slowly introducing juicy morsels about those neighbors not in the inner circle. Renee's genius was to let each of The Lookers think that she was sharing secrets with her, and her alone, so their hearts would race with guilt whenever Renee's name came up in polite conversation.

Stacia Tate Curran was Renee's most important client, and her most distasteful. She was proud to say she cleaned for one of the Tates but left out the fact that Stacia was married to a black man. It stuck in her craw that Weldon and his children were so respectful and pleasant to her. She hated them, yet was careful to make Miss Stacia think that she was a loyal servant. If she pocketed the occasional pile of loose change or dollar bill, no one was the wiser.

That Monday morning, Stacia greeted Renee at the front door. She was concerned about what Eulalie said about Kitty and Seth

Haskell at the cookout. If something was going wrong between Kitty and Seth, Renee would know. "You coming from the Haskell's house?"

"Sure are," Renee replied. "Got to spend some time with that sweet dog Daisy too."

"Everything okay over at Kitty's house?"

Renee stepped into the master bedroom. "Miss Kitty was out." She returned a few minutes later with an armful of sheets and towels. "You'll never guess what I found under Betty Oliphant's girl's mattress yesterday." Stacia looked up from typing up the minutes of the most recent homeowners association meeting and waited. "Drugs! I found a whole baggie of pot, right there, tucked under the bed skirt. I bet her mama has no idea she's even smoking that stuff."

Stacia left her tall glass of iced tea sweating on the counter and followed Renee into the laundry room. "Shameful. I remember that girl selling me Girl Scout cookies. Do you think Betty suspects?"

"She's not paying no attention to that one. Miss Betty is all about the little boy these days. He's taking all sorts of drugs for his fits."

"Really? He is awfully high-strung." Suddenly the little boy's enthusiasm for jumping off the high dive that summer took on a different significance in Stacia's mind. "Are you sure?"

"I know my prescription drugs. Like that Eileen around the corner. She's having all sorts of trouble getting pregnant. There are hormone pills in the medicine cabinet and one of those special thermometers next to the bed."

"That is too bad." It was important to Stacia to keep up with what was going on in her community, but it also felt wrong to know something so personal and painful about Eileen. She and Weldon had struggled with infertility, and it had left scars on their relationship. Stacia made a mental note to spend some time with Eileen soon. She handed Renee the bottle of detergent. "I hope things work out for them. Infertility can be hard on a marriage."

"Yes ma'am, it sure can."

Stacia nudged the conversation toward the dirty laundry she wanted to hear about. "Still," she sighed dramatically, "it's better than being single."

"Spect so," Renee replied. She didn't sound convinced.

"I worry about Marni Kaur," Stacia said, baiting the hook. "She's all alone, with her son at his dad's so much these days."

"She's been having fun though. She's got a new man."

"Really?" Stacia wanted to tug the line, but she felt she needed to reel Renee in slowly. If Stacia seemed too eager for the information, Renee could suspect she really cared about what they were talking about. She stepped back into the kitchen and pulled the iced tea pitcher from the refrigerator. Renee followed her with a mop and a bucket of hot soapy water.

"This one gives her presents, but he don't stay over like the last one."

Stacia jumped up and sat on the counter so Renee could mop where she was standing. "Want some tea?"

Renee was all too eager to stop working and took the proffered glass. "He doesn't leave a toothbrush there or nothing."

"How long has she been seeing him?"

"A month maybe." Renee took a long sip of iced tea then, with a twinkle in her eye, said, "She bought all new underwear."

"Well, I hope she doesn't get her heart broken again. She told me her ex-husband and his new wife just had a baby," Stacia said as she stirred her iced tea with a long silver spoon. She sighed dramatically. "It seems you hear about marriages breaking up more and more these days."

Renee sloshed water across the kitchen floor and into Baillie's kibble. "True, true."

Stacia tried another route. "It's nice to still see happy couples. Take Kitty and Seth Haskell. They're an awful nice couple."

Renee snorted under her breath. "I think Miss Marni would like to do something about that. He's brushing his teeth in the guest room bath these days."

Seth Haskell! What an idiot!

"I'm sure there's a good reason for that," Stacia said as she jumped down and picked up the dog's food. It would upset Baillie's stomach if she ate kibble with dirty water in it. "Still, we probably should keep that information to ourselves."

"Of course Miss Stacia, you know I only tell you things 'cause you're the homeowners association lady and need to know these kinds of things."

"Well, all right then," Stacia replied.

❧

Stacia noticed Kitty's green Volvo near the tennis courts later that morning. She left her bag beside the pool fence and set out across the parking lot in nothing but her bathing suit to get to the bottom of this sleeping in separate bedrooms thing right away. With each tentative step, the gravel burned a sharp reminder into her bare feet of the compromise she made regarding the Overlook Swim & Tennis parking lot. Pavement would have been much easier on the feet, but gravel had better drainage so close to the bluff. It was also more economical for the homeowners association to maintain.

The parking lot had been the only compromise Stacia had been willing to make when it came to the pool and it still stung. She didn't care that the location, high on the ridge with a panoramic view of the lake, was impractical and took up two of the most lucrative lots in the subdivision. She had a clear vision for what the pool was going to be like and she would not budge. When she stood in the shallow end of the pool, she wanted to have the sensation that she could reach out and touch the surface of the lake. If that meant cutting all the trees down and grading the lot to within inches of the bluff edge, so be it.

The grading subcontractor had fought her tooth and nail. The man actually patted her on the head when he told her it was impractical to position the Overlook community pool on the ridge. He wanted to build the pool and tennis courts, along with a small playground, in the center of the subdivision like every other Walk, Chase and Court. When she didn't relent, he called Weldon and advised him to "keep his little lady in line." That subcontractor was promptly fired. Stacia gave another grading company the lucrative Overlook contract.

Stacia slipped inside the fence and was surprised to see Kitty practicing alone. *I thought I was the only person who liked to practice alone. Kitty is usually so social.* Kitty startled as Stacia let the gate clang shut behind her. She quickly wiped away the tear hanging off the tip of her upturned nose. "Hey Stacia," Kitty called tremulously. "Going for a swim?"

"I've got the Wilmington Open Water race on Sunday. Amy Lathorp turned fifty-one this year so I've got a shot at taking the fifty and under title."

"I've seen you out in the lake a few times," Kitty replied distractedly. She pulled a sweat towel from her bag and dabbed her face. Her eyes were swollen and red.

Crying while hitting tennis balls alone? This is bad. Very, very bad. Stacia picked up a ball from along the fence and tossed it into the hopper. *I can't believe Eulalie was right about Seth and Kitty being in trouble. I hate it when Eulalie is right.*

"You okay, Kitty?"

"Sure, why do you ask?" Kitty said as she tipped the practice machine back on its wheels and began pushing it toward the shed.

"Your eyes are all red and puffy."

"It's nothing. Allergies."

Kitty Haskell! You are such a terrible liar. "Leave that. Rory can put that away when he gets here."

"Where is Rory anyway? I thought the bylaws said the tennis pro had to be on the premises whenever the courts were in use." Kitty fumbled with the shed doors.

"His little girl —"

"Bernice?"

"She's going to First Street Elementary this year."

"That's wonderful! I heard she was having trouble in school."

"She just needs a little extra help. She has a slight learning disability," Stacia snapped. "Anyway, they don't provide bus service to the school, so Rory's hours are going to be slightly different for a while until he works out the transportation issues. He's hoping to find a teenager to help him with the afternoon pick up in exchange for private lessons."

Kitty pushed the practice machine into the shed and worked the pad lock. "You got her in, didn't you?"

Stacia blushed and adjusted the leg of her swim suit. "I made a few phone calls."

"Good for you. All those hours of PTA and school board meetings should be good for something." Kitty picked up her racquet. "Still, I wish I'd known Rory wouldn't be here. I thought he would be here to help us."

"Us?"

"I was supposed to meet Marni to get in shape for our round-robin but she stood me up."

Stacia felt a sour lump sink in her belly. *She doesn't know?* Puzzle pieces were beginning to fall into place in her mind and she didn't like the picture they made. "Wow," she sighed and backed out the gate.

"I know, right?" Kitty locked the gate and put the hide-a-key back. "I don't know what the deal is with her lately. I've called her twice about helping me with homecoming and she hasn't called me back."

Stacia looked at Kitty and felt a flash of protective rage wash over her. "Forget Marni, I'll help you with homecoming."

"But you don't even have a kid at Nance this year."

Stacia waved her fingers dismissively at the fact that she didn't have any position at the high school that year. "Don't you worry about that. I'll take care of everything."

Stacia had told Kitty that she was going to take care of everything and, damn it, she was going to do just that. The sharp stones did not bother her on her walk back to the pool; she was focused on forging a plan to deal with Seth Haskell. She let the rhythm of swimming lap after lap help her think through the situation. By the time she pulled off her goggles and stood at the shallow end of the pool, Stacia knew that keeping Kitty happy had to be her first priority. If something unfortunate had to happen to Marni, or even Seth within reason, Stacia was willing to sacrifice them.

The sun felt warm on her shoulders. Stacia ran her fingertips along the celadon tiles of the infinity pool edge and congratulated herself on how well they blended with the lake in the distance. Along the opposite shoreline, a few leaves high in the river birches had turned yellow like subtle golden highlights in a woman's hair. Time was getting short. She had to deal with Marni that day.

Stacia pulled herself out of the pool and sped home to get dressed. She called the Lakeview Real Estate office and learned that Marni was waiting for an appraiser at Deirdre and Liam's house. *It's good that they've decided to put the house on the market and move on. Still, I wish they'd listed it with an agent other than Marni. I'll have to speak to cousin Quentin to see if he can do anything about that.*

Five minutes later, she pulled up in front of Deirdre Logan's light brick ranch and walked up the circular driveway. Apparently, Deirdre had already let the landscapers go. Red dirt showed through the mulch in front of the bushes, grass was growing in the cracks in the driveway, and there were weeds in the lawn. Stacia paused on the front walk and watched Marni deadheading the begonias running up to the front door. Unflattering wrinkles strained the fabric across the back of her black tunic each time she bent forward to toss the dead flowers behind the bushes. Stacia thought Marni should lose a few pounds instead of trying to use an all black wardrobe to hide the extra ten pounds around her middle.

Marni quickly stood up when she saw Stacia standing behind her. "Hey, Stacia. I'm sorry, but Deirdre isn't home right now."

"Good. I came to see you," Stacia said. She shook a stray begonia petal off her hot pink sandal before stepping forward and jabbing one tiny finger into Marni's shoulder. "I'll get right to the point. Cut it out with Seth Haskell."

Marni stepped back knocking her cigarette ash off her pretentious colored cigarette. "How did you know?"

"I have my sources."

"Did Deirdre tell you?" Marni shook her foot where the ash had landed on her white mule. "Typical Deirdre, she'd do just about anything at this point if she thought it would get her back in your good graces."

Deirdre knows? Stacia turned and looked out into the cul-de-sac. *This is worse than I thought. I wonder who else knows.*

"It's not important who told me. People tell me things all the time." Stacia took another step toward Marni. "How long have you been carrying on with Seth?"

"Long enough," Marni retorted with an arch sneer. "Little Miss Perfect doesn't make him happy like I do."

Stacia rolled her eyes.

Marni's voice rose an octave as she said, "All that fancy cooking and impeccable taste couldn't keep him at home when he can have me."

"I'm sure he wants you for your rotten cooking. Look sweetie pie, you are not the first woman Seth Haskell has dallied with, nor will you be the last." Stacia turned back to face Marni. "Did Seth tell Kitty about the affair?"

"It's not an affair," Marni cried and stamped her foot. "Seth is going to leave Kitty any day now."

"For you? I don't think so," Stacia scoffed and started walking away.

"He's just waiting for the right moment to tell her."

"Seth's stupid, Marni, but he's not that stupid. Kitty's the best thing that ever happened to that man."

Marni ran after Stacia and grabbed her arm. "You're wrong! He wants to be with me."

Oh Lord, you're just as stupid as he is.

The appraiser's truck pulled into the driveway and Stacia waved. "Hey, Luke!" she called. Stacia brushed Marni's fingers from her arm and jeered, "You listen to me, you break it off with Seth Haskell today or you will never sell another house in this town."

Marni stepped back and almost fell into a bed of monkey grass. "You can't tell me what to do!"

"Watch me."

Stacia stopped and chitchatted with the appraiser for a few moments before continuing down the driveway. She didn't want him to think anything was amiss and it never hurt to be friendly with the people that established the property values in Overlook.

ℰ

Weldon was laying out pieces of white bread like playing cards along the island when Stacia walked into the kitchen. He had jars of peanut butter and jelly in front of him. "Hey honey," he said with a grin. Weldon always seemed pleasantly surprised to see his wife during the day. "You're just in time to give me a hand with these sandwiches."

"Are you feeding an entire kindergarten class?"

"Brett's got a crew starting to clear a road on the other side of the lake. There are no safe places to eat over there, so I volunteered to bring sandwiches over." He smiled sheepishly at his wife. "I thought PB&J was a good idea. No mayo to go bad and everyone likes peanut butter."

"Of course it was," Stacia replied and kissed Weldon on shoulder. "I'm sorry I'm in such a foul mood. I'd be happy to help. How about we complete the child's lunchbox motif? I'll cut up some apples and oranges and see if we have any unopened bags of chips."

"There are tons in the pantry. You need to stop buying so much food now that Lana's not here to eat it."

I'll do no such thing! She'll be back. Stacia found a Tupperware container that she wouldn't mind not getting back and started cutting up apples.

"So, why the foul mood?" Weldon asked. "A kid poop in the pool?"

"No, no, no, I had the pool to myself." Stacia tossed some sugar and cinnamon into the container of apples and gave it a shake. "No, that part of my day was fine. I just ran into Kitty Haskell. She was obviously upset about something. Then, I remembered something that Eulalie said to me at Brett's birthday party about Marni Kaur having a new man in her life, and well, let's just say I put two and two together and got three."

Weldon stopped spreading peanut butter down the row of bread slices. "Really? Marni Kaur? She doesn't seem like Seth's type."

"I know, right?"

"The guy has always had a wandering eye although, I thought he went for the young ones." Weldon had told Stacia that he had seen Seth around town over the years with assorted young women on his arm. The women were usually just under thirty, young enough to still have perky breasts and no stretch marks but old enough to know not to expect anything more from him than dinner and the occasional bauble. "Maybe he's going for middle-aged housewives now because his daughter is almost as old as the girls he used to go out with."

"Eww, that's a disturbing thought," Stacia said with a shudder. "But Marni? Why Marni? She's one of Kitty's best friends."

"With friends like that—"

"Anyhoo, I had a little chat with Marni and told her to quit it with Seth."

Weldon slapped the sandwiches together and swept them into a paper bag. "Does Kitty know?"

"I'm not sure but I'm going to talk to her at the soccer game this afternoon and see what I can find out."

TEN

Kitty assumed smashing a tennis ball a few hundred times would enable her to pinch off her emotions, roll them in a neat bundle, and swallow them whole. It had not. Her time on the tennis court merely left her mentally and physically hurting. After a long shower, she rubbed muscle ointment on her burning shoulders and back, before slipping on clean panties and a bra. *I shouldn't have hit so many forehand shots. I should have used my back hand more.* She pulled on a pair of bell bottoms and a kelly green seersucker tank that played up her auburn hair. She looked at herself in the mirror and ran her hand over her flat belly. *Not bad. At least I don't look like a woman who's being cheated on.* She leaned over the vanity and dabbed some magic potion around her swollen eyes. *Passable.*

She stepped into the closet to look for her blue loafers with the kelly green piping and tripped over her slippers. Kitty kept her slippers beside the bed, however, every week, Renee moved them to the center of the closet before she vacuumed. Kitty picked up the slippers and threw them into the bedroom with an exasperated grunt. She took a deep breath and blew it out slowly. *Let it go. Let it go. They're only slippers. It's not that important.*

She wandered downstairs absently picking things up and putting them down again. Everything in their house felt out of place, but they were exactly where she and Seth had put them. She ended up in the living room. Renee had only vacuumed half of the room. Four straight tracks marred the rug in front of the television, but there were still tufts of Daisy's fur between the couch and coffee table. She pulled the canister vacuum out of the hall closet with an air of resignation.

The cord caught on the leg of the new couch making the vacuum tip over. The dust bin fell open and spilled dirt and crumbs across the parquet floor. Something deep inside Kitty cracked. *That woman is totally worthless. She can't even replace the bag?* Kitty left the pile of dirt in the middle of the foyer, clicked in a new bag, and dragged the vacuum into the living room. Kitty grabbed a small linen pillow from the low leather couch, whacked it a few times against the hard arm then hurled it toward one of the high-backed navy side chairs. *She can't vacuum up the dog hair, but she can move the pillows. What kind of idiot puts ecru linen pillows on an ecru couch? Come on Renee, we are talking basic color theory here!* Kitty grabbed the oversized chintz pillow with dramatic orange and cobalt silk tassels from the side chair and tucked it into the corner of the couch. *There, that looks much better. I told that dolt of a saleswoman that the Schumacher print would really pop against the light couch. Plaid blue pillows, my ass!* Kitty pulled out the crevice tool from the vacuum and sucked all the dust and dog hair from under the couch then, in a frenzy that cost the life of a small vase, moved on to vacuum the drapes, the crown molding and book shelves. Now the room was as clean as the maid should have left it.

Exhausted, Kitty collapsed on the couch and hugged the chintz pillow. She almost felt happy. She flicked on the television and tuned in to a re-run of *Perry Mason*. She had seen them all at least once so it didn't matter if she came in halfway through the investigation. When the police detectives questioned why an Upper East Side socialite would kill her wealthy husband and risk a life in jail, she giggled. A commercial for Mutual of Omaha Insurance came on and brought Kitty back to reality. She got up to get a TaB and remembered the package of MoonPies she'd hidden inside the stock pot at the top of the pantry. *Oh screw it, what does it matter if I get fat. Obviously, Seth already doesn't find me attractive enough.* She shook open the step stool and retrieved her stash. The gooey cookies were delicious and pushed her troubles with Seth out of her mind far better than playing tennis had.

Two hours later, the phone ringing in the kitchen roused Kitty from her sugar and murder stupor. She hauled herself off the couch and untangled the twisted cord before answering. "Mom? Can you bring my blue socks to the game later?"

Shit! Bobby's game. "Sure honey, I'll put them in my bag right now."

"Thanks, Mom."

Kitty shoved the MoonPie bag inside an empty milk carton in the trash and splashed some water from the kitchen faucet on her face. *I don't want to be the Mommy today. I don't want to cheer on the sidelines. I want to lie here and eat cookies and watch TV.*

And that Blaire Morton. I am in no mood to listen to her brag about her perfect kid and perfect life. I'd like to slap that smug little smirk right off her face.

Kitty looked out the window to the deck and saw Daisy dozing on Seth's teak chaise. Renee had put the dog out of the house while she was cleaning and neglected to let her back in. Kitty automatically ran out to shoo the dog off the chair before her claws scratched the finish, when a solution occurred to her. She ran her hand along the warm fur of the dog's side and recalled that Blaire Morton was allergic to dogs. Blaire referred to Molly's dog, Dana, as the 'dander bomb.' Bringing Daisy to the game would allow Kitty to stay away from The Lookers without anyone calling her antisocial.

"Daisy, how would you like to go watch a soccer game?"

The dog raised her head and smiled with canine enthusiasm. Kitty threw Daisy's short leash into a tote bag along with Bobby's socks, then ran upstairs to quickly slap on some make-up and jewelry. Before heading out to the soccer field, Kitty opened a bottle of Perrier and took a swallow of the bubbly water. She replaced it with vodka to help her get through the afternoon.

Molly Blevins didn't sit with The Lookers. Kitty wasn't sure if that was because The Lookers disapproved of Molly, or if Molly disapproved of The Lookers. When Kitty arrived at the soccer field, Molly was already at the far end of the field in her faded folding chair with the distinctive duct tape trim, with Dana at her feet and a paperback in her hand. Kitty felt the fluffy mysteries Molly read by the dozen were a waste of her time. Kitty slogged through the National Book Award winners, as well as all the runners-up, each year whether she enjoyed the books or not.

As a rule, Kitty stood at midfield with the other Lookers. While the boys competed on the soccer pitch, the mothers sat in a tight formation and competed over whose child was more successful on the field or in the classroom. When they exhausted their children's accomplishments, they vied for who had the nicest pocketbook, the biggest diamond tennis bracelet, the best haircut. Kitty was normally happy to scrimmage with the best of them. Not today. She swung her chair over her shoulder, looped Daisy's leash around her wrist, and marched down to the far end of the field.

"Hey, Molly. I saw your VW bus and thought I'd come find you," Kitty said as she dropped her folding chair and shook it open. Daisy and Dana sniffed each other like old friends.

"You in a better mood?" Molly asked. She looked over her shoulder at The Lookers who were all staring at Kitty, heads inclined. "What's going on?"

"Nothing much," Kitty said breezily. "It's such a nice day. I thought I'd bring Daisy with me."

Molly looked pointedly up at the sky. There was a bank of dark clouds moving in from the west. They would likely get rain before dark. "Well, it's good to see Daisy," Molly replied. She rubbed the dog's ears and gave her a big hug. Her faded black T-shirt was covered with golden fur when she sat up. Kitty pulled Daisy away from Molly and pushed her backside down until she lay down. She leaned over Molly and brushed some of the hair off her.

"Kitty," Molly laughed. "Relax. I have to change into a dress and heels as soon as we get home anyway."

"You and Tom going out for dinner tonight?" Kitty scratched Daisy behind the ears and wondered if she and Seth would ever go out for dinner again. Probably. Kitty didn't have any illusions of any real change in her role as Mrs. Haskell. She would continue to sit beside Seth at his business dinners looking pretty, while he talked about greens fees and how so-and-so might actually win the Masters that year. A void seemed to be opening up in the pit of her stomach. It could have been the prospect of her emotionally empty, embittered future, or it could have been the package of two-year-old MoonPies.

"No," Molly scoffed. "Tom and I never go out anymore and certainly not in the middle of the week. He has his shows." Molly brushed some golden hair off her cut-offs. "I have a board meeting at The Arts Center. Want to come with? You know way more about how to choose art exhibits than I do."

"But you're an artist." Molly taught watercolor and oil painting classes to senior citizens two mornings a week.

"And I'd be happy to contribute a piece," Molly said. "But this wrangling back and forth about who gets a show and who doesn't drives me crazy. I can't judge what's good and what's bad."

On the other side of the field, the team broke from their pre-game pep talk, and the coaches met in the center of the field to go over last minutes issues with the referees. Bobby came bounding toward them, all arms and legs. Kitty reached into her tote bag and tossed the blue socks to Bobby. "Thanks, Mom!" he called and sprinted back to the bench.

"Good throw, Kitty," Molly said.

"My sister was the star of our school's softball team, and I used to help her practice. I developed a pretty good arm after a while."

"You didn't play softball too?"

"Field hockey."

"I would have liked to see that. Did you wear one of those little kilts?"

"We did. Sister Ignatius was always accusing Mary Francis Angelini of hemming her skirt too short." Kitty giggled at the images rolling through her memory. "One time, Mary Francis wore a bright red leotard under her uniform so when she lunged for the ball, her little black and white skirt flew up and everyone could see her red rear end. She got suspended, but it was totally worth it."

Molly giggled along with Kitty. "We didn't have field hockey in central Ohio."

"It's not all that different from soccer. You've got forwards and defenders; you pass the ball back and forth."

"And I thought you could follow these games because you'd read the rule book." Molly opened her tote and offered Kitty a can of Cheerwine soda.

"No thanks, I have my water here." Kitty drained half of her spiked water in one fortifying draught. "And I did read the rule book. If I have to sit out here in the blazing sun or the pouring rain all the time, I want to know what I'm looking at."

Molly twisted her long salt and pepper hair on top of her head and secured it with a leather thong. "It's hot out here today but not as bad as it was when they were doing that soccer summer camp. Did Bobby get anything out of that?"

"I don't know," Kitty replied. The Lake Tate team got the first goal and Kitty jumped up to cheer. "I think he enjoyed it. I'm sure they picked up some technique." Seth had wanted his son to have a leg up on the other boys and signed Bobby up for the intensive three week pre-season camp. Had he consulted Kitty first, he would have known that all the Overlook boys were attending the camp. Bobby had only gained an advantage over the players without the means to train with private coaches and receive individualized conditioning routines.

Connor Kaur dove to the ground and blocked the ball from going into the goal. Kitty jumped up and down and whistled in support. It was much more fun watching the game from the end of the field than over with The Lookers. She searched the sideline for Marni so she could congratulate her on her son's save but couldn't find her black head in the sea of blondes.

Kitty turned to Molly. "Do you see Marni anywhere? I want to talk to her about—"

"Look!" Molly jumped up and started clapping. "Bobby has the ball!"

Kitty moved her head toward the field, but she wasn't paying attention to the game anymore. "You know, I still can't believe she stood me up this morning. She could have told me if she had other plans when she called the other day."

Molly stopped clapping, and stared at Kitty. "She called you? What did she say?"

"Nothing really. She left a message with Seth." A cool breeze blew Kitty's hair into her eyes. "They must have had a chat, because she left a message that I should get someone else to help with hospitality for the homecoming dance since Becky isn't going. I hadn't even told Marni that Becky decided not to go."

"Becky's not going to the dance?"

"No. She doesn't have a date and she really doesn't care for dances. They don't play the music she likes. She gets bored after about a half an hour."

"I was that way too. It seemed like a lot of work just to stand around sweating in a goofy dress."

"Kids don't dress up for dances like we did. I used to spend hours sewing myself cocktail dresses and finding the right pair of gloves. Now they go in droopy prairie dresses."

Possession of the ball changed and they sat back down in their chairs. "How is Becky?" Molly asked. "Has she decided where she wants to apply?"

"Seth wants her to live at home and get a business degree, but she wants to go to school up north."

"That sounds exciting."

"Seth keeps telling her that college is a waste of money. Then again, Seth's time at UMass was a drunken blur of sleeping through classes and what he called "artsy fartsy bullshit." The only redeeming parts for Seth were sports and girls. He doesn't want his Becky to be like the girls he went to school with."

"Becky's not like that."

"He says it's stupid to educate a pretty girl. He actually used me as an example. He said, "you got an expensive education and you've never even had a 'real job.'"

Molly lightly shoved Kitty's arm. "You know that's not true."

Kitty rubbed her arm. It was getting more and more tender as the day went on. "I know, but it still kills me when he says things like that." Kitty paused for a moment before continuing, "I want Becky to study whatever she is passionate about. This is probably the last decision she will ever make without needing to think about anyone else."

I just don't want her to do what I did. I gave up my dreams when I married Seth. Huge mistake.

Kitty scanned the parking lot for Seth's Mercedes. "Speaking of Seth, where the hell is he?"

"Will you relax," Molly said. "You'll give yourself an ulcer."

"He better get here soon. It's almost half-time and he said he would try to come watch the game this afternoon. I wish he wouldn't get Bobby's hopes up like that."

"Tom's not here either," Molly said. "He doesn't even pretend he's coming. He says these games are boring."

"They are boring. That's not the point." Kitty craned her neck to see the parking lot on the far side of the field.

"I hope Bobby appreciates that you're here."

"I'm his mom. I don't count."

At half-time, Stacia bore down on them from the concession stand like a tiny lime green and hot pink missile. When she arrived she nodded at Molly and mumbled a hello.

"Stacia," Molly replied in a voice devoid of affection. The two women were always pleasant to each other if not entirely friendly.

Stacia turned a shoulder to Molly and spoke directly to Kitty. "I have been looking all over for you."

Kitty waited for Stacia to say something more, but she didn't go on. A tense silence descended over the women and Kitty could feel animosity coming off of Molly in waves. Kitty blurted out, "You were looking for me?"

"Yes, I ... do you know ... um ... do you know anyone who would be good for membership this year?"

"I'd be happy to help with membership," Molly interjected.

"That won't be necessary," Stacia said to Molly with a hollow smile. "We've got it covered." She turned back to Kitty and continued, "Are you all set for the parents' night next week? Why don't I ask a few gals to help you sell cookies?"

"Okay, if you think that would be best," Kitty replied. She wasn't sure if Stacia didn't trust her to do a good job on her own, or if she was trying to be helpful.

Stacia squat down and petted Daisy for a moment. "Daisy seems to be enjoying the game."

"I hope it's okay that I brought her. Molly always brings Dana. She seemed so restless in the yard that I just threw her in the car."

"No no, it was a good idea. Maybe I'll bring Baillie one of these days," Stacia said as she stood up.

Kitty envied how gracefully Stacia moved. She involuntarily sucked in her stomach and stood up straighter. Stacia propped her oversized white sunglasses on the top of her head. She leaned in and asked in a pregnant tone, "So, how is Seth these days? Are you okay?" A wave of panic washed over Kitty.

Could Stacia know about Seth? No. I'm just being paranoid. Get a grip, Mary Katherine.

Molly stepped into the void left by Kitty's silence. "Yeah, how's that elbow feeling? Will you be okay for the round-robin?"

"Tennis?" Stacia asked.

Thank you, Molly! Kitty noticed Molly staring daggers at Stacia. They seemed to be having an intense, yet wordless, conversation. Kitty wondered what was going on between the two women that she didn't know about. She didn't have the energy to really care. She had her own problems to worry about. "Pretty good. My tennis elbow seems to have healed up nicely."

After another minute of staring down Stacia, Molly seemed to win the exchange. "Have you got the round-robin schedule ready yet, Stacia?" She asked. "I'd love to watch our own Chris Evert over here win again."

Stacia took a step back and pulled her sunglasses back over her eyes. "I don't know yet. We may have too many people dropping out this year."

"I hope you aren't expecting Debbie Manning to play this year," Molly said.

"Of course not." Stacia tilted her chin in the air and looked out over the field.

"Why not?" Kitty asked.

"I'm sorry, Kitty. I assumed you knew," Molly said. She took a deep breath. "Debbie's got cancer. She found out last week."

"Leukemia," Stacia added.

"Oh my God, poor Debbie."

"Yes, she'll be missed," Stacia sighed.

"She's not dead yet, Stacia!" Molly snapped. "There are treatments."

"Of course, I meant from the round-robin." Stacia glanced over to the group sitting in chairs near the midfield. "Well, I should be getting back. Call me if you need anything, Kitty."

When Stacia had walked out of ear shot, Kitty flopped down in her chair and said, "Wow Molly, you're awful feisty today."

"That woman just irks me sometimes. You know The Lookers are just going to write Debbie off now."

"You think so? They've known Debbie for ages. She and Deirdre have been bridge partners for at least three years now."

"Don't even get me started on the whole Deirdre thing."

"What's the story with Deirdre? I saw her talking with Stacia the other day, and then I haven't seen her since. I hear they're losing their house."

"Exactly. We've all heard that they're losing their house. It doesn't matter if it's true, or not. They'll have to move now." Molly looked over Kitty's shoulder. Her face flushed with rage as she said, "Remember Kitty, you can't always believe everything you hear." Molly jumped up and stormed off toward the ladies room.

Kitty started after her just as Seth appeared behind her and put his arm around her. His shirt was damp with sweat. "You missed the whole game," Kitty whispered through a smile.

A smirk tickled the corners of his mouth. "I'm here now, aren't I?" He waved to Bobby on the other side of the field. Bobby's face lit up when he saw his father. He morphed into an eager pre-schooler waving to his Daddy from the Christmas pageant stage.

The final whistle blew and Bobby and Molly's son, Ethan, lugged their equipment bags over to where Kitty was standing. Kitty gave Bobby a hug. *When did Bobby start smelling like a man? He used to smell like grass and sunshine after a game.* Seth put his hand up to give the boys high fives.

"Hey, where'd Molly go?" Seth asked. "She missed the final minute."

"Yeah, but she was here for the first eighty-nine," Kitty replied.

"I think she went to the car, honey," she said to Ethan. He packed up his mother's chair and slung it over his shoulder before joining the crowd walking up the steps to the parking lot.

Kitty made a show of fumbling with her tote bag to see if Seth would notice and help her. He didn't. Kitty was tempted to tell Bobby that his father had missed all but the last few moments of the game, but what would be the point? She didn't want to upset Bobby merely to make Seth look bad. He did that well enough on his own.

Seth turned and challenged Bobby to a race to the car. Even with his equipment bag over one shoulder and heavy backpack over the other, Bobby easily won. The afternoon sun made his fine blonde hair, so like his father's when he was young, glow as he thrust his fists in the air in triumph. Seth was still struggling up the grassy slope.

Kitty sprinted up the slope past Seth and gave Bobby a quick hug. He preferred her not show her love in public. "Can you catch a ride home with your father? I never made it to the grocery store today. I'll swing by and pick up some pork chops."

Bobby handed his equipment bag to Kitty. "Can you put this in the Volvo. It won't fit in his car." By the time Seth struggled to the top of the hill, Kitty was half way across the parking lot to her car.

❧

The kitchen was empty when she came in with the bags of food. The low rumble of sports radio emitted from Seth's office. She could hear water running signaling that Bobby was still in the shower. Kitty put the pork chops and green beans with roasted garlic in baking pans. She would broil them when Becky came in from practice, yet the idea of sitting down to a family dinner right now made her want to scream.

She needed to think away from the house. She retrieved that morning's track suit and her running shoes from the laundry room and scrambled down the path Bobby had cut through the buffer zone before Seth got a chance to notice she had come in. At first, she sprinted to release her pent-up anger but soon slowed to a jog. She peeked through the trees into her neighbors' kitchens. Few of the houses in Overlook had blinds in the windows that faced the lake. People wanted an unobstructed view of the water. They didn't consider how much a passerby could see when the lights in the houses were on. She ran nearly all the way around the outer loop and saw family after family eating together or watching television together. She wondered if any of them were truly happy.

Kitty stopped a few hundred yards from their house and waded through the poison ivy that defied the gallons of brush killer the groundskeepers sprayed on it, to sit on a tree downed in a recent storm. The leaves above the water line were still green. A cloud of mosquitoes hovered over the water, as if weighed down by the humid air, and then drifted into the brush. At the far end of the lake, near the dam, the remnants of the sunset made the towers of the coal plant appear to be burning. The birds suddenly stopped chirping in the trees. There were several minutes of utter silence before the tree frogs took up their nightly chorus. Kitty dipped her fingers in the dark water. *This would be a good night for roasting marshmallows and skinny-dipping. I haven't gone in a lake, never mind skinny-dipping, in years.* The community pool was cleaner and free of snakes yet Kitty still felt there was something magical about swimming in water where she couldn't see the bottom.

When Kitty and Rose were girls, their mother sent them to camp for the month of July to get them out from underfoot. Rose complained incessantly about the daddy long legs and organized games. Kitty loved it. Every morning, Kitty and her cabin mates would pick their way over tree roots and patches of slippery moss to the lake for a swim. The girls each wore a heavy grey sweatshirt over their swimsuit emblazoned with the Nipmuck name for tiny Lake Webster in a bright blue spiral. The Native Americans had named the lake Chargoggagoggmanchauggagoggchaubunagungamaugg meaning: you fish on your side, I fish on my side, nobody fishes in the middle. They waited until the last possible second to pull off their sweatshirts and run into the water. The cool morning air made the water feel warm and thick. They swam between high wooden docks playing games of chase until they were exhausted and couldn't tread water any longer. Although the water was shallow, the girls refused to put their feet down; the lake bottom was slimy and they were liable to step on an unsuspecting fish or frog.

After their swim, the girls raced back up the hill for steaming platters of pancakes and bacon and fluffy scrambled eggs piled high on the wide dining hall tables. As a girl, Kitty didn't appreciate the beauty of the old field stone building with its high rafters and fireplace large enough for a man to stand inside. It was just a place to eat and spend rainy afternoons playing board games. Every year, on the last night of camp, the older girls would swim across the lake to the boys' camp for a bonfire and farewell sing-a-long. It was a mile-long swim in the dark but no one thought twice of jumping into the murky water and heading for the distant shore.

My youth is behind me now. I doubt if I could even make it across this little cove today.

A bat fluttered over Kitty's head looking for his dinner. Soon his brothers and sisters were swooping in an intricate ballet over the water. She watched them play until the lights came on in the Hendricks' yard across the cove. Greg Hendricks was home from work. Kitty waved but he didn't see her; she was invisible on her leafy perch. He walked in the house and kissed his wife. *They look happy from this distance. I wonder if they really are.*

Kitty took off her running shoes and socks and threw them on the bank before scooting further out on the fallen tree. It held her weight without moving. She slipped her feet beneath the surface. The water beckoned to her. *I wonder how many stones Virginia Woolf had to put in her pockets before she knew she would definitely sink?*

ELEVEN

Stacia spotted Marni's baby blue Cadillac several cars ahead of her in the school drop-off line, the bumper sticker emblazoned with her face and the real estate company's name crookedly affixed to the trunk. Stacia made a mental note to speak to her cousin Quentin about pushing more clients toward the sweet young agent in his office rather than Marni. As she watched, Marni's son Conner crawled out of the car and walked into the school. He didn't say goodbye to his mother. Marni didn't turn to watch him walk inside either. She merely threw her cigarette out the open window and pulled out into traffic.

Stacia turned to Marcus and asked, "How's Connor Kaur doing these days?"

"Okay, I guess," Marcus replied without looking up from his notes. He had a math quiz that morning. "I only see him at soccer. We don't really hang out anymore."

"Why not?" Stacia crept forward in the line.

"He isn't in the A track anymore with Bobby and me. He's kind of a stoner now. He almost failed English last year."

Stacia wished Marcus luck on his test and drove home contemplating what Connor Kaur's slipping grades could mean. Was Marni such a poor mother that it was affecting her child's performance? Was Connor really on drugs? Was he a bad influence on the other boys?

She was glad to see Weldon still sitting at the kitchen counter reading the newspaper when she came in. He looked up with a smile. "There's an article here about your race. They've received over two hundred entries."

"Great! Way to make me even more nervous." She took a sip from his coffee mug. "Can we get you a new mug at parent's weekend?"

Weldon's face lit up. "Maybe we can get one that says UNC parent."

Stacia replaced the old cup at her husband's elbow. She liked how proud he was of Lana. Stacia took her coffee cup from the drain board and filled it with fresh coffee. "You won't believe what Marcus just told me in the car. "She took a sip. "Connor Kaur smokes pot."

"That's too bad," Weldon sighed.

"I don't want Marcus to play with him anymore. Marni's trashiness is rubbing of on him."

Weldon put the newspaper down and looked at his wife for a moment. "Do you think we should send him to Magnuson Country Day instead of Nance next year? They have an excellent soccer team and he'd make some good connections there."

"No." Stacia slammed her coffee cup down on the counter top. "I will never send my child there. That's Bitsy's school."

"When are you going to get over your thing with Bitsy Magnuson-Evans?"

"When she stops being a bigot."

"Rise above, honey. Rise above." Weldon went back to reading the paper. He wasn't interested in hearing Stacia rant about Bitsy yet again.

Stacia's fingers shook with decades old rage as she lit a cigarette. She stepped out to the patio to smoke until the thought of Bitsy no longer made her want to scream. The Magnusons and the Tates had lived across the street from each other on Loralei Lane for generations. Bitsy was only a year older than Stacia so the girls were invariably compared to one another. Happy Magnuson sent Bitsy to Magnuson Country Day School where she could board her horse. Stacia went to public school. Bitsy failed at ballet where Stacia was always the lead in all the youth ballet productions. The comparison went on endlessly until Stacia's accident. While Stacia spent months in rehabilitation, Bitsy gained ground by becoming a Kappa Delta and returning to Magnuson with the handsome Chip Evans on her arm. Decades later, Bitsy still refused to acknowledge Weldon and acted embarrassed for Stacia whenever they saw each other. Stacia wanted to wring her skinny neck like a hen that wouldn't lay.

⊱⊰

The sun didn't rise Wednesday morning as much as the sky lightened behind the clouds. Kitty wasn't going to let a little rain keep her from her daily jog. Nevertheless, she did change her route and ran on the street instead of the raised wooden paths along the water. No one else would be foolish enough to be out in the rain; if she slipped on the slick wooden surface, she could be lying there, hurt and alone, for hours before help arrived.

She ran out Azalea Lane and the mile up Overlook Parkway to the main road without seeing a soul. It was too early for people to be heading off to work. The early morning dog walkers would have thrust the dog into their yard to do its business and gone back to bed. She was soaked to the bone by the time she reached the granite sign at the entrance to Overlook. *Maybe I should be running in a bathing suit or one of those little outfits triathlon people wear. A triathlon. That could be fun. But I could never do that. Seth would be mortified to have people see me in one of those suits.* She turned back toward home. The cacophony of raindrops on the pavement blended into a soothing white noise that allowed Kitty to relax her mind and let her feet fly back down the streets like the water streaming down the gullies on either side of the road.

She ran into the parking lot of the Overlook Swim & Tennis Club in order to circle back to the house. Stacia's Jeep was parked outside the pool fence. *I can't believe it; she's actually practicing in the rain. How can she tell when she is above or below the surface in this downpour?* Kitty peeked through the fence and saw Stacia approach with long even strokes, soundlessly flip, and swim back to the shallow end. Kitty could tell that she could keep going like that for hours if necessary. Kitty jogged in place and watched Stacia do three more laps. *Wow, she never gives up, does she? A training regimen like that takes so much discipline, and she does it all alone. No one would know if she skipped a day because it was raining. I should be that strong.*

A muffler backfired behind her. Kitty turned to see Seth idling at the entrance to the lot. He tooted the horn and waved. She jogged over as he opened the window enough to talk through it but not enough to get his shirt wet. "You look like a drowned rat." The rain that had felt refreshing a few moments before now just felt wet. "I've been driving all over the place looking for you."

"Great, that muffler probably woke up half the neighborhood. I just got that replaced last year."

"Do you mind switching cars today?"

"Sure," Kitty said. Seth started to close the window and pull away. Kitty thrust her hand in the window to keep him from closing it. "Wait a minute, why? What's wrong with the Mercedes?"

"Nothing," Seth replied. He pushed the buttons on the radio changing the station from NPR to the AM sports channel. "I was just wondering if you could take it in for an oil change. Maybe get a sticker."

Kitty stopped jogging and groaned, "You waited until the last day of the month to ask me to take it in? Do you know how long the wait is going to be?"

"What do you have to do today?"

"Things." Kitty didn't have anything pressing going on. That wasn't the point.

"You don't have to do it this morning," he said as he cranked the window closed. Kitty snatched her fingers out before he pinched them. "You could go this afternoon. I won't be home for dinner, so you don't even have to cook."

That's right, our children don't need to eat. Totally unimportant.

Kitty was about to say something about setting a bad example for their children, but just then, Blaire Morton emerged from her driveway towing her garbage can. Seth raised an eyebrow and smirked at Blaire's hastily donned rain boots and slicker before shutting the rain-streaked window.

"Hey, Kitty," Blaire hailed. "Jogging in the rain?" Dirty water splashed up to Kitty's waist as Seth stepped on the gas and sped away.

"Yup, got to keep my girlish figure," she replied. The muffler's roar got further and further away as Seth slowed for each of the five speed bumps between her and the entrance to the neighborhood.

Back at the house, she showered and got dressed before making sure Becky and Bobby were getting ready for school. Amid the hustle and bustle of packing lunches and signing papers, Kitty put the kettle on for tea and stared into the empty white tea cup in her hand. When they registered for china, she'd picked out a pattern with hand-painted flowers. Seth liked a plain white basket-weave pattern. They got the white dishes. Kitty did all the cooking yet, except for the bright yellow tea kettle her cousin Marie had given them as a housewarming gift, she hadn't chosen any of the things she touched everyday. Their entire life had been designed to Seth's liking. They lived where he wanted, ate what he wanted, dressed as he wanted.

Kitty had submitted to it all. She never considered if any of it was what she wanted. Her opinion had not even been discussed.

I am a complete idiot. I have given that jerk the last twenty years of my life. I do everything for him. And for what? A philandering asshole of a husband. But what can I do now? I'm stuck. Seth knows I am not about to leave him and give up everything we have together. I haven't had a job since we were married. Who would hire me now? She thought back to her days at the Worcester Art Museum. That was the last time she felt valued. She missed that girl.

The kettle screamed and she poured water in her cup. She inhaled the scent of the grassy herbal tea she drank because she had read it would prevent aging, and heard her mother's voice in her head saying 'you made your bed, now lie in it.' She poured the tea down the sink. They would have coffee at the Mercedes dealership.

She yelled for Bobby to meet her in the garage and went out to push discarded bags of potato chips and donuts aside so Bobby could put his backpack on the back seat of Seth's car. *I can't take this thing to the dealership looking like this.* She blasted the air conditioning as she swept up the pistachio shells that had missed the paper sack Seth used as a trash can and threw away the empty deli wrappers littering the floor of the back seat. *Seth is obviously not entertaining his woman in his car.* A Thermos that she hadn't washed in months rolled out from under the seat. Kitty mentally thanked the manufacturer for putting such an excellent air-tight seal on its product and tossed it in the garbage can.

Bobby stepped out of the garage with a half-eaten English muffin in his mouth and a bag in each hand. "Why are we taking Dad's car?"

Kitty took his backpack from him and slid it into the back seat. "It needs to be taken in for service today."

"Did you get my cleats out of the Volvo?" Bobby considerately stored his muddy cleats in a grocery bag in Kitty's car so he didn't track mud into the house. They usually dried enough overnight for him to bang off the loose mud and put them in his equipment bag the next morning.

"I'll have to swing by your Dad's office later and get them for you."

She dropped Bobby off at school, drove an hour round trip to Seth's office to retrieve the cleats and was at the Mercedes dealership before ten o'clock. The dealership tried to make the waiting room pleasant to spend time in by providing plush chairs, plenty of current magazines, and hot coffee, but they still had the blaring televisions tuned to game shows. Kitty could not abide screaming contestants making fools of themselves.

That morning's deluge had lightened to a steady shower that Kitty could handle with the gargantuan golf umbrella she found in Seth's trunk, so she strolled the half a mile down the road from the dealership to Pinkie's, a sweet pig themed cafe and gift shop. The cafe served North Carolina barbecue as well as crispy bacon and quiche Lorraine. The shop carried everything pink and piggy from banks to aprons with giant snouts on them. She treated herself to a pulled pork sandwich with a full order of hushpuppies and a tall sweet tea. If she was going to waste a whole day doing errands for Seth, she was at least going to enjoy herself. Before she left, she bought a pink chiffon pie for Debbie Manning. She had been meaning to drop by and see Debbie ever since Molly had told her about Debbie's cancer diagnosis.

The car was ready when Kitty returned from her jaunt. She had just enough time to visit Debbie before going to pick Bobby up from school. When she rang the doorbell, she was surprised to see Stacia open Debbie's door. "What are you doing here?" Kitty asked. She got a glimpse of piles of dirty dishes and baskets of laundry spilling out into the hallway, before Stacia stepped out on the front porch and closed the door behind her.

Stacia pulled long green rubber gloves off her tiny hands and tucked them in the pocket of an apron that came down to her ankles. "What are you doing here?"

"I brought Debbie a pie. I thought she might like something sweet."

Stacia took the pie. "I'm sure she'll appreciate that," she said in a whisper. "She's sleeping right now. I'll be sure to tell her you dropped by."

"How is she?" Kitty could smell disinfectant wafting off of Stacia.

"She had a chemotherapy treatment earlier this week so .... she's very tired today."

"Should I come back later?"

"No, that wouldn't be a good idea at all," Stacia said quickly. She shifted the pie to her other hand with a sigh. "So, what's going on with you? How's Seth?"

Stacia's bright blue eyes felt like they were piercing Kitty's skull. She quickly looked at her watch. "Look at the time, I've got to run some errands before picking up Bobby. See you later, Stacia." Kitty beat a hasty retreat down the driveway and back to her house. Still, she couldn't help wonder why Stacia was cleaning Debbie's house instead of the maid.

TWELVE

Pastor Bob told another one of his inane jokes about the twelve apostles. Kitty's soul ached to listen to such drivel. She looked across the sanctuary at the wall of Tates. It had a hole in it. Stacia's father was there along with her brother and his wife, but Stacia, Marcus, and Weldon were missing. Kitty stared out the window and watched the cars go by on the off ramp in the distance while Pastor Bob got to his point. *Where is Stacia? Oh my goodness, that big race is today. Her father didn't go to watch? That's not a very Christian way to act.*

Kitty looked over at Mr. Tate again. He had the same sharp features and blue eyes as Stacia. *Interesting though how the family left their space open instead of sitting closer to each other. I wonder if anyone would respect my absence like that? Probably not.*

She glanced over at Seth sitting on the other side of Becky and Bobby. He was doing the jumble in the children's bulletin. *I wonder if Seth would even notice if I was not here. A robot could take my place. As long as his meals are made and his children are carted from place to place, he doesn't care. Not even at that, he doesn't eat at home much anymore and Becky can drive herself around now. I'm no more than Bobby's chauffeur.*

When Pastor Bob stopped blathering and the congregation stood for a hymn, Kitty scoot behind the children and said from behind a sweet smile, "I can see you doing the puzzles, you know." She put her hand on Seth's arm in the same way her mother did whenever Kitty stepped out of line in public. Seth tried to pull away but couldn't without attracting attention. The outwardly innocuous squeeze at the right pressure point cast lightning bolts of pain down his arm and rendered him helpless. "Take the children home after this ridiculousness and make sure they eat a good lunch."

"Where are you going to be?" His eyes flit to the people around them, most of whom were not even pretending to be singing.

"I am going to take Rose on a field trip." Kitty didn't know she was going to call her sister and take a day trip until the words came out of her mouth, but, as soon as she said it, she knew that a day away from Seth was exactly what she needed. Stacia was competing in the open water swim she had been training for all summer and, damn it, someone was going to be there to cheer her on. When the congregation started to sit down, Kitty pretended to have a coughing fit and stepped out of their pew. The entire balcony watched her go.

At the bottom of the stairs, Kitty stepped out of her pinchy black pumps and ran barefoot across the parking lot to the pay phone on the corner. She had to dial Rose's phone number four times before she answered. Rose kept her phone next to her bed, far from the living room. "Mary Katherine? Is that you?" Rose said breathlessly.

"You know it is," Kitty sighed. "No one else ever calls you." Kitty dropped her shoes and slipped her sore, swollen feet back in them.

"It's about time you called to apologize."

"I'm not."

"I didn't call you on Wednesday to punish you," Rose said.

Thank God for small favors.

"You're the one that needs to apologize for being an unsupportive bitch." Kitty pulled the phone booth door closed.

She heard the rattle of ice cubes in a glass. "You really should be nicer to me. I am your only blood relative."

"No," Kitty replied. "I'm your only blood relative. I have two children."

"Well, you still should be nicer to me—"

"Oh put a sock in it, Rose. You're just mad because I kicked you out before you got your leftovers in the Tupperware. Did you actually have to cook something, you big baby?"

"You know I hate cooking."

"Boo hoo hoo." Kitty fanned herself with the church bulletin still in her hand. "Hey, how about you and I go on a little adventure today? My friend Stacia is swimming in a big race at the beach this afternoon."

"A friend of yours is in a race?"

"I have friends, Rose," Kitty grunted, "and they're still ambulatory." Rose laughed and Kitty heard the sound of a drink

88

being put down on the bedside table. "So you want to go for a ride? I thought we could grab some lunch then go watch the race."

"If that's what you want, I guess I could manage." By the time Kitty arrived at Rose's townhouse, Rose had packed a basket of supplies. Heaven forbid they get caught without extra bottles of water, a tube of sunblock, hard candies, or a sweater.

A few minutes into the hour and a half drive, Rose asked, "Should we stop at a Big Boy for lunch? Mother liked Big Boy."

"Mother's dead," Kitty replied. "She doesn't get a vote."

Rose stiffened and snapped, "Then you choose, little Miss Smartypants." She stared out the window at the fields of yellowing tobacco leaves. Kitty turned the radio on to a classical station.

Twenty miles further down the road, Rose muttered, "You are so full of it."

"Excuse me?" Kitty turned off the radio.

"You give me grief about doing whatever Mother wanted, but you're no different. You let Mother tell you what to do as much as me. I'm just more honest about it. Oh yeah, you moved away and pretend you are someone else, but you're still little Mary Katherine McSweeney from Narragansett." Rose smoothed a stray lock of graying hair back into the bun at the nape of her neck. "I know you hear her voice in your head as much as I do."

"Yeah, like a ghost."

"Shut up! She was all I had. I'm all alone now."

"You don't have to be alone. Are you dating?" Rose scoffed and turned the radio back on. "I envy you," Kitty said. "You're free."

"Yippee," Rose sighed as she brushed imaginary lint off her polyester pants. "So what are you going to do about Seth?"

"I don't know."

"Well, when are you going to know?"

Kitty slammed on the brakes and was nearly plowed over by an eighteen wheeler. Rose screamed as Kitty took an exit ramp at seventy-five miles an hour. She yelled, "I. ... Don't. ...Know," as she tore into a small strip mall and screeched to a stop.

"Are you trying to kill me?" Rose yelled at her sister. She jumped out of the car. "I don't know what to do with you. Mother would know. She would know what to do with you. She always knew what to do."

Kitty jumped out of the car as well and glared at Rose over the hood. "No, she didn't. She was just as lost as the rest of us; she just acted like she knew what she was doing."

"She'd have a plan at least. She always had a plan," Rose sniveled.

Kitty slammed the car door. "You have got to be kidding me. Do you think she planned on dropping out of high school and having me? Do you think she planned on marrying an alcoholic?"

"He wasn't an alcoholic!" Rose cried. "He just ... Oh my God, that's why you are being so awful about Mother. You think you're like her, don't you?" Rose turned around and leaned on the car door. "You're nothing like Mother. She was strong. You're just a spoiled brat." Rose started sobbing. "You had options she never dreamed of having. She had no education—"

Kitty pulled a packet of tissues from her purse and threw it at her sister. "I haven't had a job in eighteen years."

"You are a capable woman, Mary Katherine. Someone would hire you if you tried."

"And do what? Don't you see? I rolled the dice with Seth and lost."

Kitty stepped into the cafe at the end of the strip mall and sat down in a booth. She watched Rose try to get back into the locked car, then stand in the blazing sun staring at Kitty through the cafe's window as she sipped a tall glass of sweet tea.

The cafe was charming. There were only four yellow leatherette booths in the window and a high counter with swiveling stools set around an antique soda fountain. The only other customer, an old man eating a mound of shrimp and grits, winked at her. Rose eventually came inside and silently picked at a garden salad while Kitty munched on fried shrimp, slaw, and hushpuppies. She was happy to enjoy her food without the burden of conversation. After their plates were cleared, Rose slammed her glass of tea on the linoleum table and demanded, "So what are you going to do?"

Kitty didn't respond.

"The way I see it, you got yourself into this marriage, so you've got to make it work." Rose pulled out an ancient tube of pink lipstick and used the back of a knife as a mirror. "Whatever happened to 'for better or for worse'? Well, this has 'for worse' written all over it. So what if your husband is a philanderer? Big deal."

"He gave me the clap!"

"Oh, get over yourself. You need to quit your whining and put on your big girl panties."

The waitress returned with a giant piece of coconut cake and placed it in front of Kitty.

"Should you be eating that?" Rose asked. "That skirt is looking a bit snug as it is."

Kitty stuffed a huge chunk of cake in her mouth and talked through the soft crumbs. "I'll buy a bigger skirt." She looked at her watch. "The race doesn't start for another hour. Let's go into that cute little boutique on the other side of the street and get a little something."

"I don't know, that looks expensive. Won't Seth mind?"

"I don't care," Kitty replied with a twinkle in her eye. She finished every morsel of sweet cake, then marched across the parking lot with Rose teetering behind her. In the exorbitantly expensive boutique, Kitty bought a pair of pink Bermuda shorts, a blouse, a pair of canvas espadrilles, and a huge floppy hat that she wore out of the shop. Her boring black pumps that pinched her toes went in the trash can with the snug skirt.

♋

A mile or so from the beach, Rose spotted a sign marked Open Water Swim - Spectator parking. They followed the signs to an abandoned golf course where young men in matching bright yellow T-shirts had people park on a sun and salt-ravaged green. "I didn't realize this would be such a production," Rose said as they joined a line to board a shuttle bus. "We should have brought chairs."

"Neither did I," Kitty replied. "I was expecting a few dozen people to be lined up on a pier to watch the swimmers go by." She looked at the people around her. Everyone else seemed to know the rules of the game - color coordinated shirts, beach sandals, folding chairs slung over shoulders, and binoculars hanging around necks. She felt overdressed and under supplied.

The shuttle bus dropped the sisters at the top of a dune where an observation platform had been constructed. While the other spectators greeted old friends and set up their chairs under canvas pavilions, Kitty and Rose wandered over to the railing at the edge of the platform. The beach below swarmed with latex clad people.

"There are hundreds of them," Rose exclaimed. "Which one is your friend?"

"I don't know. They all look the same." Kitty pulled out the hat she bought at the boutique and put it on. "You'd think I'd be able to spot her. Stacia's got to be the tiniest woman in the race."

The man standing a foot or two away from Rose removed the binoculars from his face and turned to them. "Stacia Tate-Curran?"

"Yes," Kitty said with a smile. "Do you know her?"

"Everyone on the circuit knows Stacia. She is relentless."

Kitty sensed that this man didn't mean that as a compliment. *That sounds like our Stacia.* "She has been out on our lake practicing every day all summer long. She really wants to win this time."

"She probably will," the man sniffed. "My wife, Amy, moved up an age group and really slacked off this year. Without Stacia nipping at her heels, she lost all her motivation to get up and train." Kitty stared out at the water beyond the breakers and thought about how important it was to have someone to compete against. *Who do I compete with? Who don't I compete with?*

Rose tapped the man on the arm with her bottle of sunblock. "What are the tents for?"

The way he smiled at her reminded Kitty that her sister was indeed still attractive to men. She resolved to find her sister a guy. "Each swimmer has to go through a series of checkpoints before they enter the water. First they check in, then they get numbered—"

"Numbered?" Rose asked. She picked up the man's binoculars and peered through them. He didn't seem to mind.

"They draw a number on their arms and legs so the officials can know who they are at the finish gate."

"Like marathon runners?" Rose pointed toward the beach. "I think I found her!" Amidst the mass of black and grey sheathed women, Stacia stood out like a scarlet ibis in a flock of cormorants. "Where did she ever get that god-awful pink suit?" Rose grunted.

"That's her husband's doing," the man said. "These races scare the living daylights out of Weldon, so she wears a suit he can spot from a distance."

"She wears a psychedelic orange practice suit," Kitty giggled. "I can see her from the shore when I'm jogging."

"Kid's sizes come in all sorts of colors."

Kitty looked around the platform. "Where is Weldon? The race should be starting soon."

"He'll be out in one of those." The man pointed to a pile of kayaks at the edge of the water. "He always volunteers to be an official. It keeps him from worrying so much."

A voice said something garbled over the PA system, and the competitors lined up behind the start line. There was more unintelligible talk and then the air was rent by a blast of sound. En masse, the swimmers ran into the waves. Kitty's motherly instincts worried about them getting trampled, but the swimmers knew what they were doing as they high stepped through the surf and dove beneath the breaking waves. They swam straight out from the beach and around a tall, inflated buoy in a tumult of flailing arms and splashing legs. Kitty now understood why Mr. Tate didn't come to watch; there was no way to tell one swimmer from the next.

It wasn't until almost two hours later that they saw the swimmers again. First, a handful of muscle-bound young bucks came stumbling out of the water and collapsed on the sand just inside the finish line. Kitty was wishing she was on the beach to make sure the young men got some cool water to drink and an orange slice when Rose started jumping up and down. "Look! Between that kayak and the life guard on the surf board, I can see her pink rear end." A moment later, Stacia stood up in the water and staggered up the beach. Two burly life guards were waiting for her at the finish line. As soon as she stepped through the balloon arch, they each took one of her arms and led her toward the first-aid tent.

"She won!" Kitty cheered. "She was the first woman to come in!"

Stacia stopped on the sand below them and vomited twice as the lifeguards held her up. When she was finished, they carried her into the first aid tent.

"I don't think we'll go congratulate her quite yet," Kitty whispered in Rose's ear.

"I can't stand this sun too much longer, Kitty." Kitty wiped a bead of sweat from Rose's cheek. She was getting pink despite a liberal application of sunblock. "Can we go then? I'm sure she doesn't want to see you right now anyway."

Kitty looked down at the beach. The first of the other women were coming in now along with the pack of men. They looked as worn out as Stacia had. "I'll call her tomorrow. We can go." As the two sisters boarded the shuttle bus back to the parking lot, Kitty turned to Rose and said, "Thanks for coming with me today. It was great to see Stacia do that. It makes me want to try a race sometime."

THIRTEEN

Stacia opened her eyes the next morning in a panic. "Von!" she gasped, bringing Weldon running from the chair on the other side of the bedroom. Geysers of pain shot through her legs when she tried to move. Everything hurt.

"Okay, okay, you're okay," Weldon said as he helped her sit up. He propped her up on some pillows and handed her a small pile of painkillers.

It hurt to lift the glass to her mouth. It hurt to swallow. It hurt to lean back. Stacia looked around the room, taking in the muted green Chinoiserie wallpaper as if seeing it for the first time.

"You thought you were waking up in the hospital again, didn't you," Weldon said and took the water glass from her. Stacia moaned and tried to turn on her side. She gave up after two attempts. Her hip flexors were not cooperating. She would have to wait for the drugs to kick in before trying to get up. "Why do you do this to yourself?"

"Because I can," Stacia groaned.

Weldon sat on the edge of the bed and gently rubbed Stacia's legs with long even strokes. The pressure of his hand through the sheet was painful, but it also felt wonderful. She could feel the muscles fibers slowly relax. "Were you thinking about Von at the end of the race again?"

"You know I was. Somewhere in the third kilometer my shoulders and thighs were burning so much. Then, they stopped burning and I went to this other place in my head. I kept seeing Von and the other girls. They were all in their tutus and happy and excited for me to keeping going." She winced as she rubbed her shoulder. "I could kinda see your kayak off to the side, but not really."

94

Weldon pulled her left arm out to the side and massaged her shoulder as he slowly manipulated the ball and socket joint. Both them were lost in their memories of Weldon's little sister for several long minutes.

The phone rang downstairs in the kitchen, bringing them both back to the present. "That's probably Kitty Haskell again," Weldon said. "She called last night and Marcus told her to call back this morning."

"You took him to school, right?" Stacia said as she tried to sit up more. Between the painkillers and Weldon massaging her muscles, she was able to move. Slowly.

Weldon nodded and offered a supportive arm, as Stacia threw her legs over the side of the bed. She lifted herself to her feet tentatively. "What did Kitty want?"

"You're not going to believe this. She drove down and watched the race." Stacia snapped her head around to see if Weldon was fooling with her. A searing pain shot through her neck and down her spine that made her see stars. Weldon helped her sit back down and rubbed her neck until she could move it again. "Yeah, I meant to tell you on the ride back before you conked out. I was talking to Roger Lathrop after the race while you and Amy were getting dressed. He said he met one of your friends and her sister. He said she was a skinny redhead that talked like JFK. That must have been Kitty. I didn't know she had a sister."

"She moved down here a few months ago, after their mother died." Stacia tried to stand up again and shuffle to the bathroom. "I guess I should go over there and thank her for driving all the way down there," Stacia said from the bathroom. "Did you see her on the beach?"

"No, I didn't know she was there until Roger told me. Are you sure you want to go over there? Maybe you should stay in bed today."

Stacia shuffled back into the bedroom. "As much as I would like to lie very, very still, we both know that would be worse in the long run. I need to move around a bit and get some of this lactic acid out of my muscles." She took a pair of panties out of the drawer and attempted to put them on but couldn't lift her leg high enough to slip her foot through the leg opening. She turned to Weldon and said, "Come on, don't just stand there and watch me. Give me a hand here."

"I wanted to see how long you would fight before you asked for help."

Two hours later, after a long hot shower and several more pain killers, Stacia let Renee into the house then slowly walked up Overlook Boulevard with Baillie. The little dog was acting strangely lately. Any time someone other than a member of the family came near her, she cowered under the kitchen table. That morning, as Stacia was chatting with Renee and getting caught up on the neighborhood information Renee felt Stacia should know about, the dog had crawled under Weldon's recliner. Stacia had to coax her out with a doggie treat. Stacia laughed off Baillie's odd behavior as related to the new medicine she was taking, however, she was concerned.

At first, Stacia chalked it up to a kidney stone and the dog being upset by Lana being gone. Then, she started peeing in the house. The veterinarian wasn't very helpful. He gave her some antibiotics and told Stacia to keep her off the carpeting until her medication got the infection under control. He wouldn't guess at why Baillie flinched when her belly was rubbed. Stacia worried that the dog had developed cancer. They had been through that with Baillie's father, Byron, and didn't want to put the kids through that again. Lana was settling into college life nicely and Stacia didn't want her calling home to check on an ailing dog. Marcus, on the other hand, would have to watch Baillie's decline firsthand. It had broken his little seven-year-old heart when Byron died, but he had been consoled by throwing all his affection on to Baillie. Stacia didn't have a new puppy to thrust into his arms this time.

Their progress up Overlook Parkway was impeded by Stacia's ponderous gait, between a shuffle and a crawl, and Baillie stopping to dribble out a few teaspoons of urine every few yards. Stacia considered picking Baillie up and carrying her, but the prospect of bending over was too daunting. "We're quite a pair, aren't we girl?"

By the time they finally reached the corner of Azalea Lane, Stacia was looking forward to sitting down somewhere soft with a cold glass of iced tea. Eileen Simmons stood at her mailbox across the street from Kitty's house. It was a small street, only five houses shoehorned onto a promontory in the lake so everyone got some lakefront. Stacia couldn't avoid at least saying hello. "Hey Eileen," she called from the other side of the cul-de-sac.

"Hey, Stacia." Eileen replied. She crossed her arms in front of her chest and Stacia suspected she was embarrassed to be caught in old cut-offs and a faded Wolfpack T-shirt. "I've been meaning to call you about the round-robin." Eileen tugged at her t-shirt. "I'm not going to be able to do it this time. I'm dealing with some stuff and I'm going to have to sit this one out."

Stacia recalled Renee telling her that Eileen had started taking prenatal vitamins. Stacia braved the pain of stepping off the curb to walk across the street when she saw Eileen was blinking back tears. "Anything I can do to help?"

"Thanks, but I don't think you can do anything to help me with this problem."

At that moment, Baillie proceeded to urinate on top of Stacia's foot. "Geez, Baillie!" Stacia haltingly lowered herself to the curb and pulled a tissue from her pocket to dab the urine off. She was wondering if she could run leather sandals through the washing machine when she noticed Eileen was gripping the mailbox with white knuckles. From this angle, she could see a bloodstain blooming on Eileen's bottom above the tell-tale bulge of a thick maxi pad.

Oh no!

Stacia immediately forgot her shoe and aching muscles. She took one look at Eileen's pale face and fluttering eyelids and jumped up. She grabbed Eileen's arm. "Are you okay? You're bleeding pretty heavy."

Eileen tried to pull off a casual smile. "How embarrassing." Eileen tried to look at her backside but as soon as she let go of the mailbox, she started to faint. Stacia caught her and gently leaned the young woman against the mailbox post.

"Eileen, honey, how long have you been bleeding like this?"

Eileen tried to stand up on her own. "Not long, less than an hour. I'll be fine," she moaned.

"Sure, sweetie," Stacia said as she half-led, half-carried Eileen back to the house. Stacia knew all too well what was happening. She had three miscarriages between Lana and Marcus. "You'll be fine. But we need to get you to a hospital right now."

In the kitchen, Stacia pulled out a kitchen chair and sat Eileen down. "Now, Sweetie, where's your purse?"

"Front hall." Tears slowly slid down Eileen's cheeks like drops of lost hope. "It's not just spotting, is it?"

"I don't think so. We'll let your doctor decide that. Right now, we've got to get you cleaned up a bit." Stacia handed Eileen a dish towel to dry her tears and said, "You just sit here for a minute. I'm going to get you a clean pair of pants then we'll get in the car."

Stacia found a clean pair of underwear and some of Jim's sweatpants in the laundry room, stripped Eileen's clothes off her and redressed her as if she were a toddler. She supported Eileen on her throbbing shoulders and led her to the car. "It's okay, honey. You'll be okay. Really." When they got to the hospital, Stacia called Weldon. She told him to call Eileen's husband, Jim, and tell him what was going on, then to go to Eileen's house, get rid of all the evidence of blood and save Baillie from where she had tied her up in Eileen's backyard. She knew Weldon would handle the situation. He had been as devastated by their fertility problems as she had been. He would be a soft shoulder for Jim.

For the rest of that day and the next, Stacia was completely focused on Eileen and Jim. She held Eileen's hand through the necessary medical procedures when Jim couldn't bear to watch, then she held Jim's while he cried in the waiting room. She was confident that Weldon would take care of Marcus and keep their household running. She didn't give a moments' thought to such trivial things as The Lookers or PTA meetings.

FOURTEEN

The first round of progress reports had gone home. Now that Little Johnny was failing English, the parents who couldn't be bothered to attend the open house filled every seat in the junior high school's auditorium. Late comers stood along the walls like fence pickets. The smell of parental dread and impatience was stifling in the auditorium.

Kitty slipped out of the required general PTA meeting as Blaire Morton wound it down. When The Lookers realized Stacia was a no-show, they had quickly thrown together a few remarks. No one in the audience seemed to care that there were no printed budgets or flashy overheads. They were antsy to meet the teachers and get home to their dinners.

It was a relief to get out to the cool lobby. Kitty hustled over to the bake sale table to check on the sixth grade moms Stacia had recruited to help stand behind the hospitality table and shoo away errant toddlers. The other moms had baked dozens of chocolate chip cookies and brownies to sell for a quarter apiece freeing up Kitty to concentrate on her cupcake creations. For a dollar, a child could have a chocolate cupcake frosted to look like a ladybug, a yellow cupcake with spiked rainbow frosting, or a vanilla cupcake with glitter-encrusted fondant butterflies alighting on clouds of buttercream.

"No, dear," Kitty said to one of the other moms. She could not seem to keep their names in her head. "Put the brownies and cookies at either end of the table and the cupcakes in the center. You want them to be visible, yet out of the reach of little hands. You can't rely on these people to pay for their children's messes." She rearranged the table to show her wares to their best advantage. "There, that's better," Kitty said with a satisfied smile.

A sound like cattle lowing in the distance signaled that the PTA meeting was over. The next ten minutes were chaos while Kitty and her two volunteers sold cookies, cupcakes, and brownies as fast as they could grab the money out of sticky fingers. Then, the PA system crackled overhead and the herd was driven down the halls to hear the teachers' canned speeches about homework logs that wouldn't be maintained, fundraisers to pay for mimeograph ink, and how they don't have time to teach new material because they need to spend six weeks testing the children on what they didn't learn the year before.

A woman approached the table while Kitty was arranging the dollar bills face up before counting them. Kitty did not immediately recognize her. "Oh Kitty, these are too pretty to eat! My Rachel would love these for her birthday party."

Rachel? Rachel Manning?

Kitty deftly tucked the bills inside the money box and scanned the woman's face. "Debbie! Good to see you," Kitty said with a watery smile. "How are you feeling?" The chemotherapy treatments had ravaged Debbie's pretty face. Her skin was the color of poached fish, and she looked snakelike without brows or lashes beneath a flat brown wig.

"Like three day old dog shit on the bottom of your shoe." A shudder shook Debbie's wig and Kitty could see a grey patch of scalp above her ear. "Thanks for bringing over that pie the other day. The kids loved it."

"I'm glad they liked it. I'm sorry I wasn't able to stay and visit. Stacia said you were resting."

"Resting? More like in a drug-induced coma." Debbie seemed to gather herself for a moment before asking, "Where did you get such cute cupcakes?"

"I made them," Kitty replied. "They're German chocolate cake with a cherry filling and a stiff buttercream. The ladybug is made out of fruit leather."

Debbie examined the edible art carefully. "That's an awful lot of time to spend on stuff for a PTA bake sale."

"It's my contribution to the school. I'm hospitality chair again this year."

Debbie glanced over at the other women, sweeping up cookie crumbs from the far end of the table, before leaning closer to Kitty and whispering conspiratorially, "I see that Marni isn't here. I admire the way you're keeping up such a brave face. I think I would have scratched her eyes out."

"Marni?" Kitty choked out.

Debbie snorted derisively. "I hope you raked Seth over the coals in private."

Seth? And Marni? The scales fell from her eyes – Marni not returning her calls, Molly changing the subject when Marni's name came up, the meaningful looks between Stacia and Molly. *Debbie knew too? They all must know!*

The room started to spin. Kitty dropped her hands to the table squashing a butterfly cupcake under her palm.

"Shit!" Debbie gasped. "I assumed you knew."

"Oh my," Kitty half-laughed and half-cried. She picked up her pocketbook with her clean hand. "Excuse me for a sec, I should go clean this up," she whispered and marched out the front door of the school.

Oh ... My ... God.

Kitty stumbled to her car and sat inside for several minutes with the air conditioning blowing in her face. She tried to breathe. She didn't cry. She was too angry to cry. *Marni! I'm going to kill her. How dare she? This goes against every rule in the book!*

She wiped her frosting covered hand on the passenger seat. She would have to clean that mess up too. *And Seth! What was he thinking? No wonder he won't talk to me about it. Marni gave him the clap!*

Kitty's hand flew to her mouth as she thrust back against the car seat. *Oh no, Dr. Bukalis. That's why he made me come in and get an exam. The doctor knew I had gonorrhea because he's Marni's doctor too. He knew exactly who Seth got it from.* She started laughing hysterically until a couple snuck out a side door and got in a beat-up pick-up. They were leaving after only visiting one or two teachers. *Cheaters.*

Oh crap, what if someone sees me? I must look a mess. Kitty started the engine and roared out of the circle.

She slammed her foot on the accelerator. The car was flying as fast as her thoughts. *I bet he thought I would never find out. He wasn't so far off. I didn't know, although everyone else did.* She nearly hit a parked car as she zoomed down Overlook Parkway, into their cul-de-sac, and up their driveway. *Thank goodness the kids aren't home yet. I don't want to be the Mommy right now.* She almost side-swiped Seth's car as she squealed into the driveway. *Crap! What am I going to say to him?*

Kitty pulled the car in beside the Mercedes but didn't get out right away. She needed to plan her next move. *I've got to play this cool. It's not just some floozie at the office anymore. This is serious. He won't leave me, not for the likes of Marni. But still. I need to maintain the upper hand. If he thinks, even for a minute, that he's dumping me for that little tramp, I will take him for everything he has. And more.*

Kitty could feel anger swelling up inside her like magma. She took a deep breath. *No. I have got to be calm about this. I am going to go in there, and I'm going to speak to him like a mature adult.*

No yelling. No drama.

Kitty took another deep cleansing breath and got out of the car. She pulled the heavy garage door open and screwed a smile onto her face before opening the door into the kitchen.

Seth was standing in the middle of the room, a beer in one hand and a Pop-Tart in the other. "Hey honey," he said spraying crumbs onto the floor.

Kitty punched her husband squarely in the nose.

The volume of blood splatter from one well-placed right hook surprised her. Time slowed. An image of Quincy, M.E. hitting cantaloupes with a wrench to test blood splatter patterns flashed through her mind. The beer bottle fell to the floor and shattered in a puddle of glass and foam. The Pop-Tart landed in the puddle as Seth's hands flew to his nose.

"What the hell!" Seth choked. Blood and pastry dribbled out the side of his mouth. He looked at his bloody hands. "You broke my nose!"

"Marni Kaur? Really?" Kitty threw her keys at him. They bounced off his shoulder and clattered to the floor. "It wasn't enough to cheat on me? You had to humiliate me as well? Marni?"

Seth stared at Kitty across the gulf of the kitchen floor as the mantel clock, a wedding gift, struck seven long chimes in the living room.

Seth's nose dripped on the floor. "Who told you?"

"Debbie Manning. Apparently, the whole neighborhood knows." Kitty handed Seth a dish towel for his nose. "You obviously have not been very discreet," she spat at him.

"Oh my God, I'm going to have to go to the emergency room," Seth whined.

Kitty pointed out the open door to the garage and yelled, "Get Marni to take you!"

She stood rooted to the center of the kitchen floor until she heard the Mercedes roar to life. Then, like a quivering jello mold left out in the sun, she slumped to the floor in a sticky mess.

She knew better than to express her anger like that. She should have felt shame, but she felt nothing. She watched the drops of blood slowly soak into the hardwood flooring. *What have I done? I am a terrible wife but—*

She knew she should get a rag and clean up the mess but she couldn't do it. She reached out and connected a few of the blood droplets with her finger. *But it felt so good.*

She formed a smiley face in the blood. *I should have done that ages ago. Well, maybe not punch him in the nose - that was wrong - but punched him. Maybe in the arm. Or a good kick.* She giggled. *Right in the balls.*

Listen to me! What would Mother think?

Kitty reached up and pulled the phone from the wall. Rose picked up on the first ring. "Rose, thank God you're home."

"Where else would I be, Mary Katherine? And to what do I owe the honor of your phone call?"

"Shut up, Rose. I need help." Kitty gulped back a sob. "Seth ... gonorrhea ... Marni!"

"Your friend?" Rose snorted. "He got the clap from your friend?"

"Oh, Rose," Kitty wailed. "I did something awful. Blood. All over the kitchen."

All reproach drained from Rose's voice. "Where are the children?"

"I think they're getting a pizza."

"Good. Don't let anyone in the house. No one. Start cleaning up the blood. Use lots of bleach. I'll be right there to help you move the body."

"Body?" Kitty paused then erupted with laughter. "Rose! I didn't kill him. I just punched him in the nose."

"What?" Rose screamed into the phone. "The nose? That's all?"

"Oh Rose, I love you." Kitty tried to quell her laughter. "You never fail to think the worst of me. But thank you for being willing to help me hide the body." She hiccuped. "If I ever do kill someone, I'll know who to call."

Rose harrumphed on the other end of the phone.

Kitty stood up and got herself a glass of water. "So what was your plan? I know you had one."

"Steal a wheelbarrow from a work site, put the body in a trash bag, wheel the body down to someone else's boat, hot wire the boat, dump the body in the center of lake, return the boat and the wheelbarrow. No links back to you."

Kitty hiccuped again. "All that, in less than a minute?"

"A girl's got to be quick on her feet in a crisis."

Kitty gulped down the glass of water. "You are a scary woman, Rose."

"I'll take that as a compliment." Rose paused. Kitty could hear ice cubes rattling in a glass. "We could do it you know. We could kill that Marni and get away with it, if you wanted to."

"Don't be absurd. I wouldn't kill someone over a cheating husband and a venereal disease. Maim maybe, but not murder."

"So what are you going to do?" Rose asked.

"I don't know. The kids will be home any minute. I've got to clean up this mess. I'll call you back later."

Kitty heard Rose pouring liquid into a glass. "I meant what I said about that Marni."

"I love you too, Rosie."

❧

Twenty minutes later, the kitchen was spick and span and Kitty was on the couch in her pajamas watching NOVA with the dog when Becky's VW screeched to a halt in the driveway. Car doors slammed and Becky came running across the deck. She burst through the sliding door yelling, "Mom!"

"Honey, I'm right here. What's the matter?"

"Mom, are you all right?" Becky jumped across the coffee table and landed on top of her mother. Daisy let out a yelp and ran out the still open door.

"I'm fine. Or, I was. You're crushing me."

Becky smelled of chlorine and pizza. "Connor came into the pizzeria and told us that you and Dad got into a fist fight. His mom took Dad to the emergency room." Becky inspected her mother. "Where did he hit you?"

Kitty pushed Becky off of her. "Your father would never hit me!" She straightened her pajama top and tried to figure out what to say. "We had a disagreement and his nose became bloodied."

"You punched his lights out?"

"Good for you, Mom," Bobby said from the door. He was loaded down with his soccer bag, Becky's swim bag and a pizza box. Becky jumped up and unburdened her little brother.

"Thanks, Bub," Becky said. "Did Connor say anything else?"

"Just that Dad seemed really upset when they left Connor's house." Bobby turned to his mother. "So what happened? Who told you about Dad and Connor's mom?"

The air seemed to have been sucked out of the room. *They knew too? Was I the only person who didn't know Marni was sleeping with my husband?*

"Debbie Manning."

"Bitch," Bobby said.

"Bobby!" Kitty stood up and walked into the kitchen. She needed to put the counter between her and her children. "So, why didn't either of you say anything to me about this? Did you think it funny that your mother was being made a fool of?"

"Frankly Mom, I didn't think you really wanted to know," Becky replied. She tossed the pizza box on the kitchen table. "It's not like he was hiding it very well. We just don't talk about things like that in this family."

FIFTEEN

The next morning the alarm clock chirped in Kitty's ear as if it were any other morning. She had the sensation that a small animal had died in her mouth. She tried to roll over to hit the snooze button, but her arm was pinned to the mattress. Someone was breathing behind her. At first, she assumed Seth had rolled over on her arm but as the fog in her head was replaced by a pounding behind her temple, she remembered punching Seth. *Who is this next to me? What did I do last night? Did I try to get back at Seth by having sex with a stranger?* She searched her memory. *Doubtful. But possible.*

Kitty opened one eye, fully expecting to see a strange face staring back at her. Daisy was lying diagonally across the bed, snoring. Bits and pieces of the night before came back to her. After shooing Becky and Bobby off to their rooms, she had discovered the wine rack was empty. She'd dug a crusty bottle of grenadine out of the back of the liquor cabinet and made herself a Tequila Sunrise, then five more. That explained the fuzzy feeling in her mouth and the sticky orange patch on her nightgown.

The sounds of Bobby brushing his teeth filtered through the wall. A wave of nausea rolled through her as she tried to push Daisy off her arm. Her stomach lurched at the memory of Seth's blood splattered across the kitchen floor. Bobby closed his bedroom door and clomped down the stairs with his oversized feet just like every morning.

I need a drink.

I'd better get Bobby to school first.

After a quick shower to get the sticky sensation off her skin and brushing her teeth twice, she pulled on a pair of sweatpants and one of Seth's old T-shirts. There was no hope of zipping up her tight jeans over her bloated belly. *Why did I drink so much last night?*

She descended the stairs with trepidation. *What must the children think of me, drinking myself into oblivion?* Becky was standing in front of the open refrigerator with her back to Kitty. "Morning, honey," Kitty whispered. Her head was still pounding.

Becky looked like she was off for a carefree day of yachting in red shorts and a navy and white striped T-shirt. She wouldn't let her parents' crumbling marriage interfere with her exemplary school attendance record. She was very much like her mother in that way. "We're out of orange juice," Becky scolded.

"I'll get some after I drop Bobby off," Kitty replied as she glugged down her third glass of water.

Twenty minutes later, Becky had left for school and Bobby sat in the back seat of the car. Kitty promised to clean the frosting off the passenger seat before she picked him up that afternoon. He kept up a running commentary on the condition of his cleats, how tedious he found algebra class and the English paper that was due the next day, all the way to the junior high school but he didn't say a word about the previous evening's events. Neither did Kitty.

She pulled into the drop-off line, glad to no longer be moving. Marni's giant Cadillac, with her smarmy real estate bumper sticker, was parked in the circle. Women hung off the open window as Marni flapped her arms like a whirlygig. Kitty's stomach lurched again. Blaire Morton spotted Kitty and waved. Her slick coral lips curled around a Cheshire Cat smile signaling that she was saying something particularly cruel about Kitty to the crowd.

"You can stop here, Mom," Bobby said. "I can walk across the grass." Before he climbed out of the car, Bobby did something he hadn't done since kindergarten; he leaned over and gave his mother a quick kiss on the cheek. "It'll be okay. I'll see you after practice." It would have been easier to accept if he had stabbed her in the chest. *This is so wrong. A child should never have to comfort their parent. I should be stronger. Hide my pain better.*

She did an illegal U-turn and roared away to a chorus of blaring horns. She didn't notice Molly tailing her until the brown VW bus pulled into the driveway behind her. Molly popped out of the driver's seat yelling, "What the hell is wrong with you? You could have killed yourself driving like that. You almost took out a dumpster on Lakeview."

"Sorry, I'm a little distracted this morning." Kitty slammed the car door and walked inside the garage leaving the door open behind her.

"I know, you were the lead story on the grapevine this morning," Molly called after her.

Kitty went inside and hung onto the counter. The room was spinning and she was afraid she was going to vomit all over the breakfast dishes. She closed her eyes and held her hand over her mouth, willing the contents of her stomach to settle down.

Molly followed her into the kitchen and closed the door. "What exactly happened last night? Someone told me you hit Seth over the head with a frying pan."

"Really?" Kitty chuckled through her fingers. "A frying pan?"

Molly helped herself to a cup of coffee from the pot on the counter and poured a cup for Kitty. "You okay?" Molly asked as she retrieved the milk from the refrigerator. "No frying pan?"

Kitty turned around. Her stomach had calmed down. "I punched him in the nose, but that's it."

"That's too bad. I was having fun picturing that." Molly pushed the cup of coffee toward Kitty. "Drink that. You look like you could use some coffee."

Kitty took a deep breath and inhaled the nutty aroma of the coffee. She had planned on having a screwdriver when she came in, but the coffee seemed more appealing now. And, they were out of orange juice. She took a sip and let the coffee's warmth fill her chest before grabbing Molly's arm.

"So. How long have you known?"

"Known?" Molly bit the inside of her lip.

"Marni. How long?"

Molly touched Kitty's hand on her arm. Her eyes were apologetic. "A few weeks. But, I wasn't absolutely sure. I saw them eating lunch at the Capitol Grille. I was in the back room with a bunch of people from the Arts Council so I don't think they saw me."

"They could have just been eating lunch."

"I could tell. It was the way they were sitting close, eating off each other's plates, smiling too much." Molly thoughtfully took a sip of her coffee and wrinkled her nose. "I know the signs. I used to follow Tom on his little trysts. "

"Tom?"

"Oh yeah." Molly brushed a long grey hair out of her eyes. "There's been four women over the last couple of years. That I know of."

"Why didn't you ever say anything?"

"Talking about it won't change anything." Molly took another sip of coffee then dumped it down the sink. "Your milk has gone around the bend."

"Why didn't you leave him?"

"There's no point in leaving him. Maybe when Ethan is on his own." *Poor Ethan. I bet he knew just like Bobby knew. Neither of them should have to live like that.*

"Why didn't you tell me? You're my friend."

"I almost did a few times. You didn't seem to really want to know." Molly helped herself to the crusts of Bobby's toast still on the counter beside the sink. "I was hoping it would be over before you ever found out. These things usually run their course in a few weeks."

Kitty spoke into her coffee cup. "Like a bad virus."

≪∘≫

Molly didn't stay long. She'd left the dog in the back of the bus and Dana had a talent for urinating on the one spot on the seat covers that leaked. Kitty closed the door behind Molly and stood despondent in her kitchen. The tall oak cabinets mocked her; their wood gleamed from where the cleaning crew had rubbed polish on the doors but cobwebs hung off their corners and a half inch of grease laden dust clung to the molding above the doors.

She pulled the notepad off the side of the refrigerator. She was in no shape to do much about her marriage at this point, but she could make a shopping list. She needed orange juice, milk, some kind of meat for dinner - *Maybe lamb chops. I love lamb chops. Seth hates lamb. But he won't come home for dinner. Will he ever come home? Home. Is this still his home? Whose home is it? Mine? His? Anyone's?*

She crumpled up the list and threw it toward the garbage can. It landed a foot from the cabinet where the garbage can hid behind a sliding panel, as if a piece of wood could hide the stink of the Haskell's refuse. An empty bottle of cranberry juice and a wad of wax paper sat on the counter above the trash cabinet. *Gee Becky, you choose today as the day you don't throw away your trash?* Kitty walked over and yanked on the

109

handle. The cabinet didn't budge. She pulled harder. Something was stuck behind the panel. *What else can go wrong around here?*

She pulled the junk drawer out, placed it on the floor and peered into the opening under the counter. The empty orange juice container and tequila bottle were wedged up against the cabinet wall keeping the panel from sliding open. Kitty reached in and pulled the bottle of tequila out through the junk drawer opening and tossed it in the sink. *What was I thinking throwing that in the garbage? It should be recycled.* She retrieved the orange juice bottle and ran a sink full of hot water. She scrubbed the bottles and the milk jug until every trace of their previous contents were gone.

That's my problem, I wasn't thinking. I've been doing everything I can not to think about what Seth did to me. To us. She carried the bottles out to the recycling bin in the garage. It was already overflowing with curvaceous green and clear wine bottles. *Did I drink all this wine in one week? I can't let anyone see these. They'll think I'm an alcoholic.* Kitty heard her mother's voice in her head saying those same words about her father and proceeded to vomit a foul brew of coffee, orange juice and old grenadine all over the bottles and cans in the recycling bin.

When they were girls, Kitty and Rose were not allowed to have friends in the house. Mother didn't want anyone to know that their father came home from his job as a vice-president of a large insurance company and proceeded to drink until he passed out every night. She didn't want anyone to smell the stench of whiskey and despair that permeated the brown plaid couch in his den. Mother made him wear buckets of cologne to work in order to cover up the smell of alcohol leeching out of his pores because 'people might think he was alcoholic.' Her father was an alcoholic. They all knew it, yet they never talked about it. It was easier to pretend it wasn't happening.

Once her stomach was empty, Kitty felt marginally better. She wheeled the recycling bin into the backyard and hosed the contents down. One by one she removed empty wine bottles, an empty vodka bottle and, of course, the tequila bottle, and separated them from the other recyclables. She paused several times to take long drinks from the hose and rest. After she rinsed out the bin, she put the aluminum cans and milk jugs back inside for the monthly neighborhood recycling drive. The evidence of her transgressions would need to be disposed of elsewhere.

A couple of empty boxes from the garage seemed like a solution to her dilemma, until she realized she was too weak to pick up the boxes once they were filled with the dripping glass bottles. She had to take all the bottles back out of the boxes and move them to the back of her car in several trips. By the time she finished, she was dripping with sweat and smelled like a still. She draped one of Bobby's old jackets over the top of the boxes in case anyone peered into the car before she was able to dispose of them.

The sun was high in a cloudless blue sky before Kitty gathered her little remaining strength to drive across town to the new Magnuson recycling center. After much protest from the local tree huggers, the city had set a line of old dented dumpster in an abandoned parking lot where people could bring glass bottles, cans, and old newspapers. Kitty suspected the city emptied the dumpsters into the dump with rest of the trash but she was willing to go through the motions on the outside chance the items did get recycled. She waited in the air-conditioned tomb of her car while a young Hispanic woman with a car full of children dutifully separated her paper from her aluminum cans and glass. *Did Mother do this? Did she drive across town while we were in school to discreetly dispose of Dad's empties?*

When the other car pulled away dragging its back bumper, Kitty quickly threw the bottles into the dumpster hoping to finish before anyone else came to use the recycling center. Grass a foot high grew from the cracks in the rutted pavement and the stink of urine made Kitty wish she was wearing rubber boots instead of Keds.

How could I let this happen? How could I be so much like my father? As soon as things got difficult, I went straight for the bottle. I always thought Mother was the one that made Rose and me the way we are. I obviously picked something up from Dad. Alcohol makes your troubles go away, at least for the moment.

What was he so unhappy about? I never even bothered to ask him. Most of Kitty's memories of her father were through the filter of what Mother said about him after he died. Her mother spoke about Kitty's father as if he had been feeble minded, but it was obvious she loathed him. He had stolen her future and youth but, even if the Church would allow it, Mother would never have been a "divorcée," that would have been too scandalous. She arranged their public life to keep their private home life a secret. As far as anyone knew, he was an insurance executive, father of two beautiful daughters and dutiful husband to Mary Jo McSweeney.

I'm not sure why Dad hated Mother, but I'm pretty sure that's why he drank. And, she let him. She didn't try to stop him. That's just the way it was in our family.

Kitty thought about what Becky said the night before, they didn't talk about those kinds of things in their family. Kitty threw the last bottle into the dumpster. It broke against the back wall with a satisfying smash and shower of glass.

This has got to stop before I end up like my father. I don't want to be so desperate that I drive off a bridge too.

I'm just going to have to face up to what's happening with Seth. I don't like it. It's ugly and messy, but it's my mess to clean up.

She pulled out of the parking lot and into Charlie's market to buy the things on her shopping list. As much as she hated to admit it, Rose was right; the prices in Charlie's were much cheaper. In the checkout line, she reflexively thought about how she would need to lie to Seth about where she had bought groceries then, shook herself. *What the hell am I doing? Screw Seth. What does it matter where I buy the damn orange juice? It's the same brands, just a different name printed on the bags.*

Back at the house, she saw Seth everywhere - in the dishes he picked out, in the couch he picked out, his sports magazines on the coffee table. She felt all her nascent resolve oozing away. The liquor cabinet was calling to her. She needed to get out of that house before she started smashing things. She pulled on her running shoes, without bothering to put on sunblock, and scrambled through the backyard to the lake front path. She ran as if pursued by doubt until her T-shirt was soaked and her sweatpants clung to her thighs. The smell of alcohol, bitter and wretched, spilled out of her and was eventually replaced by her normal animal-smelling sweat.

On the far side of the neighborhood lay the boat slips for the Overlook residents who did not have waterfront lots. Instead of running past the gate as she normally did, she kicked off her shoes and socks and jumped the low fence. She sprinted down the long dock between the ski boats and jumped in with a yelp. The water welcomed her in a tender green embrace. She opened her eyes under the water and watched the sunbeams play with the tiny fish just under the surface as she slowly sank into the murky depth.

It's nice down here. If I can't make it work with Seth, this would always be an option.

With one strong kick, Kitty popped up. Surfacing for air felt as if she was taking her first deep breath all day. The weakness of that morning was gone. She pulled herself out of the water renewed and clean.

SIXTEEN

Weldon had a pot of chicken soup simmering on the stove and a baguette warming in the oven when Stacia brought Eileen and Jim in from the hospital. Eileen threw her arms around Weldon and burst into tears when she saw the fresh flowers he had arranged on her kitchen table. "I'm sorry," she said between sobs. "You guys have been so great. I don't know how we could have gotten through the last couple of days without you."

Weldon stiffened in Eileen's arms. "It's just a few flowers," he replied. "I wish I could do more."

"They're so beautiful," Eileen blubbered.

"I think I should take you upstairs, sweetheart," Jim said as he peeled his wife off of Weldon. "I think those tranquilizers the doctor gave you are kicking in." He offered a wane smile of thanks to Stacia and led Eileen up the stairs to their bedroom.

"I'll make her a tray," Stacia called after them. "She should put something in her stomach."

"Thank you, Stacia," Eileen said from the landing and started bawling anew.

Stacia turned to her husband with a wry smile. "Please tell me I wasn't like that."

"Oh no," Weldon replied. "You cried so much you couldn't speak at all."

Stacia swatted him on the arm. "The flowers are very nice. Did you have any trouble at Soup Stop?" She started opening cabinets and drawers looking for a tray and bowls in an unfamiliar kitchen.

"Only trying to pick out what kind of soup to get. Too many choices. I ran into Blaire Morton and she said that the lentil soup was

114

the best, so I got the chicken noodle. I picked up a container of that cream of mushroom that Marcus likes too."

"How is my baby?" Stacia asked. She pulled the bread out of the oven and sliced a thick slab to take up to Eileen.

Weldon stopped ladling soup into bowls and turned to look at Stacia. "He didn't call you?"

"About what?"

"The coach at Magnuson Country Day wants him to try out for their team."

Stacia nearly sliced her finger. "No way. They'd eat him alive at that school."

Weldon placed a bowl on the tray. "Marcus wouldn't be the only black kid there."

"I know, the Tiftons and the Willet girl go there. The Country Day kids are just plain mean. Stacia picked up the tray as Eileen wailed in the distance and water ran through the pipes overhead as if the whole house was crying. "Marcus can go to Nance with the other Overlook kids. He'll be fine."

"Speaking of other Overlook kids, you haven't talked to anyone at all for a day or so, right?" Stacia shook her head and worriedly looked up at the ceiling. "Then you don't know about Kitty, do you?"

"Oh damn, I never thanked her for coming to the race. I got so tied up with Eileen, I never even got a chance to call her."

"She found out about Seth and Marni." Stacia put the tray down as Weldon chuckled to himself. "Marcus told me that when she found out, she went home and beat him to a pulp. I didn't know our Kitty had it in her. Good for her."

"Who told her?"

"I don't know."

"Jesus Christ, I stop paying attention for two days and this whole place goes to hell in a hand basket." Stacia walked through Eileen's dining room and looked across the street to the Haskell's house. "So what happened? Is Kitty all right?"

Weldon stood behind her in the dark dining room. "Apparently. I don't know the details; I'm getting my information from a fourteen-year-old boy. Marcus just told me that Marni took Seth to the emergency room to get stitched up."

"Poor Kitty, she must be beside herself."

SEVENTEEN

A storm front passed over the Piedmont that night washing red mud off streets and refreshing parched Bermuda grass. Determined to start cleaning up the messes in her life, Kitty spent the next morning on a ladder wiping down the tops of cabinets and door frames. Cleaning up the mess that was Seth would need more than Murphy's Oil Soap and elbow grease. At lunchtime, she took Daisy out on the deck and shared a turkey sandwich with her. The empty holes in the garden reminded her of the holes in her marriage that she still needed to patch. She leaned back in the teak chaise and scratched Daisy behind the ears.

"Where has he been sleeping, girl? Has he been staying at Marni's house with Connor in the next room? Would he do that?"

She went inside and found a message scrawled in Bobby's spiky handwriting. Seth had called and left a message saying he was okay and not to worry. She stepped over to the wall phone and dialed Seth's office.

"Hey, Mrs. Haskell," his perky little secretary answered. "Awful about Seth's bike accident, huh?"

"Bike accident?" It occurred to Kitty that Seth would have had to tell his secretary something to explain his nose. He certainly wouldn't have told Suzie that his wife had punched him.

"He's lucky he didn't break his collarbone flipping over the handle bars like that. At his age, he needs to be more careful with—"

"Suzie! Is he in?"

When Seth picked up, Kitty blurted out, "What are you wearing?"

"Who is this?" Seth asked. He sounded tired.

"It's your wife."

"Kitty!" She heard him snap his desk chair to the upright position. "Thank God."

"Who were you expecting? Marni?"

"No, I told Suzie not to put Marni through. I told her I have sales meetings all day today."

Poor Marni, he's already lying to her. Serves her right.

"The last time I saw you, you had blood dripping down the front of your shirt." Kitty blushed remembering the fat drops of blood soaking into Seth's white shirt. Those stains would never come out. "What are you wearing? You must look awful."

"I got Marni to run into Belk and pick me up a new shirt. It's poly-cotton—"

"Poly-cotton? Really?"

"—and yellow."

"Yellow? You look awful in yellow. It makes you look jaundiced." Seth didn't say anything but she could hear him playing with the nodding bird toy on his desk. He played with it when he was nervous. "How's your nose?"

"It's fine. It wasn't actually broken."

"Oh Seth, I'm so—"

"Sorry?" Seth guffawed.

"I shouldn't have—"

"Kitty! You had every right to smack me. I deserved it!"

"But....I—"

"Kitty, take a breath," Seth said. "Who knew you had such a good right hook? I wouldn't want to meet you in a dark alley."

"Seth—"

"It's probably all the tennis."

"—Why didn't you come home last night?"

"I didn't think you wanted me there."

"Seth, it's your house. We need to deal with this in private. So come home." Kitty hung up the phone and burst into tears.

That afternoon, Bobby had another soccer game. Kitty didn't want to go. She didn't want to face The Lookers and all their veiled comments on the state of her marriage. She didn't want to do any of the things that were expected of her. She would go anyway. She was a good mother.

Daisy hung her head out of the open passenger-side window. They had taken the car to get cleaned and detailed on the way to the field and the interior now stunk of upholstery cleaner. The men had blasted the undercarriage with their high-powered hoses making the brakes squeal whenever Kitty slowed down. Some problems couldn't be fixed with a good cleaning.

Kitty pulled into a parking spot overlooking the soccer field and let the dog out. She planned to tell anyone who tried to get close enough to talk to her that Daisy had an awful case of fleas. If that didn't keep The Lookers away, she would watch the game from her car. Either way, she was going to be a good mother and support Bobby. Within seconds, Seth pulled into the spot beside her. She wondered if he had been lurking on a side street waiting for her to drive by. Kitty tried to appear unfazed as she opened the tailgate to retrieve her folding chair as Seth climbed out of the Mercedes. He was wearing a pair of slacks that were too long for him and a yellow patterned dress shirt with a sheen. From the way he held his shoulders, Kitty could tell it was itchy.

He popped the trunk. "I went to Sears at lunchtime and bought myself a camping chair. That place sells everything." He bent over and looked under Kitty's bumper. "I could hear you coming a mile away. You really do need to get that muffler looked at."

"I did." Kitty peered into the Mercedes' trunk, filled with white and blue bags. "What all did you buy?"

"This and that."

Kitty rolled her eyes. Seth rustled through several bags and pulled out a square pink box. "Look, I bought you a present."

Kitty opened the box and pulled out a pair of pink boxing gloves. Seth flashed her his best aren't-I-adorable smile. Kitty threw the box back in the trunk. "Don't push your luck, buddy. I said you could come home, but I'm still really miffed at you. One wrong move and I may be forced to hit you again."

"You would never do that."

"Try me," Kitty said as she shoved Seth's new chair into his chest. She stopped short and demanded, "Are those new sunglasses?"

"Well, yeah," Seth said, quickly turning back to the trunk. "I needed bigger ones."

Kitty reached over and lifted the large aviator frames from his face. Blue and green bruises were blooming under Seth's eyes. "You look awful," Kitty groaned.

"It'll clear up in a few days," Seth said and repositioned the glasses. *Just like the infection.* "That doesn't make it all right."

Seth hoisted his new chair onto his shoulder. "Check out this awesome chair I got. It folds up into this little bag and even has a detachable foot rest."

"Why would a chair need a foot rest?"

Seth slammed the trunk and took Kitty's chair from her. "Shall we stake out a spot on the sideline?" He started walking toward the field.

"Wait," Kitty yelled at Seth's back. "I need to get Daisy's leash." She took her time getting the dog's leash out of the car and pulling a cardigan over her sleeveless blouse. The early October day had been sunny and warm but Kitty suspected it would get chilly as soon as the sun slipped behind the trees. Her cardigan also covered up her still bloated belly.

Kitty and Daisy paused at the top of the stairs and watched Seth set up their chairs at the shady end of the field. From the way he was holding his head, Kitty could tell he was keenly aware of The Lookers watching him like a pack of hyenas. Kitty tugged the hem of her sweater down, ran a hand over her hair and led Daisy down to the field. *Time to put on the show.*

The home team was running laps around the perimeter of the field while they let the opposing team warm up. Bobby stopped in his tracks and watched Kitty sit down next to Seth. "Smile, honey," Seth said through a goofy grin. "We are being watched."

"I know," Kitty replied. "Bobby just spotted us from the other side of the field." Marni's son, Connor, ran into him and knocked him to his knees. Bobby stood up and pointed to his parents.

"I'm really hating you right now. Those two used to be friends." Kitty watched the two boys exchange a few words. They didn't seem to be arguing or being ugly to each other; they stood there, heads inclined, until their coach barked at them to keep moving.

The boys were not the only people staring at Seth and Kitty. Stacia spotted them talking in the parking lot. Even though she hadn't yet had an opportunity to talk to Kitty, Stacia was prepared to rush to Kitty's side at the first sign of trouble. After Kitty walked down to the field, Stacia climbed out of her Jeep and watched Kitty and Seth for a few moments from top of the hill. They appeared to be talking amicably enough although Stacia noticed Seth was leaning toward

Kitty where Kitty was sitting ramrod straight with her eyes fixed on the field. Kitty's only movements were to occasionally run her fingertips over Daisy's back.

Stacia felt partially responsible for Kitty finding out about Seth's affair with Marni the way she did. If she had been at the school that evening, she would have been able to control the situation. Now everything was flying apart. After her conversation with Weldon, she had made a few phone calls and pieced together how Debbie Manning showed up at parents' night in a drugged-up stupor and spilled the beans. The scuttlebutt was that Kitty hauled off and stabbed Seth with a kitchen knife. That was obviously an exaggeration since Seth looked very much alive and well. *What is going on? Weldon said Kitty kicked Seth out. But here they are at the soccer game? What is happening?*

Stacia lifted Baillie out of the car and attached a thin, white leather leash to her pink collar. She had left Eileen napping while Jim worked from home that afternoon so that she could watch the game. She brought Baillie in case Kitty needed some support. Stacia knew that if the other Lookers saw her and Kitty walking their dogs around the field, they would know whose side they were supposed to be on. The little dog sniffed at a red mud puddle. Her little white face was muddy when she looked up at her mistress. "Look at you," Stacia sighed. "Daddy just took you to the groomer yesterday." The condition of the schools fields and parking lots annoyed Stacia every time she drove in. She had petitioned the school system to pave the lot and fix the drainage issues on the north side of the field. They didn't seem to share her sense of urgency.

Mud completely doused Baillie as Marni skidded into a spot at the end of the lot. *Oh no you don't! I may not totally get what's going on with Kitty and Seth, but I am certain no one wants to see you.* Stacia picked up Baillie and held her at arm's length as she rushed over to Marni's car.

Marni's copious bangles jangled loudly through the closed window as she waved at Stacia with a smug smile on her face. Stacia motioned to Marni to open the window. "Before you bother to get out," Stacia said. "You might want to look and see who's sitting together down near the east goal."

Marni scanned the spectators. Her hand flew to her lips. "I don't know what you're talking about." Her face turned the same shade of scarlet as her fingernails.

"Quit it, Marni. It looks like you didn't get your hooks into Seth Haskell after all." Marni's eyes teared up. Stacia flicked some mud off the lemon yellow cardigan she was wearing over her green and yellow paisley sheath and said, "I told you to stay away from him. Why don't you just go on home now and try to sell some houses while you still can? I'll make sure Connor gets a ride home."

"But—"

"Put the car in reverse, Marni," Stacia growled. "Go. Away. Now."

Marni considered her options for a moment then put the car in reverse. As she pulled away, Stacia waved and shouted, "Bye bye now!" loud enough for The Lookers down by the field to hear. They all turned in unison and watched Marni pull out of the lot.

Stacia gave Baillie's ears a scratch and murmured, "Come on Baillie, let's get you cleaned up then go see what the hell is going on with the Haskells." Stacia took Baillie into the bathroom and gave her a quick bath in the ladies' room sink before scooting around the back of the goals, effectively bypassing the flock of Lookers gathered at center field.

"Hey, Haskells," Stacia hailed. "Great day for a game, huh?"

"Sure is," Seth replied enthusiastically. Kitty just smiled briefly. *Okay, Kitty doesn't look too happy, but she's here and with her husband.* "Seth, what do you say we take the dogs for a stroll on this lovely afternoon?"

Seth checked with Kitty for permission. Kitty handed him Daisy's leash without taking her eyes off the field. "I'll be right back."

As soon as they were away from the field, Stacia whacked Seth's arm with the end of Baillie's leash. "What is your game?" she hissed. "You're here with Kitty like everything is fabulous but Weldon saw your car in Marni's driveway this morning. And, if he saw it, other people saw it."

Seth swung around and looked at Stacia incredulously. "It's none of your business where I park my car."

"Yes, it is. You and your wife live in my neighborhood. Your wife is my friend. Your mistress also lives in my neighborhood. Therefore, it is my business."

"This is a personal matter between my wife and I."

"Not anymore, fool. By acting like such a dumb-ass, you've involved other people. Don't you care about how this could affect the community?"

"Butt out, Stacia."

121

"Excuse me?" Stacia gasped as Seth pulled Daisy's leash and turned back toward his new chair.

"I think I will go sit with my lovely wife now."

EIGHTEEN

Kitty watched a slick of olive oil encroach on an island of soap bubbles. The dirty pots and pans had disappeared under the reflective surface. She stood back from the sink and listened to Becky and Seth arguing upstairs.

"Taking the SAT one more time is a waste of time," Seth yelled. "You could get into a decent school with the scores you have now."

"But I want to go to Brown or Dartmouth. If I can get better than a 740 on the math, I might get in," Becky said. "I should at least try."

"You should be trying to get a triple A time in the two hundred breast. That would get you a shot at the 1980 Olympics. Smarty pants are a dime a dozen, but people will pay for a good breaststroker. You shouldn't even be applying to those schools, anyway. You need to be looking at state schools."

"Just because you went to a state school...you don't...Argh!"

"College is a waste of good money. Look at your mother."

"Shut up!" Something heavy thumped to the floor. "I don't know what you said to convince Mom to let you back into this house but she's an idiot for believing anything you say!"

"Watch it, little girl!"

The house shook as Becky jumped off her bed. Kitty recognized the sounds of Becky physically pushing Seth out of her room. "You're the one that better watch it!" A door slammed and the house fell silent for a moment before heavy footsteps slowly moved down the hall and into the guest room.

Kitty lifted a casserole pan from beneath the water and pestered a baked on noodle from the corner. She had made Bobby's favorite dish, Mrs. Pinto's macaroni and cheese. The secret was to use three types of hard cheese, as well as cottage cheese and ricotta, and toss the bread crumbs with some grated parmesan before sprinkling them on top. No one could resist its creamy goodness, but the noodles always stuck, no matter how much Kitty buttered the pan. Dinner had gone better than she feared. Bobby seemed happy to see his father there and had kept up the conversation. Becky had grit her teeth throughout the whole meal. Kitty was willing to overlook that.

Kitty scrubbed the last of the cheese off the edge of the oval casserole pan and propped it in the sink to dry. It was a workhorse of a pan, white ceramic over cast iron, and had been scrubbed clean hundreds of times. Kitty had been using the same pots and pans since she received them as wedding gifts and probably would for another twenty or thirty years. She thrust her hand again into the soapy water to search for the dishrag and felt the tip of a paring knife slice through her glove. Scalding water rushed through the hole. She jerked her hand out of the water and peeled the glove off her hand. *Crap, that was a fairly new pair.*

On tall metal shelves in the garage, Kitty kept packs of paper towels, rolls of aluminum foil and bottles of detergent purchased on sale. She pulled out a packing crate filled with boxes of rubber gloves. Knowing she had a ready supply was a comfort. When her mother punctured a rubber glove, she would have patched it with electrical tape and made it make do.

As she pulled the fresh pair of yellow flocked gloves out of their box, she noticed that Seth had left the door to the Mercedes ajar. She climbed in and let the scent of leather and Seth's cologne waft over her. *This really is a nice car. I deserve a car like this.*

The phone rang in the kitchen. Kitty jumped out of the car and got to it by the third ring. Marni's voice bellowed through the ear piece, "If you think I am just going to wait around all night for you to show up, Buddy. You've got another thing coming." A wicked smile spread across Kitty's face. She had spent years listening to Marni. She knew when she was desperate. *Advantage Kitty.* "Kitty won't make you happy the way I can. You better get over here. Now!"

Kitty slammed the receiver down. She heard footsteps move down the hallway and stop at the top of the stairs. "What is going on down there? Did I hear the phone?"

"It was just a sales call, Seth. I took care of it."

"Are you almost done? There's a Bond special on tonight to celebrate the new one coming out next summer. *Live And Let Die* is starting in five minutes," Seth yelled down the stairs. "Bring me one of those brownies when you finish. And a beer! Hurry up or you'll miss the opening chase."

Kitty took the phone off the hook and left it dangling from its tangled cord.

Stacia stood on Eileen's front porch contemplating the other houses on Azalea Lane. Lives were breaking apart in this part of her realm faster than she could fix them. She was exhausted. She wanted nothing more than to go home, kiss her son goodnight, and snuggle up next to her husband. Unfortunately, Jim had asked her to come back to their house that evening to talk. He was still tied up on a sales call, but they needed to discuss what to do about Eileen. Neither one of them would come right out and say it, but Eileen couldn't be left alone right now. She wouldn't eat. She wouldn't get dressed. She barely spoke. Since coming home from the hospital, she had been curled up in a ball.

Jim's voice rose with impatience behind the closed blinds of his office. Stacia hoped he hadn't woken Eileen. She needed to rest. Stacia remembered being where Eileen was now. She knew she couldn't say anything to make Eileen feel better today, although she could try to pave the way for her to feel better tomorrow. Weldon had done a good job of cleaning up the evidence of the miscarriage, but there were little things he hadn't thought to get rid of. Stacia had removed the pre-natal vitamins from the medicine cabinet and the reminders for Eileen's doctor's appointments from the refrigerator door. She had stocked their refrigerator with enough chili and lasagna to keep them fed for a few days, and, most importantly, she hadn't told anyone about the miscarriage. Eileen needed to cry it out in private right now. If she wanted to share her grief, in her own time, she could do it when she was ready.

Stacia lit a cigarette and inhaled the beautifully noxious smoke. Stacia knew she should quit smoking, but in times like this, she was glad she hadn't yet. She stood in the dark and burned through three cigarettes as fast as she could while surveying the cul-de-sac. The Wrights in the triangular lot at the end of the street seemed to be doing all right as far as Stacia knew. They were a retired couple who played golf most days.

Angry tones drifted through the window again and Stacia moved to the far end of the front porch to peer over the fence into Betty Oliphant's backyard. Renee had told her that Betty's little boy was hyperactive, and judging from the mess of toys and childhood detritus littering the yard, that was probably true. *I'll have to recommend Betty get that child a trampoline. He needs to move more. He's probably old enough now for peewee football or even the Rambling Runners. Those programs would be great for a kid with ants in his pants.*

The Wilson's house, next to Kitty and Seth's, was dark. Renee said that Phil Wilson was traveling three out of four weeks since his start-up was absorbed by IBM and that his wife, Mindy, had taken a job that took her to Boston for months at a time. Stacia dropped her cigarette into the empty Coke can in her hand. *That marriage won't last. People who travel for business spend entirely too much time in hotel bars. A person can get into all sorts of trouble in a hotel bar.*

And then there was Kitty and Seth. Stacia pulled her cardigan around her tightly and sat in one of the white rocking chairs Eileen had placed on the small front porch. Stacia doubted anyone ever sat in them. People didn't sit out on their porches in Overlook. From her vantage point, she saw lights coming on in the upstairs bedrooms across the street. Bobby's shades were down. Becky's were open. Becky was sitting on her canopy bed with a textbook in her lap when Seth came in and sat at the desk in front of the window. *Lana would have a fit if Weldon or I had barged into her room like that and started fiddling with her things. That Becky is way too nice, just like her mother.*

She watched another few moments. Becky threw her book down and was glaring at her father. Seth stood up and crossed his arms. The argument seemed to be coming to an impasse. *I wonder what they're arguing about. Is Becky telling him that he's an idiot? I hope she is.*

Stacia pulled another cigarette out of her pocket but didn't light it. Marni Kaur's Cadillac was moving slowly into the cul-de-sac. *Marni Kaur! What are you doing here? I told you to go home. Leave Kitty and her family alone.* Stacia watched Marni circle and stop in front of the Haskell's house. They both watched Becky jump down from her bed and push Seth out of her room. Becky threw a pillow at the wall. *That is your fault, Marni. I just know it.*

Marni eventually drove away and Stacia went back inside to talk to Jim, but she couldn't get Marni out of her mind. It wasn't Eileen and her grief that woke Stacia up that night, it was Marni. Someone needed to teach that woman who was in charge.

❧

The next morning, Kitty woke up stiff but content. She, Seth, and Bobby had all fallen asleep snuggling on the couch. With the exception of Becky who had left before dawn to go to swim practice, her little family was coming together again. While Bobby got ready for school, she made his lunch and jumped in the shower. As soon as she turned off the water she heard Seth downstairs shouting, "Calm down. It's not that bad."

Now what? Something awful must have happened at the company. I hope nobody's embezzling money. If something goes bad at work, I'll feel awful for Seth. I want to stay mad at him. Good and mad. Kitty wrapped a towel around her naked body and listened.

"Marni! Marni!" Seth pleaded. "Stop crying. I can't understand what you're saying." Even from upstairs, Kitty could hear Marni screaming through the phone. "Okay, I heard you. Pull the car into the garage." She heard Seth open the garage door. "Her car is here....Then take it to the detailing place. Well, you'll have to go some time...No, I will not pay for it!"

Seth slammed the phone down and bound up the stairs. Kitty pulled the towel tighter around her chest as he stormed into the master bedroom, his face a mottled mask of rage. He had remnants of toothpaste stuck in the stubble around his lips, the bruises around his eyes had taken on a greenish cast, and his hair stuck up in the back in tufts.

"What did you do?" he gasped.

"What's happened?"

"Marni," Seth sputtered. "Spray paint...car..."

"Is something wrong with Marni's car?"

"How could you?" He covered his face with his hands. "Now look who's making this thing public!"

Kitty slowly walked toward Seth and wiped the toothpaste off his lip. "Seth, what are you talking about?"

"You...you...spray painted SLUT on the side of her car!"

Kitty heard Bobby laughing in his bathroom. She banged on the wall of the shower stall and yelled, "It's impolite to eavesdrop through the plumbing, young man." Kitty imagined Marni driving up Overlook Parkway with SLUT painted across the side of her Cadillac. "Oh my God," she chuckled. "That's awful."

"It isn't funny, Kitty! That's a company car. The real estate office owns that thing. How could you do something like that?"

"I didn't!"

"Of course you did."

In the same way she used to do with Bobby when he was a toddler, Kitty took Seth's face between her hands and forced him to pay attention. "Seth, I did not touch Marni's car." Kitty's towel fell to the floor.

"But—"

Kitty walked into the bedroom naked and began to hastily gather her clothes. "When did this happen?"

"Last night." Seth watched her in the mirror. "This morning, maybe."

"I was here, with you, all night. Remember?" She slipped on a bra and panties.

Seth looked around the room as if searching for clues as he took a sip out of Kitty's coffee cup on the edge of the vanity.

"Think about it." Kitty pulled a pair of jeans up over her hips. "We came home from the game. I made mac and cheese and then we watched the Bond movie. Bobby fell asleep with his head on my shoulder. You fell asleep sometime during the movie with your leg across my legs." She pulled a T-shirt over her head. "Are you saying that at some point during the night, I dislodged my legs from under your leg, left the house without you hearing the alarm sound, spray painted Marni's car, and then snuck back on to the couch again so you could wake up with your leg still cutting off my circulation?" She shook out her hair. "Really?"

"But—"

"I. Didn't. Do. It." Kitty threw her coffee down the drain. "Although, I kind of wish I had."

"Kitty!"

Kitty hollered for Bobby to meet her in the garage and scooted past Seth. "How many other men is Marni sleeping with at the moment? Maybe one of their wives vandalized her car. What makes you so special? She must have gotten gonorrhea from someone."

Bobby was already sitting quietly in the back seat of the Volvo chewing on a Pop-Tart when Seth followed her out to the car stammering. He looked tired. Kitty started pulling out of the garage and almost hit Marni's Cadillac parked across the end of the driveway. Bobby slid down in his seat. Kitty crawled out of hers.

Before Kitty's foot hit the driveway, Marni was running at her. Kitty ducked and covered her face but Marni's blows never landed. Before she reached Kitty, Seth picked Marni up like a three-year-old having a tantrum. Her arms and legs flailed as he held her back to his chest. "Hey! Calm down. Kitty didn't do that to your car."

"Yes she did!"

Seth dropped Marni on the damp lawn. "She was here, with me, all night." Grass stains smeared the knees of her white polyester pants suit when Marni jumped back up. Kitty wanted to wring Marni's neck as much as Marni seemed to want to gouge Kitty's eyes out. Then, Kitty spotted the car. It really was awful. The spray painted letters covered both doors on the driver's side, and whoever did the damage had also scribbled on the hood and windows. It was a mess, but that wasn't what caught Kitty's eye. The L in SLUT had a little loop in it that Kitty recognized from PTA agendas. Seth had said the paint was orange. It wasn't orange, it was tangerine, the same tangerine paint that she and Stacia had used to make a banner a few months before.

"Holy crap!"

Seth was watching Kitty's reaction and seemed to read her face. He pushed Marni toward her car. "Why did you even bring it over here? I thought you were worried about people seeing it? Go to the detailing place, now."

"What about Connor? School." Connor waved from the backseat. He seemed to be enjoying the whole scene.

"It's just a little paint," Kitty said. "Your big ugly face on the bumper sticker should distract people." Marni lunged toward Kitty again and Seth blocked her with his arm.

"Ladies," he warned, "the neighbors are watching."

Kitty couldn't see anyone watching, but knew they probably were. "I need to get Bobby to school," she said, trying to sound calm and rational. Marni just stood there glaring at her. "Move your car so I can get out."

Marni seemed to be waiting for Seth to say or do something. He didn't.

Connor rolled down the back window of Marni's car and said, "Can I hitch a ride with Bobby, Mom? I don't want to be late for school again."

"Absolutely not!" Marni exclaimed.

"Do you really want to drive me to school with this on the side of the car?" he asked.

Marni turned her back on all of them and said, "Just go."

Kitty felt bad for enjoying Marni's defeat. Connor jumping out of his mother's car and climbing in next to Bobby felt like winning both a set and match. She turned to Seth. "So, are you going to go help her?"

Marni looked over her shoulder and looked beseechingly at Seth. He stood there and looked back and forth between his mistress and his wife for a moment, seeming to weigh his options, before he pushed a strand of auburn hair out of Kitty's eyes and tucked it behind her ear.

"No, I don't think I am." He waved his hand to signal for Marni to drive away. "I think I am going to stay home this morning and eat breakfast with my wife." He turned toward the house. "Do we have any bacon?"

No one said a word on the way to the junior high school. Kitty tried to shove the image of Marni's car out of her mind and concentrate on the road. Bobby and Connor stolidly stared out their respective windows. *What must Connor be thinking? This must be so confusing for him. It's confusing for me and I'm a grown woman. First Seth shows up at his house with a bloody nose, then he is staying there for a few days, then Seth is back at home and his mother is having a conniption in my driveway. The poor kid. School must be a relief.*

And Bobby. He was so happy to have his dad home last night. And now all this happened. I'm going to have to sit down with him and have a talk. But what am I going to say? I have no idea where we really stand with Seth. When they arrived at the school, the boys climbed out and walked inside as if the scene in the driveway had never happened.

On the way home, Kitty passed a gas station with a neon Krispy Kreme sign and considered going in to scoff down a box of sugar-filled comfort and momentarily forget about Seth and Marni and spray paint. She didn't know what to think. She didn't understand why Stacia would spray paint Marni's car.

As soon as she walked into her house, the phone rang. "Hey Kitty," Stacia said in a hushed tone.

"Why would you do that to Marni's car?"

Kitty could hear Stacia walk outside and close a door behind her. "How do you know it was me?"

"Marni showed up at my house this morning. I saw the car. Why would you use that paint?"

Kitty heard a match being dragged across a rough surface. "Does Marni know it was me? Well, does she?"

"No, she thinks I did it. What if the police come after me?"

"They won't. I've got your back. She won't even report it. The last thing she wants is to have something like that on the public record. How would that look to her real estate clients?"

"Why would you do something like that?"

"People like her can't be allowed to act like that, not in my neighborhood."

"It's none of your business!" Kitty pulled the phone into the dining room to watch the garbage men navigate the cul de sac. "Really, Stacia! Her son saw it. You could be arrested."

"I may have gone a bit too far." Stacia blew out a long breath. "Okay. It was kind of juvenile of me. I just couldn't stand it anymore. That woman needs to be taught a lesson."

"How did you even know about Marni and Seth? Did she go around telling people?"

"No, I don't think she actually told anybody until you kicked Seth out."

"Then, how did you know?"

"Renee told me," Stacia replied, as if Kitty need even ask.

Kitty imagined Marni bragging to the maid or, even worse, Renee walking in on the two of them in flagrante delicto. *This is mortifying.* Kitty heard the crashing of metal garbage cans against pavement through the phone. "Stacia? Where are you?"

Stacia waved from Eileen's front porch. Kitty hung up the phone and jogged across the street. "Why are you here?"

Stacia threw her cigarette in the planter. "Eileen needed some company."

"At eight in the morning?"

"She's going through a difficult time."

"Is she all right? Maybe I should bring her a pie—"

"No! Just leave her alone."

I wish people would just leave me alone. "She gets to have secrets and I don't?"

"Hey, I was trying to keep the whole Marni and Seth thing quiet ever since I found out. I had your back. If Debbie didn't spill the beans like that, no one would have had to know."

"But everyone did know! And what were you going to do? Run Marni out of town on a rail?"

Stacia's hands shook as she lit another cigarette. "Whatever it takes, Kitty. Whatever it takes."

Seth appeared in the driveway and shouted, "Hey, you coming in to eat? I'm making pancakes."

"I'll be right there," Kitty said over her shoulder. When Seth lumbered back inside, Kitty grabbed Stacia's elbow and whispered through a smile, "Look, we need to get our stories straight because I am not taking the fall for this car thing."

"There's nothing to keep straight. You don't know anything. I'll take care of Marni." Stacia looked back at Eileen's house with a worried look. "Now go eat breakfast with your husband. I've got to go check on Eileen."

I don't want to eat breakfast with Seth. I want to go back to bed and forget this ridiculous morning ever happened.

The kitchen looked like a bacon bomb had exploded; grease dripped from the gas grates onto the cook-top and speckled the wall. Another of Seth's messes that Kitty would have to clean up.

Seth beamed at her from in front of the electric griddle. "Just in time." He carried a tower of misshapen pancakes to the table and settled it next to a heap of bacon slices. Kitty appreciated that Seth had set the table with orange juice in a crystal pitcher and linen napkins in silver rings, but she couldn't ignore the pancake batter dripping down the front of the cabinets and the footprints in the dusting of flour that coated every horizontal surface. "Your breakfast is served, madame," Seth said with a flourish.

What do you want? A gold star? It's pancakes. Kitty knew Seth wanted her to shower him with praise for making a simple meal, but all she could muster was a tepid smile. Kitty took a sip from the coffee cup set at her place. It was lukewarm. She poured some more from the carafe in the center of the table. "Who is going to eat all these pancakes? Were you expecting an army of wives?"

"The recipe on the box said it makes eight servings."

Kitty considered saying something about Seth's inability to divide by four, but decided they had bigger fish to fry that morning. She sat down and took a bite of pancake. A lump of uncooked batter turned to a gummy mess in her mouth. Kitty loved pancakes, but these were heavy with guilt and preservatives. She drowned the rest of her plate in syrup.

They ate in awkward silence for a few minutes before Seth said, "So, are we going to talk about this or what?"

"Do we have to?"

Seth topped up her coffee. "We should establish a line of open and honest communication."

Kitty almost choked on a piece of bacon. "You sound like your brother, Matt."

"He said I should say that when I talked to him yesterday," Seth said. He thrust her orange juice at her. "He says women need lots of communication."

"You're taking marriage advice from a priest? What does he really know about women?" Kitty gulped down her juice, more to give herself a moment to think than because she wanted the drink. Finally she leaned back in her chair and considered her husband. She noticed that the stubble on his chin had far more gray in it than the hair on his head and wondered if he had started coloring his hair. She was struck with how little she really knew about her husband.

"Look Seth, we've always stunk at communicating, so cut the crap. Just say whatever it is you want to say so we can go back to not talking about it, okay?"

Seth folded a pancake into his mouth and smiled crookedly at her. It was the first genuine expression she had seen on his face in weeks. He took Kitty's hand in his sticky fingers. She resisted the urge to get up and wash her hands. Seth was trying to talk to her; she should at least try to listen.

"I'm really sorry about all this, honey," he said. "I never meant for any of this to happen."

"What did you mean to have happen? Did you think you could sleep with my friend and there'd be no fallout?" Seth didn't reply. Kitty pulled her hand away from him. "She gave you a disease, for Christ's sake, and you still...and why Marni? Of all the women in the whole world, you could have slept with, why her?"

"She came on to me," Seth said, as if that were a justification.

"But she's so...so...Marni. She's not nearly as thin as I am. She's not even pretty, and she couldn't cook a decent meal if her life depended on it."

"Our relationship wasn't about food, Kitty," Seth laughed.

Kitty jumped up from the table. "Relationship? It was a relationship?"

"No. You're right. It was just sex. Freaky, stuff you only see in porn sex."

"Eww, spare me the details." Kitty threw her plate in the sink.

Seth stood up too. "What I'm trying to say is, Marni doesn't mean anything to me."

"Is that supposed to make me feel better?"

"Yes?" Seth started clearing the table. "You know what I mean. If I'm going to talk to someone about my feelings, I'll talk to you."

Kitty threw a damp dish towel on the floor and started wiping up flour by pushing it around under her foot.

"You're my wife," Seth pleaded. "You're the mother of my children. You're the person I want to grow old with."

"Oh my God!" Kitty dropped the mixing bowl into the sink, breaking a large chunk off her breakfast plate.

"Look, I know I made a mistake. I never should have fooled around with Marni. I got lazy. It was just that she was willing and convenient. I should have known better. You don't shit where you eat."

Kitty backed away from Seth waving her hands in surrender. "Okay, okay, let me try to get my head around this. By your logic, which is totally screwed up—"

"Kitty! Language."

"Screw you, Seth! No. Wait. You've been doing way too much of that already."

Seth grinned at her, erasing ten years from his face. "I have to say Kitty, you are extremely funny when you're pissed off. I kind of like this Kitty."

Kitty picked up the dish towel from under her foot and threw it at him. "As I was saying, by your logic, it is okay for you to sleep with any old floozy, as long it's no one I know and I can't find out about it?"

Seth paused, seeming to search for the correct answer. "Yes?"

"No! Why would that be okay?"

"You hate sex." Seth stepped around the counter toward her.

"Okay. Yes. Yes I do." Kitty backed up into the cook top.

"I really like sex."

"Okay, I'll accept that as a given."

"Soooooo," Seth replied as if Kitty were a slow child. "I get sex from other women."

"Then why have I been letting you have sex with me all these years?" She circled around Seth to the sink full of broken pottery.

"Because you wanted to?"

"No!" Kitty yelled. Pancakes and syrup and half a pot of coffee rose up her throat. She splashed some cold water on her face. When she was certain she wasn't going to vomit, she turned to Seth and asked, "Do you mean that if I had told you, say after Bobby was born, that I didn't want to do it anymore, you would have been fine with that?"

"Absolutely. I'm not a monster, honey."

Kitty started throwing pieces of broken pottery into the garbage can. "Did you even want to have sex with me all this time?"

"Not particularly." Seth reached under the counter and got a fresh garbage bag. "It's kinda like screwing a skeleton."

"But you like me slim."

"Slim, yes. Boney, not so much."

They stared at each other over the garbage can filled with their broken china. "We should have had this conversation years ago."

"So what happens now?" Seth whispered. "Are we supposed to get a divorce?"

"Do you want a divorce?" Kitty asked.

"No, do you?"

"Not really, no. But we do need to have some new ground rules." Kitty felt lighter than she had felt in weeks. "Number one, we are never having sex again."

"Can I come back into the master bedroom?"

Kitty thought about it for a moment. "No. I like sleeping in the middle of the bed." She reached into the sink and pulled out Seth's plate. She smashed it on the edge of the Formica then threw the pieces in the trash. "By the way, we're getting some new dishes. I've always hated these." She opened a cabinet and handed Seth a plate. "Come on, this is fun!"

"Can I have a girl on the side?"

"Come on, smash it!" Kitty smashed another plate and tossed the shards into the trash. "No relationships. Nobody you actually talk to. And I never hear anything about it. Got it?"

"Don't infect the house, right?"

"Exactly." Kitty took the plate back from Seth, smashed it, and tossed it in the trash. She then handed him a pair of rubber gloves and pointed to the spilled pancake batter. "Start cleaning!"

He grabbed a sponge and began wiping up pancake batter.

"Number two, you will be home every night for dinner, go to every one of Bobby's games, and generally be a model father from now on."

Seth nodded and scrubbed.

"Number three, I want a new car, maybe a convertible, maybe red. And you can drive the Volvo with its loud muffler from now on."

"But—"

"Tell people it's better for hauling around your clubs."

Seth threw the sponge back into the sink. "Is that it?"

"No, but that's all I can think of right now." Kitty started smashing salad plates.

NINETEEN

What a week! First, Eileen miscarries right in front of me and reminds me of all that awfulness. I pray she gets pregnant again right away. I wish I could protect her from the weeks of hoping and waiting that are coming. Then, Debbie Manning tells Kitty Haskell that her husband is sleeping with that Marni! And, I can't even really be mad at her. Debbie didn't know what she was doing. That woman is hanging on to life with the tips of her fingers. What a mess!

Stacia smeared a fresh coat of poppy lipstick over her lips and pulled out of Overlook. *That Marni though. She knew exactly what she was doing. She was going for maximum damage when she hooked up with Seth. She's always been jealous of Kitty.* Ten minutes later, Stacia pulled into the parking lot of Lakeview Real Estate and jumped out.

I can't keep Seth Haskell from ruining his marriage or stop Debbie's cancer. But Marni, I can do something about.

She straightened her purple paisley skirt, marched through the bustling room of agents, and into her cousin Quentin's plush office. Stacia closed the door behind her and said, "We've got to talk about that Marni Kaur."

"Good to see you too, Ladybug." At one point, Quentin and Stacia had been more like brother and sister than cousins. After Stacia's mother died, Quentin's mother, Jean, carted her back and forth to her dance lessons. Aunt Jean made sure that Stacia and her father had a good hot meal every night and clean clothes every morning. When Curran Development broke ground on Overlook, Quentin built three houses in the first phase and used the profits to set up Lakeview Real Estate. Overlook had launched his business.

"That woman should not be allowed to represent your business," Stacia said as she flopped down in the chair across from Quentin's wide desk.

"What do you mean? She sold the most houses in Overlook last year."

"The houses sell themselves. She just goes along for the ride."

Quentin shook his head at his cousin's arrogance. "Of course they do. Does this have something to do with all the whispering I've been hearing about Marni letting that Seth Haskell stay at her house last week? What did she do, sleep with your friend's husband?"

Stacia bit her lips and blinked hard at him. Quentin knew that expression. She had blinked her way through her mother's decline from diabetes, bloody toe shoes, and relearning to walk after her car accident.

"No problem, you don't have to tell me. She's out of here." Quentin made a few notes on a yellow legal pad in front of him. "It will take a few weeks, but I'll fix it."

Stacia stepped around the desk and kissed her cousin on the cheek. "Thank you, Quentin. I knew I could count on you."

He took her hand in his and asked, "What is going on with you? Your hands are shaking. I can feel your pulse racing like a little bird's. Should I call Weldon to come get you?"

Stacia balanced on the wide arm rest of Quentin's massive desk chair and gave him a hug. "She and her son are vermin. I think he's doing drugs. I can't lose my Marcus to drugs."

Quentin engulfed his little cousin in a bear hug. "'Nuff said, Ladybug. 'Nuff said."

The work crew that erected the plastic bubble over the Overlook pool had left a mess of Bojangles' cups and muddy footprints all over Stacia's spotless stamped-concrete pool deck. She walked around the deck tossing things into a trash bag and mourning the loss of her solitary morning swims. Bubble Day marked the low point of Stacia's autumn; the time when her view changed from her beloved lake to dull white plastic sheeting. The only change of the scenery she would get until spring would be the mildew that inevitably grew up the seams.

Bubble Day also meant the beginning of the Masters indoor practice schedule. Keeping the pool open year-round was an expense the other homeowners association members balked at every year, so Stacia sold morning pool time to the local Masters swim team and four hours in the afternoon to Lake Tate Aquatics. Lana had been one of their star swimmers. Now Kitty's daughter, Becky, was their best breaststroker. Stacia wondered who would take her place. She didn't know any of the younger girls on the team.

In the past, the beginning of the Master's season at the pool had been a welcome part of the year. Once the school year was in full swing, Stacia would drop the children off then hurry over to the pool to train with the other middle-aged swimmers. A group still met every morning but few of them were Stacia's peers, either physically or socially. Amy Lathrop had recently called Stacia to say she wasn't going to train with the group anymore. She had decided to teach children how to swim instead of competing in the Daytona 5K in February. Stacia wasn't surprised. Amy had finished the Wilmington Open Water race twenty minutes slower than her previous time. She had lost her competitive spark.

Stacia tied a knot in the top of the garbage bag and walked across the parking lot to the dumpster beside the tennis courts. Scarlet sweet gum leaves skittered across the tennis courts and mingled at the base of the net. No one had used the court in a few days. In all the turmoil of the last few weeks, Kitty and Stacia hadn't organized the autumn round-robin tournament together as they had for the past decade, and no one else had stepped up to take it over.

Who's there even left to play? Marni is out. Deirdre will be gone soon. Debbie is sick. Eileen is sad. Blaire Morton could care less and Barb Hendricks only played because she couldn't come up with a good excuse not to. Without Kitty and me, the whole thing just falls apart. No one had to officially cancel it, it just isn't happening.

Stacia turned back toward the bubble. The notion of swimming endless laps every morning in the stale air with a group of middle-aged people no longer seemed like fun. After the win in Wilmington, long distance swimming didn't excite her anymore either. She needed a new challenge. She saw Kitty running every morning and wondered if that could be her next project. It would be physically and mentally difficult to learn a new endurance sport at her age, but it might be exactly what Stacia needed to help her deal with the loss of her children. That afternoon, Stacia bought a new pair of high-tech sneakers and some running clothes. The next morning, she waited on the trail for Kitty to run by. "Morning Kitty," she called when Kitty came into sight.

"Hey Stacia," Kitty said taking in Stacia's outfit. "I didn't know you jogged."

"I was thinking of taking it up," Stacia replied as she fell into step beside Kitty.

"I thought you kept fit during the winter by swimming laps in the pool."

"I seemed to have gone as far as I can go with that. I think I might want to try a new challenge."

"Life is always full of new challenges," Kitty replied with a sigh. Kitty glanced down at Stacia's new shoes. "You're going to need better shoes than those if you're going to do any serious mileage. Those don't have enough padding to protect your knees. I assume you need to baby that knee?"

"The doctors told me to avoid high-impact activities, but that's never really stopped me from doing anything. I bet my damaged knee is still better than the average fifty year old's joint." After a few minutes, Stacia's thigh muscles started to burn and her shins ached. "I was thinking about trying a marathon or a triathlon. Have you ever done one?"

"No, I haven't, but I'd love to. I've always been too afraid to sign up."

"We should do it together," Stacia blurted out. "You could teach me the ins and outs of road training, and I could teach you how to train for a specific race." When Stacia first started swimming long distances, it had been as physical therapy to rehabilitate her knee, as well as psychological therapy to deal with her guilt and grief over surviving the accident that took her best friend. Kitty was the only person, other than Weldon, that she would trust to be by her side during the hard miles of a race.

Kitty seemed to consider the proposition for a few minutes before she responded. "You know, I think I'd like that. I'd like to run in a race with the crowds cheering for me, but let's start with something small, like a 5K, but we could work up to a triathlon some day."

"Do you know how to swim?"

"Not like you, but I can swim. I'm sure it would come back to me with a little practice."

They reached the gazebo at the tip of the ridge. Stacia stopped and put her hands on her knees. "This is harder than I thought it would be. I thought I was in such good shape."

"You are, you're just using your muscles differently. Let's rest for a minute and let you catch your breath." Kitty put her heel up on the bench inside the gazebo and stretched her muscles. She looked out over the lake. "This is such a beautiful spot. Look at the way the leaves have turned. It almost looks like there is a big pile of bricks out on the island."

"There is," Stacia said between deep breaths. "When the leaves fall, you can see what's left of the Bradford Falls Mill. If you climb through the kudzu and poison ivy, you can get to what's left of the spinning machines. In the 1800s, they made poplin fabric out there. It was actually one of the biggest mills that supplied the fabric for the Confederate army uniforms."

"Why would you put a mill in the middle of a lake?"

"No," Stacia replied with a long exhale. "The lake wasn't here then. The mill and the town of Bradford Falls were taken out by a hurricane in 1927. The lake was made when they built the dam in the thirties."

"Wow, I never thought about what was here before."

"Why would you ever suspect there was anything but fish and sediment under this lake?"

Kitty started jogging slowly next to Stacia down the path, letting Stacia set their pace. "Hey, how's Eileen doing? I heard she had a miscarriage."

"What?" Stacia said, suddenly forgetting her aching hamstrings. "Who told you that?"

"I think it was Blaire Morton." Kitty looked over at Stacia. "I'm sorry to bring it up, but I remembered that you were there the other morning and you seemed to know what was going on with her. I didn't want to go over and talk to her until I was sure of the situation. I don't mean to pry."

Stacia picked up the pace and Kitty followed. "Eileen will be fine. She just needs some time." Her shins started to burn again. Running was definitely going to be a challenge. "How did Blaire even know about the miscarriage?"

Kitty slowed her pace to force Stacia to take it easy. "I don't know. She just seems to know stuff. I wouldn't be surprised if she knows about Marni's car. You should watch your back."

"I'll take care of Marni. Don't be surprised when you hear she's lost her job."

Kitty slowed her pace even more. "You didn't."

"So, back to the race idea, maybe a triathlon would be best. Biking would be easier than the twenty-six miles of a marathon. Do you have a bike?"

"No, how about you?"

"No." Stacia considered having aching gluts as well as shins. "Then again, there's no rush. We could take some time; look into getting the right equipment."

TWENTY

The late morning silence was shattered by the sound of lawn mowers and leaf blowers. Kitty put down the stack of dishes she was unpacking and peeked through the plantation shutters at the front of the house. The Green With Envy crew had descended on the cul-de-sac like an army of ants. Everyone on Azalea Lane, except for the Oliphants who never quite got the concept of living in a "neighborhood" and mowed their own lawn, used Green With Envy. A young man maneuvered a wide-bed mower across the front lawns like a gladiator riding his chariot into battle. Behind him came the foot soldiers, smaller and browner, with edgers, weed eaters and leaf blowers.

She turned to Daisy playing with a sheet of bubble wrap under the dining room table, and said, "Hold down the fort, I'm going to go out and talk to the landscapers." She stepped outside and hailed the foreman, sitting away from the exhaust fumes in his truck. "Good morning," Kitty said. "Could your people please not block my driveway? I'm expecting a cabinet delivery this morning." After Kitty had broken every one of the dishes she and Seth had been given as wedding gifts, she had ordered a full set of Portmeirion dishes, as well as a specialized cabinet to display them in. Seth had initially questioned why the dishes needed to be stored standing upright between oak dowels instead of stacked in a closed cabinet. One harsh look from Kitty convinced him to keep his mouth shut and pay the bill.

"No problem, ma'am," the foreman said with a leer. Kitty backed away and crossed her arms over her chest. She wished she had changed out of her running clothes before coming outside to speak to him. She and Stacia had run five miles together that morning and she still hadn't showered. She quickly turned to walk back toward the house.

A young man wearing a ratty, sweat-soaked T-shirt with 'Nance Baseball' on it was edging the front walk. His protective eye covering had left light patches on his tanned olive skin, his work gloves had holes in the palms, and his work pants hung off his slim frame. *Could this young man have gone to Nance High School with Becky and now be mowing lawns?* She went inside and retrieved a bottle of Gatorade from the extra fridge in the garage and returned to the front yard. She waved the bottle in front of the young man. "Hola? Thirsty? Want Gatorade?"

The young man turned off the edger and deferentially removed his baseball cap. "Gracias," he replied as he took the bottle.

Kitty pointed to his chest. "Did you go to Nance?"

"Yes, ma'am," he said in a vaguely Hispanic accent. "But no more."

"Do you ever do work after hours or on the weekend? I have some garden work that needs to be done."

The young man looked over his shoulder at the gladiator mowing circles around the pin oak in the front yard. "Oh no, Senora. You need to call main office for any changes," he replied in a loud clear voice. He handed her back the half empty bottle of Gatorade with a business card tucked under the label. "I'll swing by this afternoon and we can talk," he whispered.

Kitty fumbled to not drop the bottle and card. "I get it," she said quietly. "I'll look for you this evening."

"Buenas tardes, senora," the young man boomed as Kitty walked back inside.

She went back to clearing a space in the kitchen for the cabinet installers to work in but could not get the young man out of her head. *Is this what happens to kids who don't go on to college? I don't care what Seth says, Becky and Bobby need to get the best education we can offer them. I would hate for one of them to end up working in the hot sun for a living.*

ﻬ

That evening, Kitty was worrying over Bobby as he lay moaning on the couch. The soccer team had qualified for the regional playoffs and Bobby had gotten into a scuffle with an overly aggressive forward from the East Raleigh team. "I can't believe that kid didn't get a red card. I think he dented my shin bone," Bobby whimpered.

Kitty pressed an ice pack to Bobby's leg. "I doubt your bone is dented, Honey. But if you want I will call in the morning and get you an appointment to see a doctor."

"Can't we go see Dr. Bukalis now?"

Kitty stood up and moved to the kitchen. She started to sweep up the sawdust that the cabinet installers left as an excuse for Bobby not to see the shocked expression on her face. She wasn't planning on ever seeing Paul Bukalis again. She and Seth had come to a detente but she could never look Dr. Bukalis in the face again. Paul not only knew that Seth gave her a sexually transmitted disease; she knew he likely got it from her friend. Paul was Marni's doctor too. No, Dr. Bukalis was out; out of their social circle, out as their physician.

"I'll call Magnuson Orthopedic and see if they can take an x-ray of that leg, okay?" Bobby moaned again from the couch.

Kitty was teasing the last of the sawdust out of the corners when Becky rushed into the kitchen. "Mom, Luis Mendes is standing on our front porch and he wants to talk to you."

Kitty dusted off her hands. "That must be the young man I spoke to earlier. He's here to talk to me about doing some yard work."

"Luis Mendes is going to do our yard work? Don't you know who he is? He was only like the best baseball player Nance ever had! And he's really cute."

Kitty handed Becky the broom. "Then I better not keep him waiting. Finish up here, will you?"

"Mom, I've English reading to do and math homework."

"Then sweep quickly."

Kitty stepped outside. She would not have recognized the young man standing in the front yard in clean khakis and a white oxford as the same young man she met earlier if not for the odd tan lines around his eyes. "Hello again. Luis, is it? My daughter, Becky, recognized you from school."

"Sure did. I recognized her too. She's a swimmer, right?" The nebulous Hispanic accent was gone and replaced with an authentic central Carolinas drawl.

"Becky tells me you played baseball?"

"Yup, made All-American and everything." The young man blushed. "I'm just working for Green With Envy to make some money for school. I got a scholarship to NC State to study horticultural design, but it's just for tuition. It doesn't cover room and board, so I'm working this semester and I'll start in the spring semester."

"Horticultural design? Trimming walkways must drive you crazy."

"It beats flipping burgers, and I get to see a lot of yards up real close and think about how I would change them."

"Speaking of changing things," Kitty pointed to the yellow garden, "I need some help reworking that garden."

Luis didn't ask Kitty what kinds of flowers she wanted or what her budget was. He asked Kitty what she wanted her garden to feel like. Kitty told him about her favorite paintings of gardens and how much she hated to weed. An hour later, they had a plan. Luis would replace the detested day lilies and fussy rose bushes with a mélange of cabbage roses, poppies and flouncy perennials that could withstand the North Carolina heat and look good all season long. Kitty promised that Luis could take Polaroids of the finished product for his portfolio.

෨∘෫

When the alarm went off the next morning, Kitty found Seth lolling in the yellow slipper chair next to her bed. "What the hell, Seth! What are doing in here?"

"I couldn't sleep. It's too quiet in the guest room." Kitty pulled the comforter up around her neck. "Anyway, I came in here to look for one of your pills and you were snoring ... and ... I like your snoring."

"What?"

"It's very soothing, the way you snuffle when you're stuffy."

"That's ridiculous. No one likes to hear someone else snoring in their ear."

Seth sat up as if she had slapped him. "I do." Kitty threw back the comforter and padded into the bathroom. Seth was on her in three paces. "What is this?" He said grabbing the old oxford shirt she had been wearing as a nightshirt. With her rumpled hair, white panties and wrinkled men's dress shirt, she looked like a male movie director's vision of the morning after. "Whose shirt is this? Who is he?"

"It's your shirt, stupid. You being a cheater, doesn't make me a cheater." The shirt started to tear as she pulled away. "Let go. I need to pee."

Seth rubbed his eyes with the palm of his hand and looked around the bedroom as if still expecting to find another man in his wife's bed. He sank back down on the slipper chair.

"Renee couldn't get the tree sap stain out of the arm," Kitty called from the bathroom. "You really should be more careful about what you lean against. I was going to toss it out because I couldn't even really give it to Good Will with a whopping stain like that. It's so soft though that I kept it. I see why you like this brand so much."

"If I have to wear a monkey suit, I might as well be comfortable. Wait up, what happened to those frumpy nightgowns with all the scratchy lace and stupid little buttons?"

"They're in the drawer." Kitty washed her hands and came back into the master bedroom brushing her hair. "Why?"

"No reason. I just thought you liked that kind of nightgowns."

"No, you liked buying me that kind of nightgowns. Why would I want to sleep in granny gowns?"

"Is Bobby's leg okay? Will he be able to play in the game next week?"

"I'm pretty sure he's fine. Why don't you drive him to school this morning and you two can talk all about how unfair the referees were yesterday."

Seth leaned back in the chair, seeming to appraise her. Kitty was suddenly very conscious of the way training with Stacia had made her hips a rounder, as well as the quarter inch of grey roots in her hair and her lack of makeup. "You look good. I don't know, softer, younger."

Kitty didn't know how to respond. Was he taunting her or was he genuinely giving her a compliment? She couldn't tell anymore. Who was this man sitting in her bedroom?

"Don't you miss sleeping next to me at all?" Seth asked.

"Not really," Kitty replied. She knew she was hurting Seth's feelings but she didn't feel the need to lie anymore. Having sex with Seth had been a chore, like scrubbing the grout in the shower twice a week.

That afternoon, Seth came home with a new white Mercedes convertible with tan leather seats and all the extras for Kitty. Seth had paid for Marni to get a new paint job and told her to keep her distance. Conflicting explanations as to what had happened to Marni's Cadillac drifted through the streets like fallen oak leaves, brown and sticky. Some said she had side-swiped a client's car after their loan fell through and she got nothing after months of showing them houses. Other people whispered that she was sleeping with one of her clients and his wife had thrown acid on her car, and still others suggested that she had taken a sledgehammer to her own car then told people Kitty had done it. Everyone knew that she was always jealous of Kitty and Seth's happy family. Regardless of which story was true, it was well known that Marni had lost her job at Lakeview Real Estate. Quentin Tate had told her that her erratic behavior reflected poorly on the office. By Halloween, no one remembered that Seth and Marni had ever really slept together, and it was assumed that Marni made the relationship up out of whole cloth.

TWENTY-ONE

The Magnuson Aquatic Center was like a sauna. Outside, freezing rain lashed the building. Kitty stripped off her cashmere cardigan and straightened her cotton shell over her hips. She found a spot in the center of the concrete bleachers twenty feet above the pool deck and unfolded her padded stadium chair. Another season of weekends spent in chlorine infused air in order to watch her daughter perform for a matter of seconds had officially begun.

Kitty had already watched ten races and read three magazines when Rose dropped her bleacher cushion next to Kitty. "How's our girl doing?"

"Good. She didn't drop any time in the 200 freestyle but she was close to her best time. How was Mass?"

"Great, you should come with me next week. We could go to that place Octavio's for brunch afterwards. Seth and the kids can fend for themselves for a day." Rose opened her bag and pulled out a cheap plastic crochet hook and a ball of green acrylic yarn. Kitty was taken aback. Rose was normally so particular about her materials when she knit or crocheted. She didn't care enough about her own appearance to spend more than ten dollars on an item of clothing but Rose didn't think twice about dropping ten dollars for a skein of silk yarn to make preemie caps for the NICU ward or silk yarn for hospice shawls.

"What's with the plastic crochet hook and grandma yarn?" Kitty asked.

"Father Abrams asked me to help out with a prison ministries project so I'm brushing up on my basic technique."

"Are you knitting hats for prisoners?"

"Crochet, dummy." Rose waggled the crochet hook in the air. "We're teaching them how to crochet."

"I could never get the hang of crochet. Knitting is so much easier."

"I like it better too, but they won't let the prisoners have knitting needles. Something about them being deadly weapons so, we are using these ridiculous rubbery crochet hooks." Rose wrestled with the tangled ball of yarn in her lap. "They're useless. They feel terrible in your hand and they stick something awful to the yarn."

"Do the women get bussed to the church?"

"No, a group of us go to the prison and—"

"You go to the prison? Where is it?"

Rose stopped struggling with the yarn in her lap and looked at her sister with disgust. "How long have you lived around here? Didn't you listen in chapel at all as a child? You know - feed the hungry, clothe the naked, visit the imprisoned. Any of this ringing a bell?"

Kitty grabbed the ball of yarn and worked on a knot. "Where's the prison, Rose?"

"About an hour up the highway. Sister Lydia drives us out there in an old school bus. What a death trap that is! No seat belts—"

"The prison, Rose," Kitty squawked. The couple in front of them turned around and glared at Kitty. She smiled apologetically and they returned to watching the races. Kitty smacked her sister on the leg and said, "Tell me about the prison."

"Anyway, Sister Lydia and a bunch of us are going out there and teaching the women to crochet." Rose ceased pulling at the yarn and stared at her lap for a moment before going on. "They're not who I thought they'd be. Some of them are so young. Drugs mostly." The yarn flew through Rose's fingers as she absently crocheted. "Initially, Sister Lydia had planned to teach them how to make shawls that they could wear in their cells, but they asked her to show them how to make sweaters for their children. This young girl, Lois is her name, she can't be much older than Becky, told me she wanted to make something that her little boy could remember her by. She's lucky, unlike some of the other girls, to have family taking care of her baby while she's serving her time. Five years she'll be in there. Just for being in the car during a drug bust. Her son won't even know her when she gets out." They sat in silence, the sound of Rose's crochet hook manipulating the yarn into hundreds of tiny interlocking loops like the hundreds of interlocking days that young Lupe would have to wait until she could hug her little boy again.

The boy's breaststroke races ended and Kitty stepped to the edge of the balcony to watch Becky swim. When she returned to their seats, Rose had the heat sheet open to the time standards page on top of the yarn. "That was a double A time," she said with pride, as if Rose had swum the race herself. "Why didn't Becky swim in yesterday's events?"

"She took the SAT again. She wanted to skip this whole meet entirely, but in the end, she made a compromise with Seth and just skipped Friday and Saturday."

Rose looked around the bleachers. "Speaking of which, where is Seth? He's been stuck to your side lately."

"Down there." Kitty pointed to the pool deck. "He's trying to schmooze the scout from the school in Wilmington, but it looks like he's getting the brush off."

"I thought Becky wanted to go to Brown."

"She does. Seth thinks it's too expensive though, so I don't know what we're going to do."

Disgusted, Rose threw the crochet hook and acrylic yarn in her tote bag and took out a skein of baby alpaca yarn and a 22" circular needle. Her entire body relaxed as she spread a half finished shawl across her lap. "If Seth won't pay, use the money that Daddy put aside."

Kitty stared down at the swimmers in the pool. "I don't know, Rose. Seth thinks..."

"Can your ears hear what your mouth is saying? What happened to - I'm not going to take Seth's bullshit anymore? Weren't you the girl who lectured me about how I've got to think for myself and not let Mother, or Seth for that matter, tell me what to do?"

Kitty snapped the heat sheet closed. "Shut up, Rose and watch the races."

The 400-yard free started and Kitty's mind wandered. *Why aren't I using the money Daddy put aside for Becky and Bobby? It would piss Seth off, but I could do it. I bet Seth wouldn't have any problem spending his money on Bobby, he's a boy. So it's really just Becky that's the issue. It really is important that she get off to a good start and not make the same mistakes I did.*

Kitty turned to Rose. "You'd really be okay with me using the money?"

"Why wouldn't I be okay with it? Daddy set up that trust fund specifically to educate our children."

"But I don't feel right spending it all on my kids. Why don't we split it?"

Rose shook her head. "I know you had a toddler and were pregnant again when he died, but did you even read the will? Neither one of us can touch that money. Daddy was afraid that Mother would talk us into giving it to her, so he set it up so only his grandchildren can withdraw the money."

"Did he really hate her that much?"

"He didn't hate her," Rose protested. "He loved her. He blamed himself for who she became."

"So do you think he would want Becky to use the money for school even if Seth doesn't approve?"

Old grief welled up in Rose's eyes as she stared into the pool. "I think he would. He was so disappointed in you for marrying Seth and, you know, I never understood that."

When Kitty had told her father that she and Seth were getting married because she was pregnant, he wept. Her father begged her to reconsider. "Don't do it," he cried. "You'll end up like her and ruin both your lives." Kitty didn't understand what he was talking about at the time. She understood now.

The last time Kitty saw her father was soon after Becky was born. Although she hadn't seen him sober and smiling in years; he was that day. He grinned and laughed while he tickled Becky's little belly. Kitty had been distracted by her mother fussing over how many diapers Becky would need and criticizing Kitty's choice of wall color for the nursery. If Kitty had known that would be the last time she would see her father alive, she would have ignored Mother and paid more attention to what he was saying. By Becky's first birthday, her grandfather's drinking had truly gotten out of hand. He still managed to go to work at the insurance company every morning, but he rarely left the den otherwise. The day after Rose graduated from nursing school, he drove off the Jonestown Bridge into the Narragansett Bay. Mother insisted his tires were bare and he had hydroplaned but Kitty knew he kept his Chevy in excellent condition. The timing was too convenient for it to have been an accident. His parting shot at his wife was to put most of his money in a trust fund for Becky and any other grandchildren that might come along, and leave Mother only enough to live modestly. Kitty's mother wore black for a year but she hardly mourned.

"I was so jealous of you when you got married," Rose said. "Now, not so much. I think I see what Daddy saw in Seth. He is just like Mother. He's charming and sweet and really very lovable, but he is completely self-centered. After what he's been pulling lately, I don't see how he can make a fuss about giving Becky the money Daddy left her."

"True. It's not really his call, is it?" Kitty looked back at the pool with a sigh. "I guess I'll cross that bridge when I get to it."

TWENTY-TWO

One bleak mid-winter morning, Bitsy Magnuson-Evans sidled up to Stacia at coffee hour. The Magnusons and the Tates were the oldest families in the area as well as two of the founding families at Pinnacle Point Church. The families not only lived across the street from each other, Bitsy's father was Stacia's father's business partner. "Hey Stacia," Bitsy said with a thin lipped smile. Her fluffy blonde hair, heavy make-up, and pale blue boucle suit made her look like a giant Barbie doll. "How's your Lucinda doing at Central?"

"Lana's at Carolina," Stacia replied. She loathed Bitsy. She was a bully at the age of eight and a two-faced shrew at the age of forty-eight. Bitsy was the sole reason Stacia never joined the Junior League. She picked up a plate and placed a miniature scone on it. "Where's your Judy again?"

"She's at Vanderbilt like her Daddy," Bitsy replied with a proud smile. "Hey, I was surprised your Marvin—"

"Marcus."

"—didn't apply to the day school. I would have liked to see affirmative action working for someone we actually might want."

Kitty wanted to slap the disingenuous bigoted smirk right off Bitsy's face, but she was in a church and her father was watching from the other side of the room. "He'll be fine at Nance," Stacia said through grit teeth. She wondered how much Bitsy had to do with the soccer coach recruiting him.

Stacia teetered closer to the coffee table. "Anyhoo, we were hoping you were going to be able to do membership for out parents' council, but I guess not, huh?"

"Membership?" Stacia asked. She took a coffee cup from the trembling hands of the elderly coffee hostess. "I've been the president of our PTA since my Lana was in first grade."

"Of course you were, dear." Bitsy graced the coffee hostess with a closed lipped smile as she accepted a cup of coffee and led Stacia away from the table. "And I'm sure you would have just been such a big help. I don't know what we'll do without you." Bitsy's eyes twinkled behind her bright blue eyeliner as she caught the eye of someone behind Stacia. She turned to see a clutch of women fawning over a new baby and suddenly felt very insignificant. Her firstborn had left the nest and it wouldn't be very much longer before her Marcus would be gone too.

"I hear your sister-in-law Eulalie might take over at Tate next year," Bitsy said, barely containing her disdain.

Stacia stiffened as a plan hatched in her head. The thought of empty headed, annoying Eulalie taking her place as PTA president at Tate Junior High School had until that second infuriated Stacia. She had planned to find another Mrs. Curran, any Mrs. Curran, to take over. But, if it would get under Bitsy Magnuson's skin to have Eulalie Curran as PTA president, Stacia would use every ounce of her social capital to push Eulalie all the way to citywide PTA board chair.

"Anything's possible," Stacia replied. "Excuse me; I've got people waiting on me." She plunked her cup on the table causing the brown liquid to slosh over the edge of the china cup onto the white tablecloth, and turned on her tiny pink heel.

৯৽৽৶

It was a perfect November day in North Carolina. The sky was a clear blue, fifty degrees, no humidity. Ideal running weather. Kitty planned to push Stacia to attack the four mile loop around Overlook twice. She knew Stacia could do it just as Stacia knew Kitty could swim two miles in the pool. They were excellent training partners. Stacia was teaching Kitty to be more competitive and push herself to win their races in practice. Kitty, for her part, was helping Stacia recognize when her body was exhausted and stop. Kitty was particularly anxious to meet Stacia at the gazebo this morning. She had exciting news to share.

A few hundred yards along the path, Kitty pulled Daisy up and froze. Debbie Manning was slumped over in the gazebo up ahead.

155

Kitty didn't recognize Debbie at first; she recognized her dog. The Mannings were the only family in Overlook with a cocker spaniel; it was such an old-fashioned kind of dog. Debbie didn't seem to have heard Kitty coming. She had a knit cap pulled down over her ears and a book open in her lap. Kitty thought she may have been asleep. She considered turning back but resisted the urge to retreat. Kitty couldn't avoid Debbie forever. She hadn't seen her since that fated evening in October when she told Kitty about Marni and Seth. Debbie had left a tearful message that Kitty had left unreturned. She would have to talk to Debbie eventually and she should probably do it soon.

Stacia had confided to Kitty that the months of chemotherapy had been unsuccessful and that Debbie's cancer had come back stronger than ever. Supposedly, Debbie's immune system was dangerously weak and she was not supposed to be exposed to any germs. Kitty stopped several yards away from Debbie and called, "Hey!"

Debbie raised her head and winced before smiling broadly. "Hey," she replied. Even from a distance, Kitty could see that Debbie was gravely ill. Not only did her face look naked without eyebrows and lashes, the purple bags under her eyes were the only color in Debbie's gray face. She looked like she hadn't slept in months.

"What a pleasant surprise," Kitty said. "How are you?"

Debbie's smile vanished. She looked away to pet the dog sitting on the bench beside her. "It's such a beautiful day; I thought I'd take the dog for a walk while Renee is doing the house. I can't sleep with the vacuum going."

"Renee? The maid, Renee? I didn't know you used her too." Kitty thought that Renee only cleaned The Lookers' houses. Debbie was not one of The Lookers inner circle. She always struck Kitty as a hanger-on, and not a very good one at that.

"I didn't used to. Stacia is paying her to clean my house every week while I'm going through chemo. What a gem!"

"Wow, I had no idea she was doing that for you." Kitty wondered why Stacia hadn't mentioned something important like that during their morning workouts. She threw a sweet gum ball for Daisy to chase. "Will you be finished with all that soon?"

"For now." Debbie tugged at the edges of her jacket as if there had been a sudden chill. "What's new with you? Renee tells me that Becky's applying to schools up north."

"Um, yes." Kitty tried to remember if she had spoken to Renee about Becky's applications. She usually left the house when the cleaners were there. "I didn't realize she knew that."

"Oh yeah, that woman knows everything. If it weren't for her, I wouldn't know what was going on around here at all. Stacia never tells me anything." Debbie blushed. It brought some much needed color to her face. "Of course, sometimes Renee gets her facts wrong. I can't believe she actually believed that Marni Kaur was having an affair with your Seth."

Kitty didn't respond. She wasn't going to deny or confirm anything. She threw another Sweetgum ball for Daisy.

"You do realize that nobody talks to Marni anymore," Debbie chattered. "She's totally out."

"Really?" Kitty paused for a moment and tried to remember the last time she saw Marni around the neighborhood or even in the carpool line. She couldn't.

"Renee told me she even slashed her own tires and said you did it. I think she's regretting the whole thing now." Debbie brushed a leaf off the bench as if brushing away the idea of Marni. "But Marni is old news now. The whole thing with Betty Oliphant's daughter is all the scuttlebutt now."

Kitty threw another ball for Daisy. "The one who had to be sent off to that special school in Tennessee for detox?"

"They're blaming Betty for the girl's problems," Debbie clucked. She seemed to be winding up for a good gossip session. *Oh shut up! Poor Betty. She must be beside herself.* "But I think she didn't know what else to do. Renee told me she has been doing drugs for ages. Betty just had to send her away."

Then, it hit Kitty. *That is who spread the gossip about my husband and my friend. Marni must have bragged about her sexual prowess to the maid, then Renee nattered on to the rest of the neighborhood. They must have been rabid for that juicy tidbit.* Kitty bounced on her toes like a boxer. *I bet that's how Blaire Morton gets all her info too. She probably invites Renee to sit with her and talk, instead of cleaning like she should.*

"I don't know what I'd do without Renee to keep me entertained with all the goings-on around here," Debbie went on. "I'm cooped up in that house all the time. I haven't even been to the grocery store in over a month."

Kitty took a step back. She didn't want to breathe too close to Debbie. Who knew what kinds of viruses and bacteria could have been on Kitty's body. "Should you be out now?"

"I should probably be wearing a mask," Debbie said. "My tests were better this week though, so I think it's okay."

"Good to hear," Kitty chirped. *Poor Debbie, she has nothing to keep her occupied but gabbing with the maid. If that's all she's got left, how can I fault her?*

She jingled Daisy's leash and started walking further down the path. "Well, good to see you again. We'll have to get together for coffee sometime."

She intended to ask Stacia why she hadn't mentioned paying Renee to clean Debbie's house, or about the things that Renee was still saying about Marni, but by the time she reached Stacia's house, Kitty's thoughts had refocused on her news. When Stacia arrived, Kitty jumped up from where she was petting Daisy and yelled, "I got the job!"

Stacia started jumping up and down. "I knew it. I knew you would get the job. Who else would they hire?"

Kitty had mentioned in passing that Molly was nagging her to apply to the position of new exhibits coordinator at the Arts Center. Once Stacia found out, she and Molly teamed up to force Kitty to apply. Molly had spoken to the other board members on her behalf and talked her into buying a green silk dress that played up her auburn hair for the interview. Stacia had made some phone calls of her own to prominent Magnuson arts patrons and had coached Kitty during their morning runs on what she was going to say.

"I don't know why I'm so worked up about this piddly little job, really," Kitty said. "It's a nothing job. Unimportant. Just a way to make a little money." *Or hide a lot of money.* "Still, I'm really happy I got it."

"Was there really any question you'd get it?" Stacia replied. "When do you start?"

"Right away. They're not paying me much so they said I could work whatever hours I want. It shouldn't interfere with our training schedule."

"Of course it won't. You and I are going to win that triathlon in May if we have to train in the middle of the night." With that, Stacia took off down the trail leaving Kitty to catch up.

TWENTY-THREE

Kitty nosed her shiny little convertible into a spot at the far end of the co-op parking lot. It was a disorderly mess of abandoned shopping carts and pickup trucks straddling parking spaces. The well-organized and polite Subaru owners came earlier in the week to pick up their wild caught turkeys, locally harvested yams and bags of fresh chestnuts. At four o'clock on the day before Thanksgiving, the co-op was overrun by crazed shoppers in search of that one illusive special ingredient to impress their relatives at Thanksgiving dinner. In other years, Kitty would have been there on Tuesday morning checking off her purchases on a long list organized according to the stores illogical setup. This year, she had far less to buy, only a fresh turkey and a few stalks of Brussel sprouts. Rose had volunteered to bake all the pies, as well as the potatoes and a dish of their father's fruited stuffing. She had whined to Kitty that she had to visit six bakeries before she found one that made Anadama bread, but that it had been well worth it. Kitty and Rose had a date to venture out to Millie's Moravian Meat Market & Breads to sample Millie's signature sugar cake that weekend. Their adventure would have to wait until the weekend, Kitty was far too busy with her position at the Arts Center to go anywhere during the week.

What had started out as a small part-time diversion had rapidly blossomed into a more than full-time obsession. In her first three weeks, she had already cobbled together an installation of wooden Christmas ornaments carved or turned by local artisans. It was thrilling to drive around the Piedmont visiting workshops and interviewing each of the twelve woodworkers. The write-up for that installation was what brought Kitty to the co-op so late in the day.

She had spent the entire day with the printer transforming her words and pictures into an exhibit catalog that could be printed on the cheap. She would have given her left arm to simply send her pictures and text to someone and have a lovely glossy bound catalog delivered a few days later. She had ruined a beautiful pair of camel-colored wool slacks with printer ink that morning.

She reached behind the passenger seat in search of her canvas shopping bags and spotted Marni Kaur standing twenty feet away opening the trunk of a beat-up blue Chevy. The real estate agency's big Cadillac was a thing of the past. Stacia had mentioned that Marni had lost her position at the agency to a new young agent and was planning to put her own house in Overlook on the market in the new year. Then, the week before, Bobby had come home and told Kitty that Connor had been caught smoking marijuana behind the school and was going to live with his father. Bobby was sorry to see him go, but Kitty suspected he was relieved. Their friendship had become awkward.

Kitty hurriedly scooted down behind the convertible's leather headrest. She could see Marni perfectly in the space between the headrest and the seat. As Marni struggled with the sticky lock, Kitty could see her stretch pants straining against her growing girth, her roots were showing, and she was missing her signature scarlet manicure. Marni bent over to lift a canvas bag out of her cart. It had the Catawba Marathon logo emblazoned on the side, and it matched the one Kitty was clutching in her fist.

Kitty's heart twisted in her chest as she recalled the day she and Marni received the bags as a volunteer thank you gift. They had spent a long day standing in the middle of the road tossing Dixie cups of water to exhausted runners as they flew by during the annual race. Neither Kitty nor Marni had fully understood what they had signed up for. The volunteer coordinators had laughed at them when they showed up in high-heeled sandals and white capri pants. It rained off and on the whole day forcing them to both stand in the mud during the downpours and suffer through hours of blazing sunshine and oppressive humidity. By the end of the day, their shoes were ruined, they were covered with mud, and were as punchy as sorority sisters.

I miss my friend. How could she do that to me? To us? I can't believe she actually loved Seth. It wasn't about Seth. It was about me. She only wanted him because he was mine. She wanted to knock me down a peg.

Well! Look at you now, sweetheart. Was a few weeks with Seth worth losing your son? Your job? Your home? Me? Kitty was tempted to run over and shake some answers out of Marni but she didn't. She simply watched her ex-friend get in her car and drive away.

The second week of December, The Lookers received a slightly different type of invitation to Kitty's annual Christmas cookie swap. She still asked that everyone bring ten dozen homemade cookies to share, although she knew most of her guests would buy their offerings from Hoppin' Frog Café, as well as a check for twenty dollars made out to one of the charities on the list Kitty included with the invitation. This year, instead of setting up five different Christmas trees throughout the house, each decorated with a different theme, Kitty set up folding tables covered with pine boughs on top of red tablecloths in the garage. She simply put a pile of shallow cardboard boxes at one end of the tables and encouraged her guests to fill them assembly-line style. By the end of the afternoon, every one of The Lookers had a varied assortment of Christmas cookies to take home to their families and the chosen charities were a thousand dollars richer.

After several mugs full of mulled wine, Blaire Morton pulled Kitty aside and said, "Great party, Kitty! These chocolate things are fab! Where'd you get the recipe?"

"Thank you, Blaire," Kitty replied as she grabbed Blaire's elbow to steady her. "I like them too. My friend used to call them pizzettes, but I may be remembering that wrong. It was a long time ago when she gave me the recipe."

"Well, they're delicious. I always admired your sugar cookies, but they were so pretty, no one ever wanted to eat them."

Kitty tried to catch Stacia's eye on the other side of the table to signal her to come save her from Blaire, but Stacia was deeply in conversation with Eileen from across the street. Kitty watched as a wide smile spread across Stacia's face and she gave Eileen a quick hug. Kitty wished she were part of that conversation instead of dealing with Blaire.

Blaire refilled her mug from the crock pot full of mulled wine. "Great idea, doing this in the garage. This has been way more fun than picking our way around your dining room table trying to cram cookies into those tins you used to give us. Don't get me wrong,"

Blaire said with a hiccup. "Those tins are darling and it's great the way you went to the effort to find ones that went with each of our decors but, come on, how many Christmas cookie tins do any of us really need?"

Kitty took in Blaire's flushed cheeks and wobbly stance. She looked around the garage and noticed several of the other women hanging on to the edges of the tables to keep their failing balance. *Holy crap, they are all falling down drunk. How did I never notice that this group is all a bunch of booze hounds?* She took a bite out of one of the coconut macaroons Blaire brought. It was far too sweet. A sip of coffee from the cup in her hand allowed Kitty to swallow. She reached across the table to refill her cup from the carafe next to the simmering pot of mulled wine. *Coffee. They're not different. I am. I'm drinking coffee, instead of wine. Last year, I was just as piffle as Blaire.*

"So, where's Seth today?" Blaire asked. She popped another pizzette in her mouth. There wouldn't be any left for anyone else soon.

"I'm not sure," Kitty replied. "I didn't need him to help out here, and he said he had to work today."

Blaire rolled her eyes and took another sip of wine. "He has to work on a Saturday in December, selling golf equipment? Really, Kitty?"

୬֍

Although the holiday season was a blur of parties and celebrations, neither Kitty nor Stacia let their busy schedules interfere with their training. Three days a week, they ran eight miles before Kitty went off to the Arts Center and the other mornings they swam in the Overlook pool. Stacia was surprised how much she liked having a training partner who was as competitive as she was. Kitty challenged Stacia to mini races on their runs that kept her engaged and helped her forget how much her shins hurt. For her part, Stacia patiently pushed Kitty to improve her freestyle stroke and do a flip turn smoothly. The more they trained together, the more Kitty reminded Stacia of Von. Stacia and Von had also pushed each other to be excellent. Stacia didn't envy how Von's long lithe legs made her leaps magnificent, and Von didn't bemoan the grace and speed of Stacia's pirouettes. They had each other's backs. Stacia had that same feeling toward Kitty. She wanted her to succeed and believed Kitty wanted the same for her.

Nevertheless, it still surprised Stacia how genuinely nice Kitty was. One cold grey day in late January, Stacia was curled up on the couch with her incontinent little dog watching reruns of *Search For Tomorrow* when Kitty called. Stacia dabbed at her eyes with the wad of tissues in her hand before answering the phone. She had been sniveling since Weldon had left that morning and was at risk of sobbing again.

"Hey, Kitty. What's up?"

"I've got a meeting at ten, but what do you say we meet at lunchtime and look at racing bikes? The Bicycle Chain is having an After Christmas Sale."

"Are they really having a sale? Or, are you calling because I told you this morning that Weldon is driving Lana back to school this morning?"

"Both?" Kitty admitted. "Oh come on, meet me for lunch. We've been talking about getting bikes for weeks, and I'm hoping the difference in our heights will give me an advantage over you."

Stacia tossed her tissues in the garbage and said, "Yeah, but I don't weigh nearly as much as you do, so it would be easier for me to turn over the pedals." Stacia rubbed Baillie's ears and smiled at the thought of a shiny new bicycle. *That would be a good challenge.* She looked out the window. "I don't know, Kitty. It's raining kind of hard and the weather man said we might get black ice conditions this afternoon."

"A little bird told me that your sister-in-law Eulalie got a racing bike for Christmas. You wouldn't want her to take over the Tate PTA and beat you in a road race, would you?"

"You are evil, Kitty Haskell," Stacia said and turned off the television. "You really know how to hurt a girl's feelings. You know that?"

"So? Am I going to be the only one that could take on Eulalie?"

Stacia laughed under her breath and got up to get dressed. "Noon, at the Bicycle Chain."

TWENTY-FOUR

Kitty stayed home one cold March morning to work undisturbed on a grant application. She didn't have a quiet office at the Arts Center; she had a cubby hole in the main office and permission to spread out in the conference room when it was available. Most days, she set up on a card table at the back of the small gallery space so she could greet the growing number of patrons who visited. In the last four months, Kitty had organized the holiday show of locally turned wood ornaments, two showings of the Art Center's watercolor classes and a display of local quilt makers. *The New York Times* had picked up the local newspaper's story about the quilt exhibit that included excerpts from Kitty's thin exhibit guide explaining the historical significance of textile arts in the Carolinas as a female art form. Kitty was single-handedly bringing in new patrons, and the board of the Arts Center couldn't have been more pleased with her. They had doubled her meager salary and given her free rein to plan the year's exhibit schedule.

Capitalizing on the goodwill the *New York Times* article brought her, Kitty was planning an exhibit of crocheted sweaters made by the prisoners in Sister Lydia's prison ministry. It would be controversial, but Kitty felt it was important. Sister Lydia turned out to be a talented fiber artist, as well as a visionary nun. Kitty had gone with Rose and Sister Lydia to the prison to interview and photograph the women for the exhibit. Intellectually, Kitty knew the prisoners had done terrible things to land themselves in jail, but in her heart, she thought of the women as all having been led astray by men. She knew how it felt to be trapped by the mistake of trusting the wrong man. Kitty planned to display photographs of the female prisoners along with photographs of their children wearing the tiny hand-crocheted items lovingly made for them. She planned to also assemble a small booklet that would explain how each woman got to the point in her life where the only physical contact she had with her child was through her crochet hook and a ball of donated yarn. She was applying for grants from the State Correctional Department, as well as from prisoner rights organizations. The money would cover some of her expenses as well as lend credibility to the show.

Kitty was spreading out photographs of the women on the dining room table when Renee let herself in through the front door like she owned the place. She let out a yelp when she saw Kitty. "Miss Kitty! You scared the life out of me! Aren't you supposed to be at work?"

"I'm sorry, Renee." Kitty jumped up and started picking up piles of paper from the floor. "I forgot this was your day to come." Kitty hadn't seen Renee in months and frankly, she had forgotten all about her. The house never seemed particularly cleaner one day to the next.

Renee pulled the vacuum cleaner out of the closet under the stairs. "I see you've taken to using your husband's office lately."

"Yes, I needed a place to work from home." Kitty had taken over the room when she started her job at the Arts Center. Seth rarely did anything in there but read his dirty magazines. She had taken away his office privileges. Enough was enough.

Renee leaned on the vacuum and eyed Kitty like a ripe peach. "I saw that cute little Mexican was back to finish with the new garden. Better count your tools before you pay him."

"Don't be silly, Renee," Kitty said as she transferred the piles of papers to a box on the dining room table. Kitty was overjoyed with her new garden. It was everything she had asked of Luis, and more. He had been able to take her abstract ravings and translate them in a botanical masterpiece. Already, the first snowdrops and Eranthis had broken the drab winter gloom. Now, crocus and narcissus lit up first one corner and then another of the garden. Soon the poppies would start. Huge scarlet and orange blooms would nod their heads for a few weeks and then completely disappear to make way for the next round of blooms. Luis had visited the week before, to check on things and take photographs of the bloom progressions for his portfolio.

The notion that Luis would steal anything from her was preposterous. On the other hand, Kitty would not put it past Renee to steal from them. She quickly did an inventory of her house wondering if anything had gone missing in the last few years. *Would we even notice if a handful of loose bills or a piece of the silver we never use went missing? This woman has a key to my front door, and I really have no idea what she's actually doing when no one is home. She's not vacuuming. I know that much.*

Daisy ran in from where she'd been napping in the family room and nuzzled Renee's leg. *Don't be such a sucker, girl. Just because she keeps liver treats in her pockets, it doesn't make her such a nice woman.*

"Daisy remembered you were coming."

"I like a big dog." Renee scratched Daisy's ears. "Not like that fur ball of Miss Stacia's."

Kitty tapped a pile of papers on the table. *I'd hate to see Stacia's face if she heard her AKC-certified dog referred to as a fur ball.* "Baillie's a sweet dog if a little high strung."

"I have to give that one a swift kick every once in a while to keep it out from under foot," Renee snorted.

Kitty got up and shooed Daisy back into the living room. "Have you been busy lately?"

"Not so much, I have a few opening for new clients if you know anyone. You know, I don't clean for that Miss Marni no more."

"Really?"

"Oh yeah, her house is sold now anyway. You must be happy about that."

"I hadn't noticed." Kitty walked back to the dining room table. She hoped Renee would get the hint and get to work.

"Sure you noticed." Renee leaned on the door jamb. "We'll all be happy to see the back of that one. She got all snippy with me 'cause she thinks I was the one who told Miss Stacia that she wrecked her own paint job."

"What would make people think Marni did anything of the sort?" Kitty tried to sound nonchalant. She made motions as if to get back to the photographs on the table.

"I don't know how they got the idea in the first place. But, after Miss Marni gave me the boot, I may have let one or two people think that. You're still paying me, so best keep this house happy with me." Kitty's head jerked up. "Oh yeah, I saw the car. But don't worry. I didn't tell Miss Stacia who really did it," Renee said with a rapacious grin. "I never tell that race traitor the truth."

"Excuse me?"

"Oh yeah, I remember when you made that big ol' sign last year. I know the extra paint was probably right out there in your garage when Miss Becky went out that morning."

Indignant rage bubbled up from Kitty's toes. *You little parasite! Don't you say that in front of me!* "Very funny, Renee," Kitty guffawed as if Renee had just said something amusing, rather than menacing. "Becky would never do something awful like that." She grabbed her box of documents and crossed into the bright office.

Renee took a step back into the dusk of the foyer when Kitty dropped the box on the floor and spun around to face Renee. "Everyone knows that Mrs. Kaur lost control and slid into another vehicle."

"But—"

"She really hasn't been quite right lately. It really is quite sad." Kitty began to push the door closed in Renee's face. "Now, if you wouldn't mind, please make sure you move the coffee table when you vacuum. You forgot last time."

Kitty heard Renee say, "What the?" under her breath as the office door clicked shut.

Kitty sat down behind the desk and tried to calm her breathing. She had to think. In all the hullabaloo around Seth and Marni, she hadn't given much thought to how everyone else in Overlook seemed to know about the affair before she did. She knew that both Molly and Stacia had known, but they had both actively tried to keep it a secret. Then, she remembered how Debbie gushed on about how Renee kept her up-to-date on what was going on in the neighborhood. A cold draft of guilt rushed over her. She had never visited Debbie. Her only visitors were Stacia and Renee.

Kitty glared at the closed office door and recalled what Renee had just implied about Becky. *How dare she imply that Becky do anything untoward! The nerve of that woman! I wonder what other lies she has made up and threatened people with.*

Then, Kitty remembered what Debbie had said that day about Renee telling her about Betty Oliphant's daughter being sent away because she was on drugs. *I wonder if that girl has ever even taken drugs.* She heard the vacuum cleaner go on for a minute, then go off again.

What am I thinking, letting that woman come into my house and threaten my Becky? I don't think so!

That afternoon, a locksmith changed the locks to the Haskell's house and Kitty reprogrammed the alarm codes. She would not officially fire Renee for another day or two. She needed to talk to Stacia first and develop their plan of attack.

❧

The next morning, Kitty alternated between jumping in place and running in circles while waiting for Stacia to join her on the running path. They couldn't go out on their new bicycles on the icy roads, but cold wet weather would not deter either of them from their training regimen. Stacia could tell that something was on Kitty's mind and hoped Seth hadn't been caught cheating again. She wouldn't be surprised if he had. She had heard rumblings about someone named Brittany.

"We need to talk about Renee," Kitty said. Her green eyes flashed with rage in her flushed face.

"Renee? What about her?"

"You have got to fire that parasite!" Kitty took off down the path.

"Wait!" Stacia had to sprint to catch up. "Aren't we going to warm up?"

"That woman has been playing us against each other like chess pieces then sitting back and watching the fireworks."

"What? What are you talking about?"

"Renee had the gall to come into my house yesterday and insinuate that she knew that Becky spray-painted Marni's car—"

"Slow down. Becky?"

"—and she had the nerve to say that she was keeping it a secret because I was such a good customer. What's next, a horse head in my bed?"

Stacia stopped and hung her head between her knees until her breathing slowed to a normal pace. Eventually, Kitty turned and jogged back to her.

"Really, Kitty," Stacia gasped between breathes. "You can't just take off like that without letting me warm up. We're not kids anymore."

"Sorry," Kitty said. "I've just been thinking about this since yesterday afternoon. I guess I'm a little worked up." They stepped off the path behind Blaire Morton's house and sat out of the rain on the covered wooden bench next to the Mortons' empty boat slip.

Once she could speak intelligibly again, Stacia asked, "So what are you all upset about? Renee threatened you? Why would she do that? What exactly did she say?"

"She said she saw Marni's car that morning and recognized the color paint you used."

"That's ridiculous. Why would she even remember that paint?"

"I recognized it too. It was that weird tangerine color."

Stacia stared slack-jawed at Kitty. "Renee told me, that someone told her, that Marni smashed up her own car. And, I let her think that." Stacia stood up and started pacing up and down the slip. "Wait a minute. Even if she did recognize that paint, why would she think Becky did it? You, I could see. But Becky? Why would Renee say something like that about Becky?"

Kitty picked up a twig and tossed it in the water. "I think she's planning on blackmailing me with what she thinks she knows. Well, maybe not blackmail per se, but definitely hold it over my head to get something out of me." She tossed another twig with more force this time. "I don't really understand what she wants from me. And I don't really care. I just want her gone. No one screws with my kids and gets away with it!" Kitty took a deep breath and went on.

"So, I did a little research last night. I went across the street to see Betty Oliphant. Despite what Renee told Debbie Manning, and who knows who else, Betty's daughter is not a drug addict who had to be sent away. She is happy and healthy and living in California. The girl did go through a rough patch where she was running with the wrong crowd, but she is fine. She decided to take the GED test and go to art school a year early. Betty showed me some of her work. It's wonderful."

Kitty looked out over the rain-soaked lake seeming to weigh her words carefully. "Betty also told me that Eileen is pregnant."

"That is not for public consumption yet," Stacia gasped. "How did Betty even know about that?"

"Come on, Stacia. How do you think? Renee cleans her house."

"That's ludicrous. Renee has been with me for years. She's like family."

Kitty considered telling Stacia about the bigoted remarks Renee had made and decided against it. She didn't need to hear that. It wouldn't help the situation. "You let your family kick the dog?"

"What?" All the color drained from Stacia's face. "What are you saying?"

"Yesterday, Renee told me that she gives Baillie a swift kick every once in a while to keep her out from under foot."

Stacia recalled the months of nursing her beloved dog through repeated kidney infections, and how Baillie cowered in her bed whenever Renee came to clean. "That bitch!" Stacia started to walk back to the path. "I'll fire her right now!"

Kitty put her hand on Stacia's arm. "Hold on now, Stacia. We need to be smart about this. Look what she has been saying about Marni. Marni fired her, then Renee started saying nasty things about her to the others. We need to figure out a way to ruin her business and get her out of Overlook in one fell swoop. Everyone needs to fire her, but we need to make it seem like it was their idea."

Stacia could see from the twinkle in Kitty's eye that she had a plan. "Kitty Haskell, you evil genius. What do you have in mind?"

"We fight fire with fire. All we do is simply spread a few nasty rumors of our own. What is it that the Lookers value the most? Their jewelry? No. Their homes? No. Their reputations? Yes, but that's not it. These women love their children more than anything."

Stacia nodded in agreement. She would do anything for Lana and Marcus.

"So, this is what we do. You tell a bunch of people that you smelled pot smoke on Renee's clothes, and I'll tell different people that I heard that some kid over on Pin Oak Road bought some LSD from her. You watch, people will be firing her before lunchtime. Then, all you and I have to do is sit back and follow the trend."

"It'll be over before she even figures it out," Stacia said with a smile.

TWENTY-FIVE

Seth sat at the kitchen counter, nursing a beer when Kitty came in from work. Sweat darkened his Carolina blue polo shirt, although the kitchen was cool. She was surprised to see him. He wasn't supposed to be back from his latest golf junket for two more days. She was disappointed; she'd had such a wonderful day. She and Stacia had biked ten miles that morning, the azaleas were blooming in her garden and she'd been offered a consulting job. The Abbott Museum in Philadelphia had offered to pay her $10,000 to guest curate a traveling exhibit of their folk art collection and the board of the Arts Center had agreed to give her a six-week leave of absence to put together the exhibit. What had started out as a little part-time job was quickly turning into a lucrative career.

She put her pocketbook in her office and came back to the kitchen. A dead light bulb and a note from the new cleaning service on the counter saying they were now out of three-way bulbs. Kitty flipped though a pile of mail and asked, "Where are the kids?"

"Becky went to get Bobby from baseball practice."

"Are you two speaking again?"

"We talked on the phone earlier," Seth grunted.

Seth and Becky hadn't spoken to each other since her last swim meet six weeks ago. Seth had hectored Becky about the importance of her swimming well in order to secure a scholarship. Needless to say, she swam poorly. After she gained ten seconds in her two hundred yard breaststroke race, Seth had taken the back staircase down to the pool deck and had a screaming fight with Becky beside the warm down pool. Neither one of them would tell her what was said, but none of the coaches would make eye contact with Kitty after that.

Kitty was not disappointed when Becky announced the next week that she had quit the swim team.

They'd seen very little of Seth since his blow out with Becky. He stopped coming to Bobby's baseball games and had fallen into his old habit of coming in late. Kitty and the kids had not missed him. Kitty knew she should probably speak to him about his behavior, but she kept putting it off. Her new job and parenting her children kept her busy. Supervising Seth seemed like more work than it was worth.

Kitty washed her hands and started pulling food out of the refrigerator. "Are you going to be here for dinner tonight? I was going to make chicken piccata. You like chicken piccata."

"Can Becky take Bobby out? I want to talk to you alone," Seth said. He stood up and staggered around the counter. Kitty suspected the beer in his hand was not his first.

"I guess so, but I really wanted to eat with the kids." Kitty returned the package of chicken to the refrigerator. "I wanted to celebrate with them. I got that big consulting project in Philadelphia!"

"Great," Seth said as he drained the bottle in his hand. "I'm glad your little art thing is going well."

She leaned against the refrigerator and looked at Seth. He was sweating like a pig. Something was definitely wrong. "Seth? What did you want to talk to me about?"

"I, umm," Seth mumbled. "I need to tell you that—" The phone rang. He ignored the call. He put the beer bottle down on the counter and rubbed his face with his palms. He seemed to be developing a plan of attack. When he dropped his hands, his face was transformed by a clown-like grin. He reeled over to the wine refrigerator and pulled out a bottle of champagne. "Let's take a boat ride to celebrate that museum thing. Come on, it's a beautiful evening!"

"What about dinner? You really should eat something."

"Forget dinner. We'll eat after we talk."

Caterpillars of dread crawled up the back of her neck. *What is going on with you, Seth? Why do you suddenly want to talk to me so bad? I like it so much more when you leave me alone.* "Okay," Kitty said slowly. "I'll grab a sweatshirt and meet you down at the boat slip." Although the thermometer said it was 73 degrees out, the late-April air had a bite to it. As soon as the sun went down the temperature would plummet. Kitty slipped one of Seth's old sweatshirts over a pair of shorts and walked down to the boat slip. She paused on the walkway to watch Seth load the insulated wine cooler into the back of their boat. His shoulders were more slumped than they used to be, and he was developing a paunch.

There was no one else out on the lake, most of the other Overlook residents still had their boats winterized. They followed the shore line for a few moments enjoying the azaleas dancing like flamenco dancers in the fading sunlight then, headed out to the main part of the lake. Seth cut off the small outboard and let the boat drift toward the dam.

"Don't you want to go over to the island? We could beach the boat like we did when we came out here for picnics with the kids."

"No, let's just float for a while." He popped the cork out of the champagne bottle and poured a toast. "I'm really glad to hear that your little job is going so well. That makes it easier to say what I have to say."

Kitty took the plastic champagne flute from Seth and asked, "I'm not going to like what you tell me, am I? Is the company in trouble? Did you make a mistake somewhere?"

Seth's face was flushed and his eyes darted everywhere but to Kitty's face. "No, the company's fine. It's nothing like that."

Kitty leaned back against the gunwale and looked back toward the ridge. The fading light reflected off something at the tip of the ridge with a flash.

"Kitty, pay attention to me. This is serious."

Here we go. Kitty looked back at Seth. Sweat was beading up on his forehead again. *Okay, let's get this over with. The sun will be going down soon and I don't want to be floating out here in the dark. Maybe I can use whatever awful thing he's done to offset the news that Becky received her acceptance letter from Brown.*

She placed the champagne flute on the floor of the boat. "I have something to tell you too. And you're probably not going to like what I have to say either."

"Did you meet someone?" Seth asked hopefully. "Because if you did, that's perfectly okay with me. I just want you to be happy."

"No, Seth. I did not find another man. I wouldn't even consider—"

"I met someone," Seth blurted out.

Goose pimples erupted on Kitty's bare legs. "I thought we agreed we weren't going to talk about your little diversions. Why are you telling me this?"

Seth took a swig of champagne directly from the bottle. "Shelly's not just some diversion. I love her. She needs me. You don't need me anymore. Even the kids don't need me anymore." He looked over her shoulder at the opposite shore. "Maybe this time I'll do a better job."

"What are you saying? Are you leaving me?"

"I'd be very generous."

Kitty was too stunned to speak. Nineteen years of putting up with his crap, and he was going to dump her just like that?

Seth looked back to Kitty's face. "You said you had something to tell me? What did you do?" That question, coming out of Seth's mouth sounded just as punitive as it ever had when her mother had asked it.

Kitty squared her shoulders and blurted out, "Becky got into Brown, and I don't care what you say. She's going."

Seth rolled his eyes and started to move toward the motor. "I told her she couldn't go to a private school. I can't afford it, especially now."

"I'll pay for it," Kitty said, "with the money my dad put aside for her and Bobby."

"Rose will never agree to that." He sneered as he emptied the champagne bottle and dropped it in the well of the boat.

"She already has," Kitty replied. She picked up the bottle to put it back in the cooler.

"I won't allow it. It's too expensive. You had an expensive waste of an education, and look at you. You bake cupcakes and arrange quilts all day."

Kitty stood up and glared at Seth. "You won't allow it?" The boat rocked dangerously. Water splashed over the side and sloshed into the boat.

"Sit down!"

"Wait a minute. What did you mean, especially now?" Kitty steadied herself in the center of the boat. "What aren't you telling me? Why does this Shelly need you so much?" Seth looked up at her with pleading eyes. He seemed to be begging her not to make him say what came next. "She's pregnant, isn't she? You just never learn, do you?"

A sudden calmness came over Kitty as she saw a glimpse of the future. Seth would make all the same mistakes with this Shelly that he made with her. He wouldn't be faithful. He wouldn't be a better father. Kitty didn't know this Shelly person at all, but Kitty knew Seth. Shelly would be better off without Seth. She couldn't let Seth's irresponsibility ruin yet another family's lives.

She could barely see Seth anymore in the fading light as he whined, "So, you see why Becky can't go to Brown. I've got to think about the new baby. We'll have to sell the house, unless you let me and Shelly buy out your half."

Excuse me? You think I am going to just roll over and let you bring another woman into my house? Oh, Seth. You stupid, stupid man.

Kitty smiled her sweetest smile and leaned down to hug Seth. "Whatever you think is best, honey. It'll be all right. We'll work it out." He hugged her back as if relieved to get through the hardest part of such a difficult conversation. Kitty shifted her weight to kiss Seth on the mouth, then brought the champagne bottle in her hand down on the back of his skull. Seth's eyes widened but he didn't make a sound as he slumped over the side of the boat. A thin ribbon of blood floated in the water around his head.

Oh God, I've killed my husband!

She reached for the emergency flare gun strapped to the side of the boat, then stopped. *Think Kitty. How would you ever explain this? Think of the children. All the children.*

But what if he's not actually dead? What if I just knocked him out? Kitty reached down and touched the bottle shaped dent in Seth's skull. *Nope, definitely dead.*

I hope he's dead. I want him to be dead.

Oh my God, do I ever want him to be dead. But, how am I ever going to explain this?

Kitty tried to hold off the panic creeping up her spine. *I've got to get rid of the body. What would Rose do? She would have a plan.* Kitty searched the boat for clues as to her next move. There wasn't much to work with - an emergency kit, a champagne bottle, plastic glasses, the anchor. The anchor. She took off her blood-splattered sweatshirt and pulled it over Seth's head so she didn't have to look at his face. Then she unrolled the anchor line and deftly tied around his shoulders before winding the long rope around his hips and legs until there was only a few feet of rope between Seth and the anchor resting near the back of the boat. She kicked out the drain plug in the hull with the side of her Keds.

There, if they ever find the body, my fingerprints won't be on the plug. They'll think he went out for a boat ride while he was drunk, knocked out the drain plug, then slipped and smashed his head. That could happen.

Water quickly started rushing in. Within minutes Seth's body was covered. The anchor was keeping him under the water as the boat slowly sank.

Holy crap, this is going to work. I might just get away with it. I'll tell the kids that Seth wasn't there when I got home, and I assumed he had a few beers and went out. That's not so weird. He does that all the time.

The boat sank further beneath the surface of the lake. Kitty tread water and watched her husband slowly sink out of sight.

'Til death do us part.

Only then did she react. Kitty started sobbing. She floated on her back while she cried. She cried out of disappointment in Seth, she cried out in fear that she would be caught, she cried for the death of her marriage, for the death of her husband, for the death of her dreams. When she finally looked up, it was completely dark and her legs were numb.

She was disoriented. She couldn't tell where the shore was until she saw a light flash on and off high above the water's surface. It took a moment to realize the light was the floodlight on Stacia's patio. *The ridge. I can swim to the ridge.* She slipped off her sodden shoes and shorts and started swimming toward the lights in just her bra and panties. *I can do this. It can't be more than a mile to Stacia's dock. We swim two miles every time we practice. I can totally do this.*

When she was a hundred feet from shore, the floodlight suddenly went out. Kitty could barely make out the outline of the dock until she was right on top of it. When she pulled herself up and collapsed panting and shivering, she saw a pair of Lana's sweatpants and an old Nance High sweatshirt on the dark surface of the dock. There was a pink note written in Stacia's loopy handwriting tucked under the jeans.

It read - Go home and don't worry - I've got your back.

THE END

Look for the sequel to Overlook in 2016

ESCAPE PLAN

Overlook

ONE

April 1976

Seth Haskell deserved killing - Stacia Tate Curran didn't doubt that for one second. Still, she didn't enjoy seeing it happen.

It was an enchanting spring evening. The shocking pink redbuds on the far side of Lake Tate extended their delicate limbs over the water in the warm breeze. They reminded Stacia of her days as a young ballerina, watching her friends stretch in their bright costumes before leaping on stage. She picked up her binoculars with a contented smile and followed a line of pale ducklings until something disturbed the smooth surface of the lake and sent the ducklings scrambling after their mother. She retrained her focus on a boat making its way out of Tranquility Cove and frowned.

Stacia scratched the ears of the dog sitting in her lap. "Why is Seth home? Kitty isn't expecting him home until tomorrow night." Baillie looked up at his mistress and raised his eyebrows. Stacia raised the binoculars to her face again and watched the Haskells drift toward the dam at the southern end of the lake. Kitty lifted a bottle of champagne as Seth turned away from the engine.

"How sweet, he must have come home a day early to celebrate with Becky." During their morning jog, Kitty had recounted how Becky had jumped around the kitchen waving her acceptance letter from Brown University. It was an impressive accomplishment. She was the only member of the class of '76 to get into an Ivy League school. Stacia watched as the small boat rocked as Kitty stood up and leaned over to hug Seth. Stacia hoped Becky's news would help them put Seth's infidelities behind them and focus on their children; but then Kitty raised the champagne bottle and brought it down on the back of her husband's skull. Blood spurted across Kitty's face as Seth slumped over the side of the boat.

Stacia moved to call her daddy's friend Sgt. Lafferty down at the police department; however, Kitty's movements froze Stacia in place. Kitty moved toward the emergency flare, but didn't pick it up. Instead, she paused as if thinking of her next move, pulled off her sweatshirt, and wiped the blood from her face. Stacia's heart dropped. If she hadn't witnessed Kitty deliver the blow, Stacia could have continued to think of Kitty as her sweet, organized friend that made beautiful cupcakes and knew far too much about art. If Stacia hadn't seen it with her own eyes, she wouldn't have believed her friend was capable of pummeling her husband, then efficiently disposing of his body. It turned Stacia's stomach to watch Kitty wrap her bloody sweatshirt around Seth's head, weigh him down with the anchor, then sink the boat.

While Kitty floated naked and alone out in the lake until the sun sank below the coal plant, Stacia decided no good could come from reporting the crime. Whether it was a murder or a moment of passion, Seth was dead and Kitty needed help. Becky and Bobby Haskell needed their mother, and, more importantly, a murder would reflect poorly on the neighborhood. She couldn't have that. A scandal in Overlook wouldn't have been good for anyone, so Stacia did what needed to be done. She called Kitty's house and invited Becky and Bobby to spend the night at her house under the guise of an impromptu pizza party. Then, she turned on the floodlight above her patio as a beacon to guide Kitty back to shore, ran down the stairs to her dock with a pile of clothes for Kitty to run home in, and kept her mouth shut.

Kitty appreciated Stacia helping her get back to shore, however, the person she needed most was Rose. Her sister rankled at times, but Rose was the one person Kitty could depend on when push came to shove, or more accurately, smash came to blub blub. All Kitty had to say when she called was, "Rosie," for Rose to reply, "How bad?"

"He's gone."

"He left you?"

"No...I...bottle...head...blood."

A few seconds of silence on the line were followed by the sound of a heavy bottomed glass thumping on the surface of Rose's chintzy coffee table. "Well, it's about time."

"Lake...boat...sunk." Kitty could barely spit out the words.

"Holy crap, Mary Katherine," Rose snorted. "Okay, think. Is there a lot of evidence to clean up? Do I need to bring anything?"

"I don't think so." Kitty slid down the kitchen wall and sat with her splayed in front of her. "I don't know."

"Where are the kids?"

"Umm...they should be here, but they're not."

"Sit tight. I'll be right there. We'll deal with them when I get there." Ten minutes later, Rose burst through the door like a general entering a war room. "His car's in the driveway. We have to get rid of that."

Kitty hadn't moved since calling Rose. The weight of what she had done anchored her to the floor. Rose took the buzzing telephone from Kitty's hand and hung it up. "Christ, you're shaking like a leaf. Let's get you out of those damp clothes and into a hot shower." Rose eased Kitty up the stairs and into the master bathroom. She leaned her sister against the shower stall and turned the water on. As steam filled the room and obliterated their reflections in the mirror, Rose peeled the sweat suit off Kitty as if she was a sleepy toddler.

"Whose clothes are these anyway? This isn't Becky's school sweatshirt."

"Stacia. Dock." Kitty's shoulders shook as she recalled the beacon that guided her back to shore. "She saw me."

Rose froze in the middle of pulling the sweatpants down Kitty's thighs. "Someone saw you? Are you sure?"

Kitty stepped out of the sweatpants and into the shower. She stood under the hot stream of water until she stopped shaking and her toes felt like part of her body again. When she slid the shower door open, Rose had a towel ready and dry clothes waiting for her.

"How am I going to explain what happened to the boat?" Kitty said as she let her sister towel her off.

Her voice sounded far away. Kitty wasn't sure if she had even spoken out loud until Rose replied. "You sunk it, right?"

"Uh huh, I kicked out the plug and it sunk." Kitty couldn't focus on Rose. The tiny flowers on her staid wrap skirt seemed to move like insects swarming over her thighs. She vaguely felt the towel sliding down her back as she slumped forward on the vanity.

Rose yanked her upright and attacked her hair with a brush. "Look, you can freak out later. We need to deal with that car before someone notices it." Rose took Kitty's face in her hands and gently slapped her cheeks until she snapped out of her stupor.

Kitty pulled away from Rose. "Okay, okay, I'm okay." She looked at her reflection with wide eyes. "What am I going to do?"

"Well, while you were slowly going catatonic in the shower, I think I've come up with a plan." Rose folded and refolded the hand towel. "So we need to get rid of that car and explain why the boat is missing. Right?"

"He said his latest floozie is pregnant so he wouldn't allow Becky to go to Brown. She got in. She has to go. She has to."

"We'll talk about that later, okay?" Rose put the towel down and put her arm around Kitty's shoulders. "Now, does Seth ever take the boat anywhere other than out on the lake and back to your dock?"

"Slip," Kitty corrected her automatically. "We have a slip. Stacia has a full dock."

Rose gave Kitty's shoulders a quick shake. "Concentrate, Mary Katherine. Does the boat ever leave the water?"

"Sure, when it needs to be serviced." Kitty fiddled with the hem of the Fleetwood Mac concert t-shirt Rose had pulled over her head. It belonged to her daughter. "Sometimes he and Bobby go fishing on other lakes."

"But how does he move it? Is there a marina or something?"

"He uses the boat trailer," Kitty replied as if that was self-evident. She and Rose stared at each other for a moment before a smile spread across Kitty's pale face. "The trailer is under the deck. All we'd have to do is lift out the lattice and slide it out."

Rose brushed Kitty's hair behind her ear. "I think I've got it. What if we hitch the trailer to the back of the Volvo? It has one of those ball things on it, right?"

"Yeah."

"Then we drive the car and the trailer around to the far side of the lake, so if anyone goes looking for him, they'll think he took the boat out fishing and had an accident."

"They can't find his body." Kitty shuddered at the memory of blood spreading out in the water around Seth's head as he sunk to the bottom of the lake. "As soon as the police see the big dent in the back of his head, they'll know it wasn't an accident." Kitty turned and grabbed Rose's arms with both her hands. "Oh my god, I killed him. I flipped out and actually killed him."

Rose shook her sister off. "Yeah, yeah, yeah, you're a real badass." She nudged Kitty into the bedroom and pushed her down on the satin bedspread. She twisted a pair of Keds onto Kitty's feet. "But you do have a point. We don't want Seth found. And if he is, it needs to look like someone else killed him."

"Or an accident. An accident would be good." Kitty lay back and let her feet dangle off the edge of the bed. "We need to make it look like he went out on a different lake and disappeared." She flopped over onto her stomach. "Or faked his own death."

"Why would he do that?"

"I don't know," Kitty said. "I'm just thinking out loud."

"Okay, think. Where would go? Where should we leave the car?"

"Maybe somewhere near that Shelly's place in Charlotte. That way, when someone notices the car, the police will link the car to Shelly."

Rose went to the window and played with the blinds. "That's too iffy. We need to make it obvious to any idiot that he went out in his boat and drowned." She turned to Kitty. "Is drunk driving a problem with boats."

"Yeah, every year someone cracks up their boat on the Fourth of July because they've been sitting out in the sun drinking too many beers."

"Okay then, let's go," Rose said. "Let's get that car out of the driveway before your nosey neighbors notice it."

An hour later, Kitty parked the Volvo and boat trailer at the edge of a lake just a few miles from Charlotte. Before she climbed into Rose's car, she splashed a bottle of Seth's smelliest whiskey on the floor mats, so whoever found the car would assume Seth was drunk when he took the boat out on the lake.

It was a good plan.

Stacia pulled herself out of Lake Tate and perched on a fallen tree. She peeled her wetsuit off her upper body and let the warm afternoon breeze dry her skin. Her legs would have to stay encased in neoprene. Once the suit was wet, it was too difficult to pull it back on. In a few more weeks, the water would be warm enough to swim in just one of her colorful racing suits.

She took a moment to admire her lake. Spring in North Carolina was breathtaking. From the island in the center, the redbud and dogwood looked as though they were floating under the tall pines near the dam. If she looked back toward Overlook, the last of the azaleas blooming in her neighbors' yards looked like pink and coral rick rack along the hem of a dark green dress. The neighborhood appeared happy, from a distance.

Stacia pulled her right arm across her chest and leaned into the stretch. Over her shoulder, she could see the backhoes and cement trucks lumbering on the shore near the dam. A new subdivision was going in on the western end of the lake. For two decades, Overlook had been the only community on Lake Tate. When Tate Power & Electric built the hydro-electric plant that flooded the valley, a hardscrabble hilltop became a lush promontory into the lake. Stacia and her husband, Weldon, had transformed the land into a showcase of mid-century casual architecture. At the time, polite society looked askance at Stacia Tate marrying a black man, but her family's acceptance of Weldon along with his decorated military service and his sister's tragic death allowed them to tolerate him. The fact that the Curran family was one of the richest banking families in Durham and owned more land than the Tates didn't hurt either. Still, Weldon and Stacia chose to build Overlook near the technology park where most home buyers were originally from up north and less likely to care if the Tate Currans were an inter-racial couple. Now, this new Fox Chase sub-division threatened Overlook. It looked to be a hippie-dippie blend of brown wood-sided condominiums and cheap pre-fab ranches that were only one tiny step up from a double-wide. Who knew what kind of people would move into an anarchic place like that? Swingers? Druggies? The childless?

Stacia switched arms to stretch the other side of her body and shifted her gaze away from Fox Chase. She had other, more immediate things to worry about. Even after the exertion of her mile-long swim out to the island, her brain raced through all the ways Kitty could get caught and Stacia could be implicated. The Kitty Haskell situation had kept her from sleeping. She'd hoped they could talk during their morning jog, but when it came time to call Kitty and arrange to meet, Stacia couldn't pick up the phone. She didn't know what to say. Had Kitty killed Seth in a moment of passion? She had punched him in the nose when she found out he was sleeping with her tennis partner, but she was still drinking at that point. Or had it been a cold-blooded murder? Stacia didn't really want to know.

She wanted to talk to Von. She slipped her arms back in her wetsuit and zipped it up. As she kicked out into the deeper water, a familiar voice echoed inside her head. At least she killed him near the lower dam. The current will keep his body from surfacing near Overlook. Stacia smiled to herself as she started to swim back toward home. The voice of her long-dead best friend and sister-in-law was always in her head whenever she was physically or emotionally exhausted. Stacia hung on to Von's memory almost as tightly as she hung on to her guilt for surviving the car accident that had killed Von and ten of her classmates.

"Did I do the right thing helping Kitty?"

Hard to say. It'll be hard to look her in the eye after seeing her wrap that anchor around his corpse.

"I keep thinking about how he's down there near where the old town used to be. What if the boat sunk on the old school or the church? I hate to think of him decomposing where people once worshiped."

It's been decades since your grandfather flooded the valley to form Lake Tate. I'm sure the buildings have disintegrated by now. Still, you're right not to involve the police. The last thing you and Weldon need is police cars swarming around Overlook when there are newer neighborhoods popping up on the other side of the lake.

With any luck his bloated corpse will turn up near Fox Chase. Then they'd have proximity to dead bodies and a coal plant.

ACKNOWLEDGMENTS

No author truly works alone. I'd like to thank my writing friends : Rebecca White, Samantha Dunaway Bryant, Sarah Sugg, Elizabeth Carroll, Kimberley Workman, Amy Overley, Dawn Taylor, Robert Byrd, Noelle Granger, Becky Abbott, Sandy Gottlieb, Susan Mwarabu, Grace Wetzel, Stepheny Houghtlin, Sarah Wilkins, and Jennifer Madriaga. Thank you also to my biggest supporters - my darling husband Ted, my daughters Katherine and Emily, and my parents, Anthony and Janet Trippi.

ABOUT THE AUTHOR

Elizabeth Hein writes women's fiction with a bit of an edge. Her novels explore the role of friendship in the lives of adult women and themes of identity. She lives in North Carolina, in a city very different from Magnuson. *Overlook* was her first novel. Elizabeth enjoys interacting with her readers and can be found on Facebook, on Twitter @_ElizabethHein, and at ElizabethHein.com.

www.ingramcontent.com/pod-product-compliance
Lightning Source LLC
Chambersburg PA
CBHW021039130626
46552CB00005B/1926